A Jarful of M...

CHRISSIE BRADSHAW

Copyright © Chrissie Bradshaw 2016

ISBN 9781983146145

The moral right of Chrissie Bradshaw to be identified as the author of this work has been asserted in accordance with the Copyright, Designs and Patents Act 1988.

All rights reserved. No part of this publication may be reproduced, stored in a retrieval system, or transmitted, in any form or by any means, electronic, mechanical, photocopying, recording or otherwise, without the prior permission of the copyright owner.

All the characters in this book are fictitious, and any resemblance to actual persons, living or dead, is purely coincidental.

The opinions offered in this book are those solely of the author.

For Rob

Thank you for believing x

Acknowledgements

Thank you to everyone who has supported me in publishing 'A Jarful of Moondreams'. This is my own moondream come true.

Debi Alper and Emma Darwin, thank you for taking me through your self-editing course and sharing your skills.

Thank you to the RNA for supporting me through the new writers' scheme by providing an experienced reader to critique my work and a network of writing friends who have been frank, fun and fantastic.

The Border Reivers, the Northumbrian RNA chapter, have always been encouraging and I thank you and wish you all success in your writing.

My beta readers Rhona, Lisa, Pam and Rob were so enthusiastic, thank you for your time and comments; I'll ask you to do this again.

Thank you Oscar, my tenacious terrier, for helping me to sort out my plot on our beach walks.

Writers need a back up team and mine have been the best, thank you friends and family.

PINK MOON

1

Cleo Moon had almost made the fifty miles to Dunleith, the Northumbrian village that she still thought of as home, when her mobile rang. The display showed Neil's name so she turned into Church square and parked to take the call.

Before she could accept, the phone stopped ringing, damn it. Pressing ring back, she calmed herself and tried to make her voice sound upbeat.

'Hi Neil, it's me.'

'You never catch my calls!'

'I've been driving, as you should know, and I've parked up to phone you. I'm not at Mum's yet.'

'Hmm. Because of your sudden change of plan, I'm at a loose end all weekend with nothing to do.'

'Lucky you, I'll still have work to do for Monday when I get back tomorrow evening.'

'Sounds like we'll have a great Sunday night too.'

Cleo heard the sarcasm and felt annoyed. She wanted to tell him, don't come around at all then. No, that wouldn't help their blossoming relationship, she'd have to try a bit of placating here.

'Neil, I *am* sorry. I'd love to see more of you this weekend, but Mum wanted me here on my own and we'll soon have a whole week away together at half term. Maybe you could ring some friends and find something to do?' she tried to keep her tone light.

'You're sounding all 'school marmish' again. Look, if you're going to be like this, I'll just leave it this weekend.'

Well done, Cleo. That's what happens when you show people your weak spots. She'd once told him she hated it if anyone mentioned she was in teacher mode, so much for trying to be understanding.

'Maybe that would be best.'

'Goodbye then.' Neil sounded curt.

'Wait–'

What a pain he could be. She reached into the glove compartment and grabbed a bagful of jelly rings. Neil seemed to be oh so charming, until things didn't go his way.

Chewing on the jellies, she fumed. Why did she bother with relationships? They started off well but were never carefree for long. She would have to try to forget about Neil and their bumpy relationship for the rest of the day.

Cleo reversed out of the square, headed towards the brae just outside the village and took the familiar road to High Rigg trying to recall when she had last visited her mum. They spoke a couple of times a week but an actual visit; it must have been before her ski trip. She'd told her all about Neil over the phone when she got back from skiing but, since then, she'd been so busy.

It must have been some time in March. Mother's Day? Yes, she'd gone for lunch and taken her flowers and that silver pendant. She had plenty of reasons, well excuses, but she knew that it had been too long.

Her spirits always lifted when she caught sight of the trees lining the driveway and the gateway welcoming her home. She slowed down when she saw the feline shape of Pharos strolling along the driveway to check her out. He rolled over right by the car door so that Cleo had to stride over him when she climbed out.

'Hello old boy, am I actually getting a welcome?' His eyes rewarded Cleo with a gooseberry glare, as if to say 'you should be so lucky', before he led the way around the back of the house to the kitchen.

The door was half open with steam cascading out making the air pungent with spices and there, stirring furiously at a large pot, was Teri. She wore a top of sage and muted greens that Cleo had bought her last birthday over jeans. Her blonde hair was a halo of loose curls and she was barefoot as usual.

Cleo felt a surge of love. She'd missed Mum. She would definitely, absolutely visit more often.

'Darling, I'm at a crucial stage of this Moroccan chicken tagine. Come and give me a hug.'

'Hi Mum, it looks like it's all going on in here. I'm starving.' Cleo was already at the stove, her arms around Mum. It felt unfamiliar - she felt frail, birdlike. 'Have you lost some weight, Mum?'

'Have I? Perhaps a pound or two.'

'It doesn't suit you. You're thin enough.'

'I know, I know, sweetheart but I've had a lot on my mind and I can't eat when I'm... Look, grab a glass of that Merlot and we'll go into the garden room. This needs another forty minutes to simmer and you and I need to talk.'

Overflowing with flowering plants, a couple of olive trees in tubs by the door and filled with a mish-mash of comfy seating covered by throws and quilts - this family space was an eclectic mix of vibrant and faded colours, yet restful. It was so grandly named after Cleo had brought back a wooden 'le salon de jardin' sign from France after a school trip. Over the years it had become the place for 'talks' or 'news.'

Teri was looking out at the garden and the fields as Cleo settled down onto the sofa.

'What is it Mum? You've brought me here for something, and I can't think what can be so important that Alex the Great isn't in on it.'

Teri turned to face Cleo, 'Don't be like that; you know I think you're both wonderful.'

'Do you ever tell Alex to stop making insulting remarks about me?'

'All the time. Now, for goodness sake, she is your sister; stop scoring points.' Teri's frown showed concern rather than annoyance and Cleo felt a bit ashamed.

'Sorry Mum, it's just a habit when I get back here, and it's a luxury to have you to myself for an evening. So tell me, what's up? Have you met a handsome visitor to these parts? Are you going to start life anew?'

'Nothing quite as drastic but I do want you to help me with a rather exciting plan.'

'Why am I not getting a great feeling about this? Cleo searched her mother's face for clues.

'Just hear me out, darling. There's something I'd like you to do...well to consider doing.'

'I'm listening.' Cleo could sense that this was going to be a big ask. Mum was fiddling with her rings and sitting on the edge of her chair; she seemed loath to begin. 'Come on, Mum. It can't be so hard.'

'You know that I love Egyptology and I've always wanted to go to Egypt?'

Cleo nodded and waited for more.

'Of course you do.' Teri smiled and gripped the arms of her chair before going on, 'I've decided it's high time that I put that plan into action and I'm going to book an extended trip.'

'Can't it wait awhile Mum? Egypt isn't all that safe at the moment and I'd worry about you and I can see you're worried about it too. Look at you, you're all on edge.'

'I've waited long enough and I'm willing to take the risk. The trip is not what I'm feeling on edge about.'

'Then what is it?'

'I'm worried about asking you to look after Alex while I'm away. I'm hoping you'll say yes because I do so want you to take her under your wing. She can live with you and spend a few weeks at your school. There I've said it. That's what I'd like you to do.'

Once it all spilled out, Teri felt less anxious but Cleo was speechless. She cast around frantically for a good reason, any reason except the real one; that she couldn't stand to be with her sister. Her sister's arrival seventeen years ago had just about ruined her life and the less she saw of her the better.

'Mum, that's impossible. She can't just follow her A level courses at a different school and, anyway, she wouldn't want to stay with me. What about the Collingwoods? She's always with the twins, can't they have her there?' Cleo saw the sorrow in her mother's eyes and felt so mean that she immediately shut up.

'I'm not happy about leaving her with friends when she has family of her own to stay with. I've checked with school and she can take her coursework with her to another school for the month of July. It's four school weeks and I'm sure that you will be able to clear it with your own school if you try.'

Mum had done her research and Cleo knew she was right. Her school took in pupils who were staying with relatives quite regularly. She had no excuse really.

'I'm not sure I can do this, Mum. I don't know what to say.'

'Cleo my love, I'm sure that you *can* do this or I wouldn't have asked you. You don't have to say anything at all for now. Just sleep on it and think it over and you can let me know when you're ready.'

Cleo hardly tasted the delicious dinner and drank too much wine. She could accept that her mum wanted to travel. She deserved to fulfil her own dream of exploring Egypt. It was Alex at her apartment that seemed crazy. Alex with me for weeks on end? Attending *my* school for the last few weeks of term! Mum you've lost your senses. We could kill each other. She couldn't say this of course. Mum was so hopeful and she'd been through a lot. If she was honest, she felt relieved that it wasn't news that she was ill again.

How hard would it be to do as Mum asked? Bloody hard. She wished Mum would just ask the Collingwoods if they were able to help out. She could have coped more confidently with doing teen care for the odd weekend.

They'd gone back into the garden room after dinner and now Teri was making a hot drink; she had left Cleo to finish the last of the wine. Cleo could hear clattering in the kitchen which meant that Mum was stacking the dishwasher and clearing up. Mum seemed to have her plan all sewn up. She'd always thought that she would do absolutely anything for her mother, but this... it would test her big time.

Teri came back with a mug of tea and, as they finished their drinks, she talked about all the places she longed to see. As she mentioned Cairo, Alexandria, Luxor, the Sinai desert and the Nile, Cleo had never seen her so animated. Could she help Mum to do this? She wanted to give it her best shot.

'I'm off to bed now Mum, but I'll put you out of your misery first. Of course I'll look after Alex, if you're sure that's what you want. I'm willing to have her as long as you let her know that I'm going to be in charge.' After giving Mum a kiss and a long hug, Cleo went upstairs.

What had she let herself in for? She walked into Alex's room. A complete mess of clothes, books, makeup and a desk piled high with junk. She didn't really *know* Alex, hadn't let herself know her, but she couldn't be any different from the hundreds of teens that she had taught.

Cleo closed the door and stepped into her own room; clean, uncluttered and organised. She loved being back in here and under the same roof as her mum. She knew exactly which drawer her nightclothes were in and found an old pair of pyjamas to slip on. Although she had a lot to think about, the merlot had run very freely and this bed was always comfy so, as her head touched the pillow, she went straight to sleep.

Teri turned the garden room lights low and sat for a while looking out at the darkening sky; there was just the tiniest sliver of this spring's pink moon left. Her gaze was drawn towards the sheen of the tall jar in the far corner of the room. She remembered how delighted Cleo had been, on her seventh birthday, when she was as tall as their moondream jar. It was decorated with Egyptian figures walking around the jar telling their story and hieroglyphics giving more details of those ancient tales.

Teri loved turning the jar to see the stories unfold, to feel the contours of the curved side. If she removed the lid, she could peer into its inner darkness and see the secret wishes that lay hidden there. This was where they had always posted birthday and Christmas lists, wishes made on a new moon and treasured mementos of happy times; first there had been hers and then her two girls had added their own.

If only Cleo and Alex shared her biggest dream. Her biggest wish, that her girls would grow close to one another, had been popped into the jar over many moons and she'd tried all ways to bring them together but it hadn't happened. Getting her daughters to bond called for drastic measures but, maybe this time, she'd found a way.

She felt stiff as she stood up. She was forty-nine but, at times, her joints made her feel as ancient as those Egyptians on the jar. She made her way upstairs feeling lighter in spirit, Cleo had always been the harder daughter to reach, but it was done. Cleo seemed strong but she was not so resilient underneath that armour.

Speaking to Alex, almost seventeen, was as easy as breathing to Teri. Alex might already have suspicions that something was afoot, but Teri had been evasive until Cleo had been dealt with. Dealt with, what an awful way of thinking. With Cleo, her first born, there burned such a strong love, but she was always so hard to fathom. As Alex had once remarked, 'Cleo is wired differently to you and me, Mum. Just accept it.'

She reached into her bedside drawer and, although she found the box of pain relief capsules, she paused. She'd had a couple of glasses of wine, should she take one of these? If she did, she'd be out for the count until morning but if she didn't... she didn't want to be pacing the floor with her back and hip pain when Cleo was here because it would worry her. That settled it, she took one.

2

In Edinburgh, Alex was feeling glad that she had missed Cleo's arrival but what she couldn't fathom out was why her mum had suddenly decided to ask Cleo to stay over *this* particular weekend while she was away. Usually Mum bent over backwards to get the two girls together and to arrange 'quality sister time.' She absolutely dreaded those weekends and she was sure that Cleo did too. Bloody bossy boots. She was so up herself, she hadn't visited for ages and only lived in Newcastle. Fifty miles was hardly the other end of the country! Not seeing Cleo suited her just fine; it was Mum she felt sorry for. Her sister took Mum totally for granted. Cleo had never ever been a proper big sister; she just didn't feature in Cleo's world. Well, she wasn't bothered. Alex was shocked to feel tears welling in her eyes. What were they about?

'What's wrong Alex?' Eleanor looked up from her iPhone and saw the tears ready to roll.

'Nothing, something in my eye I think.'

Isabella stopped painting Eleanor's nails and glanced up. Had she noticed too? She could see the EllaBellas dart one another one of their looks.

'You can't kid us, what's wrong? said Isabella.

'I'm OK. I was thinking about Cleo. I was thinking of…of the way she treats Mum.'

'And you.' added Eleanor.

'You can't help how your sister is,' Isabella's words consoled her slightly.

'And you're lucky you've missed seeing her, to go partying with us. I can't wait to get my Alex creation on. You are so talented!' Eleanor smiled over at her and Alex was grateful the subject had changed.

'Don't move yet, Ella.' Isabella's brow furrowed with the effort needed to apply varnish without smudging, 'I just need to concentrate on this last coat.'

'Hey Alex, thinking about Cleo, which I'd always rather not; didn't our Dan have a lucky escape?' said Eleanor.

'I can't believe they ever hit it off. He must have seen the light in the end.' Alex shuddered making Eleanor laugh. The thought of Cleo ever being with Dan Collingwood was laughable. He was always so friendly towards her and actually liked *his* younger sisters. He wasn't bad looking either, for an older person. Dan was supposed to be keeping an eye on the twins while Dr and Mrs Collingwood were away for a few days, but his eye wasn't going to stretch as far as Edinburgh tonight. Just as well.

The girls were staying with the twins' great aunt Maggie who was very hard of hearing and kept her radio turned up so high that she was oblivious to the racket the girls were making as they got ready for their night out. They had all been looking forward to getting out of sleepy old Dunleith and spending a Saturday night in Edinburgh for weeks. An excited shiver of anticipation ran through Alex as she glanced at the three black dresses hanging on the outside of the wardrobe.

After commandeering her mum's sewing machine for a week, with some expert guidance from her mum, she had customised three plain black Top Shop dresses that they'd snapped up for next to nothing in the sales. By using ribbons, feathers, sequins and one or two strategic slits, each one was slightly different. She'd even successfully removed one sleeve of her own dress, making the design look asymmetric. With outfits ready and everything booked, this was going to be their most eventful experience ever.

Alex had been happy to go along with Eleanor's idea for Saturday night. Eleanor often took the lead, she was ten minutes older than Isabella and a month older than Alex, so who were they to argue? The concert alone would be an exciting trip, but the riskiest part, something they'd never done before, was going afterwards to a party night at a club they'd heard loads about. The parents would have vetoed the idea but they'd never know.

'Your turn,' Isabella patted the dressing table stool and that Alex sat down in front of her and the pots of varnish. 'The dresses are looking brilliant, Alex. Now for your nails, red or dark? You can have 'Blood in the Snow' or 'Chocolate Dip', we've both gone red.' Alex hovered over both colours. Decisions, decisions. Picking up the red, she grinned at Isabella who took the bottle, nodded in approval and gave it a brisk shake,

Alex watched as Isabella, tongue hanging out in concentration, carefully applied a base coat. She was lucky to have both EllaBellas, their twin name that had stuck since nursery, as her best friends; it more than made up for her having an absent sister who took no notice of her whatsoever.

Half an hour later, their transformation was complete,

'Hey Alex, you so look like our triplet now,' Isabella said. They were all in their dresses and Alex was delighted with her look; the twins usually looked that bit older. People told her she was pretty but, with her fine features, she looked young for her age - whereas both twins had inherited their mother's strong roman nose and striking high cheek bones. She was happy that the dress and makeup had worked magic and added a few years.

'For one night only, we're going to be over eighteens!' she announced to the mirror.

'Sshh don't let Aunt Maggie hear!' Eleanor was checking herself out in the mirror behind Alex and, as Isabella pushed them both aside for another glance at her own reflection, they were off into a mirror fight and fits of giggles.

To escape a lecture on dress length, the girls put their coats on to say goodnight to their aunt who was nodding off as she listened to the radio. They then left them on the coat stand in the hall, added scarlet lipstick and were off. It was a lovely May evening; who wore a coat to a concert or club?

It was just before midnight when Alex got to the front of the queue waiting outside The Hornet's Nest. She had been to the concert and then for a quick drink but the evening wasn't over yet.

'Weren't the band cool tonight?' asked Eleanor

'Yes, brilliant; even better than The Script,' agreed Alex.

'Don't know about that, Alex, it's a close call,' Isabella said, her carefully painted eyebrows rising a fraction.

'I just hope it's not a close call getting in here., Alex replied. 'Are we looking old enough?'

'Course we are, Bella. I managed to get into all of the pubs last time we were here and we're way older now,' Eleanor said confidently.

'Yeah, way older by two months,' Isabella, her twin reminded her.

'Two months!' nodded Eleanor and they both got the giggles.

'Sshh. Let's keep it down,' Alex started to feel uncomfortable. 'We're getting nearer, the doorman might hear you.'

Alex would have been happy enough with the

concert and then pub but she always wanted to follow the EllaBellas. It had been on Eleanor's wish list to make it into a late night session at the Nest ever since they had heard about the mix of music and partying that went on there. So what if seventeen was underage? That wasn't going to stop them from giving it their best shot.

The broad-shouldered doorman, muffled up in scarf and a long overcoat even though it was spring, glanced over and Alex noticed that Eleanor, her eyes dark and dilated, gave him a grin and a nod. Her super confident attitude was partly due to that lurid blue concoction that passed for a cocktail in the pub around the corner but mainly courtesy of the pill she had popped with it.

It had been easy to find someone with the stuff they needed to party; a legal high to stay awake all night and to make them feel friends with the whole world. Alex did want to get in there and dance the rest of the night away, but she was nervous because she still felt that she looked the youngest and might hold them back.

The bouncer didn't return Eleanor's grin; he checked his watch and went inside, probably checking to see if he could let more people in. There was quite a queue gathering behind them.

'If we don't get past the door, we'll just have to walk back to Aunt Maggie's.' From Isabella's tone, Alex guessed she was feeling edgy as she neared the front of the queue too. Aunt Maggie went to bed early so she had entrusted them with a key. The girls huddled together to avoid the night breeze that had started up and Alex cast an envious glance at the doorman's coat. It didn't look so daft now.

'I'm aching to get inside to the heat' moaned Eleanor, linking arms with the other two.

'And the beat,' added Isabella.

Alex shivered from cold, nerves and excitement and couldn't say a thing.

The doorman drew himself up, pulled his shoulders back and gave them a long stare. Did he suspect they were underage? Alex felt like turning tail and calling it a night.

They were almost in the entrance and light from the doorway shone on long, blonde hair and cat's eyes shaded by heavy lashes. They all had pale skin, a slick of red over their lips and a slash of black skimpy dress. Endless legs, even longer in high-heeled shoes, completed the look.

The Collingwood twins were identical and, even without the same coloured outfits and makeup, they were difficult to tell apart. Although slighter and shorter, Alex looked part of their trio.

'In you go girls, enjoy your night.' The doorman hadn't asked for ID. They must look old enough. Alex could breathe.

'Thank you.'

'Thanks.'

'We will!' called the three in unison ... they were in!

Straight into the cloakroom where perfumes and hairspray were thrown together into a heady mix by the hot air driers. They jostled through the crowded room to get to the mirrors for a top up of gloss and to smooth their hair.

'Are you OK now, Alex?' Isabella asked.

Alex realised that her nerves must have been on show to her friends. 'Ecstatic,' she smiled, as she searched for her comb. After combing her hair and flicking it back, she surveyed herself in the mirror. Now that they were in, they were going to have a fantastic time. 'Come on girls let's find this party,' she urged.

They opened the door to the blast of the music. The warmth of the fuggy dance floor blanketed her, the music boomed through to her soul and, for tonight, she was flying.

'Night Ladies.' The doorman looked at his watch; it was just after one, they hadn't stayed long.

'Goodnight,' Alex and Isabella replied. Eleanor was silent between them. As they led her outside, her face had a grey pallor.

'The cool air will make you feel better, Ella,' Alex said.

Eleanor didn't reply. She seemed to be finding it hard to put one foot in front of the other.

'Come on, we have a fair hike to get back so you should cool down and start to feel better on the way,' Isabella sounded confident.

Alex wished she felt the same way.

They knew that Eleanor had taken an extra pill half an hour ago. Alex and Isabella hadn't needed to top up, they were both still feeling the effects of the first one they'd popped in the pub, but Eleanor, convinced that hers hadn't worked properly, took another.

Loads of people had bought stuff around the back of the pub. It was supposed to be safe to take a couple, but when Eleanor came back to the dance floor, she felt hot and breathless and thought she might faint.

'Let's keep going. We haven't enough for a taxi so we'll have to walk,' Alex said to Eleanor, to urge her on.

They turned the corner and Eleanor stopped abruptly. 'Hold on, hold on,' she slurred, 'lemme' … she kicked of one shoe then the other … 'carry these. Tha's better.' Eleanor bent to pick up her shoes but fell over. She stayed on her knees and started retching. She tried to get up, but crumpled in a heap on the pavement. Out cold.

'Ella!' Alex shouted while trying to pick her up.

Isabella had picked up the shoes and was frozen in horror, clutching the discarded shoes to her chest.

Eleanor's skin felt clammy and, from the street light, Alex could see it had a green tinge. They needed help.

'Stay with her, Bella,' Alex called as she ran back to the corner. Thank God the doorman was still outside the club. He must have heard her running, as he turned his head and looked her way. 'Help us,' she yelled, 'you have to help. It's my friend ... come and see her!'

He moved surprisingly swiftly and Alex was relieved to see him at Eleanor's side. Taking command of the situation, he handed his phone to Alex and told her to phone 999 and give her name, stay calm and speak clearly. As she dialled, Alex watched him turn Eleanor onto her side into the recovery position, check her airway was clear and feel for her pulse. She knew about that from first aid training but hadn't thought to do it. *Please God, don't let her die!*

After Alex gave her name, his hand stretched out for the phone and she handed the call over to him. She heard him describing Eleanor's condition. She had a pulse. Thank God. He gave details of where they were. Placing his scarf under Eleanor's head and his coat over her limp body, the doorman knelt beside her continually checking her breathing and her pulse. Feeling absolutely useless, Alex put her arms around Isabella, who had started to shiver and sob uncontrollably.

They heard the wailing siren first of all and then the flickering blue light of the ambulance came around the corner. By the time it pulled up and the crew got out, their doorman had taken his coat and had disappeared around the corner.

The paramedics went to work immediately and, in seconds, they were all in the ambulance on their way to the Royal. Alex picked up the doorman's scarf from the pavement and she clutched onto it for dear life. Please God, thank you for helping us so far. Don't let Ella die.

Staff were waiting at the hospital and Eleanor was rushed through the double doors of the emergency area. Isabella gave her sister's details to someone in a white coat; what she had eaten and drank and she handed over the extra two pills to show what she'd taken. After giving her address and contact details, they were turfed out to the busy A and E waiting room.

They decided to take turns to go to the washroom in case they missed news of Eleanor. Alex was glad when she could peel away the false eyelashes and wash the heavy makeup off her face.

She couldn't help sobbing, her tears mixing with the warm soapy water and whirling away. What if Eleanor should die because of a night of fun? … more tears coursed down her cheeks. Her face was pink and blotchy from hospital soap and paper towels but she didn't care, she felt clean.

She tied her hair back, wrapped the doorman's scarf around her neck to provide more cover over her skimpy dress and went to sit and wait.

Someone, in a nurse's uniform, with a kindly face came over with a tray. 'There you go girls; you'll feel better after a hot drink,' she said as she handed them tea and biscuits. 'We called home and Eleanor's brother picked up. He is coming straight here to collect you all.'

Bella grabbed Alex's hand and her wild look mirrored Alex's feelings. Holy shit, Dan! He would be *so* not amused by this. Holding onto Bella's hand, Alex sat silently keeping watch on the doors into the treatment area and the hands of the clock and prayed that Ella would be OK.

3

Cleo woke with a start and it took her a moment to realise that she was in her old bed in High Rigg. She'd been woken by a noise, something familiar but she could not place it. She raised herself up onto one elbow and listened intently, straining to hear. Was the noise from Mum's room? She got up and slipped along the hallway to peer through her mum's door. Slow, steady breathing reassured her that all was OK in there.

As she retraced her steps to the doorway of her own room, she heard it again; heavy rain battering on her window pane. Only it wasn't raining. This time she knew immediately what it was, someone was around the back of the cottage and throwing gravel at her window. The only person who used to wake her like that was Dan.

She strode over to the window feeling more curious than scared; this was Dunleith, quiet, sleepy. Who would know she was here in her old room? Peeling back the curtains and peering into the back garden, she saw Dan's face looking up at her.

A spike of adrenalin jolted her heart so fiercely that she gasped for breath. She closed her eyes and opened them; was she dreaming? No. Standing in the garden and gesturing for her to come downstairs was Dan Collingwood. She was certain it was him, even by moonlight.

The years rolled away and she was in her teens again. She let the curtain fall. He lived in Australia, what the hell was he doing here?

Was it shock or nerves giving her shivers as she hurried downstairs? She realised she was wearing old pyjamas covered in faded teddies, a relic from years back that she had found in her drawer. Add unbrushed hair and a bare face and she was the most unready she had ever been to meet up after all these years. Bloody hell, Dan!

Cleo opened the back door and peered around it.

'Hi, Cleo, it's a good thing you're here this weekend... Can I come in?'

She opened the door a little further; the kitchen was still in darkness. Dan strode past her,

'It's an emergency or I wouldn't have woken you,' he said in a hushed tone.

Cleo turned on the light and faced him. She hadn't said a word yet; she couldn't find her voice. He stepped forward and gave her a hug.

'My God, Cleo, you're looking bloody dreadful.' He rubbed a thumb tenderly under one of her eyes, the intimate gesture taking away the meaning of the words.

The one night she hadn't removed her mascara. She must look a real mess. Dan tightened his embrace, pulling Cleo on tiptoes towards him. Heat seared through her and she was aware of just how thin her ancient nightwear was.

Silently praying, please don't let them be see-through in this bright light, she pulled back, and tried to gather her thoughts.

'Thanks a lot, Dan. If I'd known that I was having a visitor I'd have made more of an effort.' Sounding annoyed might mask her discomfort and stop the strong urge to wrap her arms around him and never let go. 'Now what's this about an emergency?'

'It's the girls. They're in bother in Edinburgh. Don't panic, Alex is OK. It's Eleanor who's needed treatment.

She's recovering and almost out of the woods. They are all at the Royal infirmary and I'm going to collect them.'

'What happened? Was it at the concert?'

'No, they went clubbing...'

'Clubbing? They weren't meant...'

'Look Cleo, we can talk in the car; we really need to get going. Grab some clothes and I'll tell you on the way.'

As Cleo got changed, swapping washed out pjs for hair-covered, cat-clicked trousers and a sweater, the whole situation felt unreal; it was as though time had dropped away. Being held by Dan had felt like coming home. After checking that her mum was sleeping soundly, she went downstairs with a pen and paper.

'I need to leave a note in case Mum wakes up. What shall I say?'

'Just say that you've decided to run off with me, at last,' he smiled.

Cleo felt the beginning of a blush as she went to the table to write 'Be back soon, love Cleo x'

Dan's hands were on her shoulders as he gently turned her round, looking serious.

'I didn't want to phone the house this late at night. I knew you were here and thought it would be best to tell you about this rather than your mum. We can decide how much the grownups need to know once we've got the girls home.'

How easy it was to fall into old ways, they'd always called their parents the grownups.

His hands, still touching lightly on her shoulders, were making the fine hairs of her skin stand on end, his presence was overpowering. Gently, Dan folded her into his arms. Had his lips brushed the top of her head? She couldn't be sure but the trembling she felt was ridiculous. She pulled back; it was unnerving to feel what his nearness was doing to her, even in a crisis.

Dan was driving his father's car, he told her that he'd

been staying with them for a week and that he was keeping an eye on the twins while his parents were on a wedding anniversary getaway to St. Andrew's.

As he slid the car into gear, he gently brushed Cleo's knee and she twitched at the touch.

'Sorry Cleo,' he apologised.

'It's OK, I'm just ticklish.' That sounded stupid and hot colour rose in her cheeks again.

'I remember.'

Oh damn it, she was blushing even more.

'I don't know about you,' he said, 'but I feel like we are back to where we were all those years ago, well... almost.'

Cleo nodded but didn't answer. She couldn't speak.

Their journey through to Edinburgh was swift because the roads were clear in the early hours.

Cleo started to feel more at ease as Dan outlined what had happened to the girls and they discussed how they would handle the situation. Both agreed that tonight was not the time for lectures. After all, they had seen enough in teaching and medicine to accept that drug experimentation was, unfortunately, part of growing up. They agreed to talk to them later about 'using' and going to clubs when underage.

'Even though we blagged our way into a few clubs?' Cleo queried.

'That was then and, besides, we were students living away from home; we didn't need to fool the grownups about our whereabouts.'

With Joe and Mary Collingwood being away and Teri unaware that there was a crisis, they agreed to keep this escapade to themselves. Surely the girls would be sufficiently shaken by this experience to learn from it.

Cleo relaxed back in her seat and listened to Dan talking about his travels, his work in Australia and the possibility of getting a consultancy at Newcastle's heart unit, he was here to look around and meet the team before deciding whether he wanted to apply for a post that was coming up in a month or two.

He asked Cleo about her career and she found herself telling him of her work as a deputy head in the inner city of Newcastle and how she had just started her dream project of setting up a unit for teen mothers and pregnant students within the school.

'It's almost underway. We've had a donation to help with the setting up of the 'TeMPs' unit, that's what we're calling it for now, and I'm presenting the case for our school setting up and running the unit, to the governors next Thursday. I'm keeping it short and persuasive but can't help changing it to add something new every time I look at it. It's got to be right.'

'Ever the perfectionist, Cleo,' Dan smiled at her and it made her stupidly happy. The miles flew by and they were soon on the outskirts of Edinburgh.

As they approached the Royal, Cleo attempted a quick hair repair and a touch of make up by the light of the passenger mirror.

Dan stared at her. 'You look absolutely fine... for this time in the morning.'

Cleo wasn't sure if that was a compliment or not.

In accident and emergency Cleo let Dan do the talking, hospitals were his thing and she never felt quite comfortable in them.

They were directed to a ward and there, in a side room, they saw Eleanor lying back in bed and Alex and Isabella sitting either side of her. They all looked exhausted.

Cleo couldn't believe their outfits. Why didn't she think to bring them jumpers? She might have guessed they'd have no coats with them.

Eleanor's face lit up when she saw her brother and the other two stood up to receive a big hug from Dan.

'Sorry, sorry, don't be mad,' started Isabella.

'Hold it, this can wait till later' Dan calmed them down.

Alex looked over at Cleo standing in the doorway; if she was surprised, she didn't show it. 'Hello there big sister,' she said, but she stayed in Dan's arms and didn't approach Cleo.

Cleo brushed the uncomfortable, feeling of hurt away.

The staff on duty explained that Eleanor had collapsed with hyperthermia, her body overheating. This could have been lack of water and the heat of the club but was likely due to taking the pills.

Although 'legal,' they were lethal. Shady manufacturers kept changing the contents slightly, therefore the drugs were not yet on the banned substances list. After a chat with Dan, the registrar was willing to release Eleanor so they could all go home.

Dan drove to Aunt Maggie's to collect their things and to leave a note for when she woke up. It explained that one of them was ill, so he had come to take them all home. It was five o'clock and dawn was breaking by the time they were on the road home. The three girls dozed in the back of the car.

'It's all very quiet back there. Shall we put some music on?' Dan gestured towards a compartment of CDs, his Dad's car didn't have iPod technology. 'They're an old selection from student days. You might remember some.'

Cleo glanced back at the girls and picked a few CDs to browse through. 'Those three have an e-type hangover, I'd say. The kids where I work call it 'thizzed.' With some, we have to try to teach them when they're like that.' Cleo knew they'd feel rough for a few hours.

The CDs brought back happy times of being with Dan. Which one was safest to play? The Fugees? Too intimate; held too many special memories. She opted for the safety of The Kaiser Chiefs.

Alex could hear the conversation, but kept her eyes

shut; saying nothing. She hadn't expected either of them to understand. She had to endure ancient music, but was so relieved that she didn't have to listen to a lecture, right now. Party beans, never ever again!

Alex was half awake and wanting to sleep as Cleo helped her upstairs at the twins' house. It appeared that she was going to stay with the twins; maybe Mum wouldn't find out she'd been an idiot. She was thankful to feel a pillow under her head. She was head to toe with Isabella and Eleanor had a bed to herself. They were so lucky that she was alright.

Alex was just drifting back into sleep when she heard Cleo talking to Dan outside the bedroom.

'Mum's asked me to take charge of Alex for a while. She needs a break and wants to explore Egypt and I'm glad she's doing something for herself for a change. She didn't exactly say she was struggling with Alex but, if this is the way things are going, she does need some help with her. Mum must hope that I can instil some sort of guidelines and work on Alex's attitude. I've just agreed to do it tonight and now I know what a task it's going to be.'

'Don't overreact, it won't be that hard. This is a one off, they all said so. I think Alex is a great kid, Cleo, give her a chance.' Dan's voice faded as their footsteps carried on downstairs.

What? Alex tried to clear her fuzzy head. Had she heard that right? Mum wouldn't do that to her. Would she? Never! She must be having a nightmare.

Dan drove Cleo back to High Rigg as the sky took on the silvery blue of morning and a slender crescent of moon, as well as a new sun, lit the sky. Mrs. Weddell was opening her shop to sort out the morning papers and did a startled double-take as they passed her in Dr Collingwood's familiar Volvo.

Dan smiled, 'Did she catch who was inside, do you think?'

'She's either seen us and she'll let everyone know that you were taking me home in the morning, local news with their morning paper. Or she hasn't and she's wondering who has called out the doctor on a Sunday.'

'I must call in for a newspaper on the way back to make sure she has her story right.'

'Dan, don't you dare,' Cleo laughed. There was never much privacy in Dunleith.

They left the village and were approaching the drive to High Rigg when Dan stopped the car.

'I'll drop you here because there is just a slight chance that your mum hasn't woken up yet; and you won't want Betty next door hearing the engine and peering through the curtains to confirm Mrs. Weddell's Dunleith bulletin.' He had his arm over the back of her seat and had turned to look at her in a way that made her insides melt.

'Thanks Dan. Thanks for sorting out the girls. Although it was a hell of a night, it's... it's been lovely to see you again.' That was an understatement, she could hardly bring her eyes to meet his. Could she trust herself, if she was caught up in his gaze? No way.

'I've missed you, Cleo. I was determined that I'd see you when I came back.'

Cleo looked into the deep blue eyes that she knew so well and knew that this was what she wanted too. They both moved forward, their lips met and she was lost in his kiss. This was what she had been longing for all night.

A bicycle bell broke the spell and they parted to see Alf Chapman touch his cap and grin as he rode by with the morning paper under his arm. They both grinned back.

'Alf's a man of few words, we're OK.' Dan gave a wry smile and then she caught his questioning look. 'What are you doing next weekend, Cleo? Any chance that we can go out, meet up away from here, and catch up on one another without the world watching?'

Shit! What could she say? She hadn't mentioned Neil. Hadn't thought of him until now. 'Sorry, I'd love to Dan but... but I'm away. It's half term and I've booked a trip to Italy.'

'That sounds great. Maybe we can meet up after that? I'm owed some time off so I'm staying here for a couple of weeks.' Dan was brushing her hair from her face, so that she couldn't hide her discomfort behind it.

'Is something wrong? You do want to see me don't you Cleo?' His eyes seemed to burn through her, scorching her cheeks as she searched around for the words that she needed.

'Yes, of course I do! More than anything.'

'I'm hearing a 'but'. What is it? Is it too late for us to give each other another chance? Is that it?'

Damn, why hadn't she mentioned Neil before now. She'd have to tell him the truth.

'No, Dan. It would never be too late. It's just that I am seeing someone else at the moment. I'm going to Italy with him. We're not that serious.'

'Not that serious but you're going away with him for a week? That sounds bloody serious to me Cleo, or you've changed,' Dan's eyes blazed into hers.

'You haven't let me finish, Dan.' Cleo grabbed his shoulders and held onto him.

'I don't need to. Here you are agreeing to meet up with me after your holiday, and all the time you know you're off with your boyfriend. I think I've heard enough. It wasn't a fling on the side I was thinking of.'

Dan leaned over her and opened the door. He wanted her to leave and he wasn't giving her a chance to explain.

'Look, Dan. I didn't know you were suddenly going to appear. I didn't know that I'd still have feelings for you. Stop being so bloody judgemental.' She was out of the car but wishing Dan would look her way. When he did, his eyes were blue ice.

'Goodbye, Cleo. Enjoy Italy.' He drove off leaving Cleo feeling angry and hurt and wanting to be back in his arms.

4

Late on Sunday morning, Teri took a mug of green tea outside; the sun was bright and trying hard to warm the flagstones and open the flower buds. She had slept soundly and hadn't woken until Cleo brought her tea after nine. Cleo had looked tired. Maybe what she'd asked of her had given Cleo a restless night.

She sat beside Pharos who had the sunniest spot on the bench. He purred and rubbed his head vigorously into her knee. Pharos had been a present, better than any diamond, for her birthday in the year that Alex was born.

Mac, her husband, had found a breeder and had secretly been on a waiting list for one of the first Egyptian Maus to be bred in England because Teri loved all things Egyptian, especially cats, and he had loved her.

Teri felt sure that Pharos had been the lucky talisman that had helped her to conceive after years of hoping for another baby. Mac had laughed at that but agreed that it had been a strange and wonderful coincidence.

Cleo came to join her; she'd showered and seemed brighter. She hesitated before moving Pharos onto the ground and taking his warm space. Teri noticed his glare of indignation before he turned, nimbly jumped onto Cleo's shoulder and then landed lightly onto the garden room roof.

'A clicked jumper again! Cashmere ... Reiss...I do try

with Pharos Mum, but look, I'm sure he dug his claws in on purpose.'

Teri leaned over to examine the beginning of a hole and dangling threads. 'I'll fix it so it won't show before you go,' she soothed. 'Now, we talked about me all last night, you must tell me how you're coping with work and what's new?'

As she heard how the plans for the new unit for teenage mums and pregnant students were progressing and saw Cleo's eyes sparkling with enthusiasm, Teri's heart swelled with pride. This project was partly for her; Cleo knew what Teri had missed out on in her teens. If she had been able to stay on at school when she was pregnant with Cleo, she would have been able to take her place at Oxford studying Ancient History. She had never stopped studying and, although she had no degree, she was an expert on Ancient Egypt.

Would she change her life even if she could? No way. She had moved to Manchester and used both her knowledge of Egypt and her creativity to make a living in designing and sewing quilts, tapestries and then she had got into creating stage clothes for glam metal bands.

During that lucky run in the eighties, she had moved to London, made a name for herself in music and art circles and made her fortune without qualifications.

She'd known Mac from the first week she arrived in Manchester and, when she moved South with Cleo and he moved North after his course finished, they had missed one another. It took less than a year for them to realise that Teri and Cleo should settle here with him and Teri should become Mrs. McAplin; well, the wife of Angus McAplin.

She hadn't changed her name and Mac hadn't expected it. She'd been perfectly happy to give up being a rising star of design. Back then, Teri hadn't wanted to attract too much attention with intrusive questions about her background anyway.

A first in history didn't matter to Teri, but she was keen on the idea of enabling young mothers to continue having a good education and the opportunities they would have. The more she heard about Cleo's work in her school, the more she thought she had made the right decision to send Alex there for a few weeks. Alex could see just what her big sister was achieving and would, perhaps, look at her in a different, more positive light.

Life was good on days like this. She would have both girls here for lunch and she just knew this summer with the girls together would be a big step forward for them all.

Alex walked slowly towards High Rigg later that morning. Her mouth was dry, she felt like death and worse but she had been glad to get out of the Collingwood's house and Dan's unfathomable gaze. He seemed calm, but what had he been thinking? Would he keep his word or would he spill the beans, or the use of party beans, to their parents?

She shuddered as she recalled facing him and the eggs and toast he had made them all. The three of them had gone downstairs when he called them an hour ago and had stuffed some breakfast down in a suffocating silence. Alex had chewed on her toast wondering how long before it would seem decent to crawl back to the girls' bedroom or slip off home.

It was Dan stating that they all needed a walk with the dogs down by the river to get some fresh air that had pushed Alex into making her excuses and heading for home, but for what?

Tears welled up and her nose started running, why did she never have a tissue? She sniffed and wiped her eyes with her scarf, not exactly hers, the doorman's scarf from last night. Her proof that their nightmare had been real. She was taking the long route from the Collingwood's but it was still only ten minutes door to door.

Her walk slowed down even further, she was going

from hell to purgatory, or was it from purgatory to hell? Whichever was worse, Cleo was it! The best scenario would be that her oh-so–busy-and-important sister had shot off back to Newcastle and her oh-so-busy-and-important life. Turning into the lane she could see the snazzy little sports car still on the drive. No such luck.

What about that conversation she'd heard last night? Cleo and her, it couldn't work. Please God, if there is a God and you are there, then please let me have the rest of today off from my crummy life.

She couldn't resist kicking Cleo's tyres as she passed. She glanced into the interior; so tidy! Nothing like Mum's Range Rover that she was learning to drive. Seats with books and shoes and wrappers and CDs that showed ... showed what? Their lives she supposed.

Walking around to the back of the house she could see her ladyship reading the paper in the garden room. Oh yes, why don't you chillax all morning and let Mum cook dinner, eh? Sure enough Mum was in the kitchen by the stove and... Whoa there it was, the smell of roasting beef. Of course, it had to be, Cleo's favourite. She wanted to scream. Why did her mum bend over backwards to please *her*?

Mum glanced up and Alex rushed over to hug her, breathing in the fresh smell of lime and clean hair and baking.

'Mum, I so love you! She buried her face into her neck and kissed her.

'Hi poppet. You missed me? Good night at the concert?' Teri, smiling, looked into her eyes and Alex saw the cloud of concern wash over her. 'Are you OK? You look peaky sweetheart? Was it a late night?'

Alex looked away and fiddled with a tatty extension that she'd forgotten to remove from her hair. Mum didn't know a thing after all.

'I am a bit tired Mum. I think I'll just go and lie down.'

'You'll do no such thing. Mum has been cooking for half the morning and we have waited for your return.'

Her sister was in the doorway looking like she was in charge, as always. Alex threw Cleo her coldest, most sullen look and ignored her remark.

'I'm going upstairs for an hour Mum, OK?' she said, still meeting Cleo's glare.

Cleo stepped into the kitchen, hands on her hips and her eyes darkening even more in anger, 'Mum, that's ridiculous, she has it too easy. Alex can help us with lunch. You shouldn't be so soft with her.'

Alex stomped upstairs. She couldn't stand to see her mum hanging onto every word that Cleo uttered. She flopped on her bed, popped her earplugs in and selected shuffle on her iPhone. Music then sleep, just an hour of oblivion.

What the hell? Her earplugs were yanked out and she was pulled into a sitting position. She looked into fearsome brown eyes as a finger pointed too closely at her face.

'Listen here, you selfish little madam. You aren't the only one who got very little sleep, remember,' Cleo hissed in her ear. 'Now you have two minutes to get off your backside and downstairs, and then you'll smile and make decent conversation at the dining table. Got it? If you don't, I might be tempted to tell mum exactly what her 'poppet' was doing last night.'

Cleo stood up grabbing Alex's iPhone from the bed, 'As for this, you'll get it *if* you behave, just before I leave. Now get moving.' She turned on her heel and swept out of the room.

Bloody hell, she had no energy to argue with *that,* thank God the dragon hardly ever came home. Alex headed for the bathroom; maybe a quick shower would warm her and wake her up. Her sister wasn't one to mess with.

After her shower, Alex made her way downstairs. Sunday lunch was served late and, although it felt a bit strained, she thought it went off OK. Cleo was polite in front of Mum and the subject of Mum taking a break wasn't mentioned.

Alex was grateful that she had time to prepare to do battle. She didn't want to upset her Mum but she had to persuade her to drop the idea of that high-and-mighty doylem being in charge of her. She even managed to clear up and stack the dishwasher with Cleo afterwards.

At long last, Cleo headed for home and left Alex's iPhone on the hall table. She could take it to the tranquillity of her room and plug into some music. As she felt her body relax into the bed, she breathed a long sigh of relief. When was Mum going to mention her ridiculous plan? Whenever it came up, she was forewarned and she would be ready to tell Mum that putting Cleo in charge of her was the most hideous idea ever.

FLOWER MOON

5

Cleo's week flew by and when Thursday arrived she was well prepared to deliver her presentation. Bearing in mind the mix of people who were governors at the school, she had spent hours on making sure her slides would get her message across to them all.

After all that preparation, Cleo was running late. Maybe she should have stayed at school instead of coming home to change. She noticed a message flashing as she passed the worktop where her phone was lying. Oh no, she'd left her phone on silent again. The text was a reminder that her taxi had arrived. Already? She checked her watch, bloody hell, talk about cutting it fine; she had twenty-eight minutes to get back to school. That's if the driver was still waiting.

A last minute touch up of her nails, with a quick-dry polish, meant she had to pick up her bag and attempt to put her phone into the side pocket with stiffened digits, *Edward Scissorhands* style. Her phone flashed again, an incoming call. Damn, she just didn't have time to answer. Blowing on the nails of her free hand, she took another glance at her watch and decided that, whoever it was, her caller would have to go to voicemail. Twenty-seven minutes to get to the room and ready to greet the governors who were attending tonight's meeting.

In the two years that Cleo had been deputy head, she

often went along to governor's meetings. None had made her feel as nervous as this one. Presenting her plan to create a purpose built unit for pregnant students complete with crèche that would serve their own school and others in the area was going to be a challenge. The project was close to her heart and she couldn't contemplate the governor's declining the idea. It was what the area, the girls and their babies needed and the plans had to go through.

Cleo ran downstairs from her apartment to her waiting taxi.

'Three minutes on your meter already, pet,' warned the driver. Cleo caught his triumphant look through the rear view mirror.

'I know, I know, I got held up. Just take me along the river route to Tyneview please, it's quickest.'

He shrugged. 'If you say so.'

Touché. Cleo knew that back route was also the cheapest. Hoping her nails were dry, she tunnelled through her bag to check her USB flash drive was still there in the small zipped pocket and then moved past her heeled shoes for later and a myriad of other daily necessities to reach a bigger pocket stashed with tubes of sweets. Grabbing a half tube of love hearts to munch on, she settled back into her seat.

It was Cleo's first chance to relax since she'd rushed down a sandwich at lunchtime while planning a cover timetable for a teacher who'd gone home sick. There hadn't been any spare staff to cover the last lesson and that Year 10 class would have been troublesome for a teaching assistant, so Cleo had covered the lesson herself and enjoyed teaching the class.

Her planned quick getaway at four o'clock was shelved when an irate mother, wearing a jeweller's shop worth of chains and studs, had come into reception to protest, on her daughter's behalf, about the school's 'rubbish' jewellery policy. She had been adamant about seeing 'one of them bosses' or she'd be reporting them to 'the civic'. An hour, two cups of tea and a few tissues later, Cleo had waved off the mother who had problems coming at her from all directions and had needed to vent her spleen on someone about something.

All this had left Cleo with just over an hour to get home, freshen up, park her car for the night and get into a taxi. She would have stayed in school until after the meeting, but she was meeting her friend Heather, afterwards.

Heather juggled a hectic family life but always kept their every-other-Thursday night catch up, so Cleo made sure that she did too and this quick turnaround was worth it. She hadn't spoken to Heather all week and they'd have loads to catch up on.

Cleo ran through all the points she wanted to get across to the school governors at the meeting that lay ahead. Her plan to open the unit was a brilliant one and one massively generous donation meant they had the funds for it. Her project would enhance education in the whole authority because other schools were eager to opt in to the facility.

She knew it was what the city needed and the rest of the school's leadership team agreed, but she had a mixed bunch of governors to convince. Her presentation had to be a success. It was because of Mum and what she had gone through having Cleo in her teens, that she was determined to get this unit up and running.

As they approached school, Cleo remembered her missed call. She checked to see who'd been trying to reach her. Was it Mum ringing to wish her luck? No, it was a voicemail from an unknown number. Whoever that was, they would have to wait.

They were an hour into the meeting before it was time for

Cleo's presentation and she had used that hour to guess who she could count on and who she would need to persuade. She thought the numbers were even so she certainly had her work cut out.

'Miss Moon, can you talk us through your proposal for refurbishing the East wing of the school? Explain what you want to use it for and go over the funding for your project?' The Chair of Governors gave her an encouraging smile, he had been very impressed when he first saw the plan and would back her.

'The East wing of the school is in sound condition but it has not been used since we opened the new sports block last year. I've done a fair amount of research and found that, with a refurbishment that is mainly cosmetic, we can utilise the wing to open an education area for teen mothers and pregnant students and run a crèche for their babies.' Cleo's power point sprung into action and showed how the wing would be transformed.

She'd added some cute baby pictures from another nursery she'd visited to try to soften the harder hearts. These were left on screen as Cleo closed with, 'This evening, I would like you to consider how much this TeMPS unit would benefit the community and to agree with this plan in principle.'

'Is it *really* needed?'

'Surely we want to discourage this sort of thing not support it.'

'Are there enough cases to warrant a full time unit?'

'Seems very ambitious to me.'

'Pie in the sky more like'

A barrage of comments, queries and objections were fired across the table.

By now, Cleo was in her stride and, as she had anticipated these responses, fielded each question truthfully but with enough background information to show the board why the unit was necessary and how it would provide for several other schools, as well as their own.

'It's alright *you* asking us to agree to this in principle, Miss Moon, but where is the money being taken from? It must be taken from somewhere' the ruddy-faced, disgruntled vice chair butted in.

'Thankfully, that is not the case. We already have a small local authority grant to refurbish the wing and the running costs, which will be shared between all the schools involved, are less than educating these young people out of school.'

Then Cleo delivered her winning stroke. 'We have also recently been given a large donation to set up this teen mothers and pregnant students unit by a generous benefactor who wants to support this community.

'How large?' boomed Mr. Vice Chair.

'Half a million pounds *large*,' Cleo scanned the table and beamed at them all.

'Well blow me down, that's a different story.' The vice chair almost cracked a smile.

'Money to burn if you ask me,' Mrs. Harris whispered loudly to the equally miserable Mr. Harris; two killjoys in one marriage.

'Time to go for the vote then,' said the Chair. 'Those in favour?'

Cleo sat down and waited as the mutterings subsided and hand after hand went up. She'd convinced more than enough of them. Her heart was doing a happy dance. Now she could start making her plans a reality.

Cleo rested her forehead on the cool mirror in the staff cloakroom and let out a long sigh of relief. She looked up and grinned at her reflection. She had done it. The governors had believed in her; that she would be able to set up the unit for teen mothers and make the changes she wanted without too much extra cost to the school. Now she had to make sure her new ideas worked.

Under the harsh light of a bare light bulb, Cleo topped up her lip gloss in the old flecked mirror. She didn't look too bad considering she had been on the go since six that morning. Her dark bob was still shining, her fringe hadn't gone flat and black trousers teamed with her new cobalt blue jacket would take her easily from governor's meeting to the Vineyard wine bar, once she had changed into some decent heels.

If only her cheeks would lose the rosy glow they always took on when she was passionate about something. Presenting her ideas and answering all the challenging questions had given her cheeks spots of colour that did not go well with her new lip colour, 'Insouciance'. She'd liked the shade, but the name sold it. She'd bought it hoping it would make her feel that way during next week's mid-term break.

Cleo rushed down the echoing corridor turning off the lights as she made her way to the main doors, her mind half on the meeting and half on next week's half term break. Seven whole days and six romantic nights touring the Italian Lakes with Neil.

Half term would give her the chance to relax and spend more time with him. They had literally fallen for each other when they bumped into each other while skiing during the Easter holidays.

Living in different towns meant that they had only spent a few weekends together since then. She had to admit that Neil didn't give her butterflies or fill her waking thoughts, but he was fun, fit and entertaining and she was willing to give their relationship time to grow. He'd apologised for being sulky last weekend and promised to make it up to her on their holiday.

Jim, the caretaker, was at the door waiting to lock up and her taxi was parked outside.

'Enjoy the rest of your night,' said Jim. Cleo saw him

glancing at her change of heels.

'I'll enjoy what's left of it, Jim. You too. See you at opening time tomorrow.' Cleo liked Jim, he was great at his job and they were usually the first staff in the building and last out.

It was almost nine when Cleo strolled into the wine bar peering into the darkened space to see if Heather had arrived.

'Hi, over here,' Heather was waving from their favourite booth. 'A couple were just leaving our space as I ordered a bottle,' she said, deftly pouring a large Chenin Blanc for Cleo and returning the bottle to the bucket to chill.

'You can't guess just how much I need a seat and I need this too,' Cleo took a gulp of her wine. 'It's been a long day.' Their booth was ideal; they had a view of what was going on yet it was far enough from the music speakers to make chatting a possibility. Cleo took another sip of chilled wine and felt the day's burdens begin to loosen their grip. As Heather's gaze left the bustling bar and came back to her, Cleo beamed.

'Love your hair like that, Heather. It suits you.'

'You're joking, right? I was in a rush after putting Archie to bed and couldn't find the straighteners in the bedlam of my boudoir so I just had to come out 'au naturel.' I'm just glad we're in a darkened booth.'

Cleo knew that Heather got frustrated with the products needed to manage fair skin that hated the sun and softly waving hair. She loved the red-gold, bordering on ginger that you would never get in a bottle. Usually Heather had it tamed into a glass-smooth sheet of toffee or worn tied back, but the curls framing her face this evening suited her.

'First of all, I've got to tell you about my successful

presentation and how I think I can actually see this unit happen.' Cleo was off on her favourite subject.

Two generous glasses later, they had almost exhausted the ins and outs of education for pregnant teenagers and the trials of juggling journalism with domestic mayhem and emptied the bottle.

When Cleo came back with a second bottle, never a good idea on a work night but something that inevitably happened when they got together, she saw that Heather had a look of glee that wasn't just at seeing a chilled wine.

'I can't believe I haven't had time to tell you this already. Guess what's happened!'

'Oh no, not again,' groaned Cleo as she slid back into the booth.

The journalist in Heather loved to spice her conversations with the intrigue of a guessing game. It was likely to be about one of her men and Cleo was happy to play along. 'Now let me see, has Archie made a model to rival Antony Gormley's 'Angel' from his Play-Doh? Or, has Mark finally agreed to a puppy?'

'No, no, it's not about either of them. It's really a guess who, I suppose. Guess who Mark is meeting this very weekend.'

'Give up.'

'One big hint then, he was the first love of a very good friend of mine.'

'Dan?' Cleo's voice sounded funny and she felt a rush of heat to her cheeks. Thank goodness their corner was dimly lit, Heather missed nothing.

'Right first time. He's had enough of being the flying doctor of the outback and he's back here sussing out the job scene. Just imagine, he may be moving back here to the North East. Don't be surprised if he gets in touch.' Heather's smile was gleeful.

'Sorry to steal your thunder, Heather but I've already met him and it was a total nightmare.'

'You never said,' Heather gave Cleo an astounded look.

'I was going to tell you but the success of tonight's project put the humiliation of Saturday night right out of my mind for a while.

You might guess that, like all things that end badly, it involved Alex.'

Heather was so gripped by the tale of Dan and Edinburgh that, halfway through, Cleo had to remind her to take a sip of her wine. Cleo loved the way Heather added 'My God' and 'Oh no' in exactly the right places. It was good to have a sympathetic ear.

At the end of it all, Heather asked, 'So you *did* still have feelings didn't you? For Dan, I mean.'

Cleo twirled the stem of her wine glass, looking for an answer within the pale liquid.

She looked up, 'For a brief moment I thought that I did. The old attraction was still there but Dan and I were over a long while ago, you know that, and we've both moved on.'

Heather's enquiring reporter's eyes were watching Cleo so closely that she had to avert her gaze as she said, 'End of subject.'

'End of conversation for tonight,' conceded Heather. They'd all been friends and dated from sixth form. Heather and Mark had stayed together, married, had Archie and were like family to Cleo. Cleo and Dan hadn't made it.

Back at her apartment, Cleo set about the comforting ritual of getting ready for bed. This was a cleansing, toning and creaming workout that gave her time to wind down. Throughout it all, she thought about seeing Dan last Saturday. He had filled out and grown into those long limbs, he still had long hair that flopped over one eye and he was just as funny and good-natured. What she couldn't stop thinking about were his kisses; they aroused feelings that nobody else had ever come close to.

Sorting clothes for the morning was another 'must' before bedtime. As she hung her light grey suit and a white silk shirt outside of the wardrobe door, she was flooded by more memories of Dan. Those intense blue eyes that could melt even her practical heart. Try as she might to turn her thoughts to work, or to the list of jobs she had to do before she could relax into a week's holiday, Dan was there.

Their split, a year after they'd both gone to different universities, had been agonising. People assumed it was because they were studying in different cities but it hadn't been that at all. The main reason that she had fallen out, but not fallen out of love, with her first love was her sister. In Cleo's eyes, Alex Moon had a lot to answer for.

It was nudging onto midnight when Cleo crossed her bedroom to draw the curtains against the city lights. She paused, it was a new moon. As a child, it had felt special to share her name with that faraway globe in the sky.

She and Mum had always remembered good times on a full moon and made a wish to put into their 'moondream' jar at their first glimpse of a new one.

This was the beginning of a Flower Moon; Mum had taught her the name of each full moon. She had always supported Cleo in everything she wanted to do and now she had to overcome her dislike for Alex to give her Mum the break she deserved.

She reached for her phone to text Mum to say the presentation was a success and saw the reminder that she had a voicemail from an unknown caller. As she listened, she went from cold to clammy and her hand tightened around the phone.

'Hi Cleo, I wanted to catch you to wish you luck for your meeting and to say I didn't mean everything I said to you last weekend. I hope you don't mind that I got your number from Alex. Take care.'

That familiar deep voice melted her heart; he'd remembered her presentation was tonight and he had called. What did 'take care' mean? Was it goodbye or was it can we talk? Alex had given him her number. Her little sister had done something right for once.

A hectic day, followed by a lot of wine, had left Cleo with a raging thirst and a dull throb at her temples so she drank a glass of water and hoped that it would make her feel better by morning. Just one more early start before her mid-term break. Troubling thoughts of spending the whole of that break with Neil and remembering the way she felt when she heard Dan's voice meant that Cleo fell into an uneasy sleep.

6

Teri stepped out into a dull, grey Friday morning, noticing the fine haze that could turn to drizzle at any moment. Their Northumbrian climate was great for the complexion but not for aching bones. If all went as planned, she would soon be somewhere hot and dry and different.

As Teri drove over to the Collingwood's, she wondered what Mary would say about her idea for the summer. She had been friends with Mary ever since they'd both been pregnant 'older' mums.

Mary, Dr Collingwood's wife and receptionist, had three children going to Cleo's school and an active part in Dunleith life so, before their last pregnancies, Teri had known her well enough to say hello and chat about village events. The Collingwood twins came along as a great surprise when Mary was forty-one. Teri had been in her mid-thirties with a teenage daughter who happened to have a massive 'crush' on Mary's eldest, when they started the same antenatal class.

That first session, they sat beside one another in the back row behind a squad of eager first time twenty-somethings to hear about the changes in approaches to labour and rearing babies.

'I don't think I need this, it was my husband, Joe, who urged me to come along. confided Mary.

'Neither do I, it was your husband who told me to sign

up too.' whispered Teri.

'He can come to the next one. I think I'll leave at the break. Having babies hasn't changed.'

'I'll make my escape with you.' They scarpered off for a coffee and became firm friends.

A steady drizzle had set in by the time she reached the Collingwood's so Teri parked as near to Fernlea Lodge as she could get. It was a large gravel car park that served the house and the doctor's surgery and she wanted to be as near to the front door as possible to save the outfit that she was dropping off from getting wet. As she was taking it from the back seat, the door opened. She waved at Mary who was standing there with an armload of laundry.

'Hi, come in, Teri. Come and rescue me from stripping beds.'

Teri hung the dress along the picture rail in the hall and left a bag with shoes and makeup underneath it. 'Is this OK here, for now? Alex asked me to bring her stuff over because she's coming round to get ready at your house tonight.'

Mary nodded taking the dress and holding it against herself. Looking at her reflection in the hall mirror, she said, 'I couldn't get away with that now. I used to wear them that length too. The twins are looking forward to the sixth form disco, even though they claim to be far too cool for it.'

'Yes, it's not got the girls as excited as Edinburgh but they'll have fun,' Teri said, as they walked through to the large kitchen.

The farmhouse table was already set with a percolator of coffee, mugs and some cheese scones. This was always a kitchen of delicious smells.

'Actually, Alex has been subdued all week and I'm pleased she's off out with the twins tonight. I've been waiting to see if she's coming down with something.'

'Dan did have to collect them all because Ella was so sick after the concert. I thought it was the excitement but they may have caught something.' Mary poured the coffee and popped a scone onto a napkin and handed it to Teri. 'We'll save on plates.'

'Mmm, thanks. Yes, Alex told me that he'd picked them up so they didn't have to bother with the bus home on Sunday morning. He's so good with your younger ones.' Teri bit into her scone.

'Did you have a good catch up with Cleo?' Mary asked.

Taking a sip of coffee, Teri waded in. 'I wanted to talk to you about that. About why I needed Cleo to myself, I mean.'

'What's wrong? Why are you looking worried?' Mary's concern encouraged Teri to tell Mary about her plans.

'You're right, I am worried. It's a bit complicated and I hope I'm doing the right thing but I'm not sure.'

Mary sipped her coffee and waited. 'Come on Teri, spill the beans.'

'Ok. As you know, ever since Alex was born, Cleo hasn't really gelled with her. She's never really taken to having a sister and you could say it's the big age gap but, when I see Dan and the way he is with the twins... the way he is with Alex even, I can't help feeling it's not just the gap.

'I can see that they're not that great with one another. When she was younger and going out with Dan, Cleo didn't seem to mind the twins when she was around here but didn't like Alex being included in things.'

Teri put her head in her hands, this wasn't anything new to her but she hated hearing it.

'I'm sorry, Teri. I don't want to upset you more. Anyway, why are you thinking of all this now? What's brought all this on?'

Teri looked up. Yes, why? That was what she really

wanted to talk over. Taking a breath, she explained.

'I want them to bond, Mary. I hope this doesn't sound silly, but now that they're both grown up, my greatest fear is that they'll never regard each other as... as true sisters, as family. I'm annoyed with myself and worried that I've let the cold war between them go on too long and, if it's the last thing I do, I want to know I've done everything I can to get them to become closer. Be honest, does that sound daft to you?'

'Certainly not!' Mary hesitated before adding, 'It might take some doing. I mean, Cleo's in Newcastle and, when she comes home, Alex comes over here as soon as she can to avoid Cleo's company.'

'Exactly.' Teri sat back down at the table and sipped her coffee. 'When I was going through all that ovarian cancer treatment, I vowed that once I was on my feet, I'd sort out the girls. I was so tired afterwards and I was trying to pick myself up at first and then time passed... It was easier to fall into old ways of managing them and sharing my time.'

'And now?' Mary topped up their mugs and returned her whole attention to what Teri was saying.

'Now I need to sort it out, if I can. I don't know if Joe has told you anything about my tests?'

'Joe doesn't ever discuss his patients' health with... Oh Teri, don't tell me you're ill again?'

Teri could see that Mary was alarmed and shrugged, 'I don't know as yet. I went to Joe with this nagging bone pain that I've had for a while. It's getting worse and I think it might be nothing or it might not be good.'

'What tests do you have to have done?' Mary looked tearful but Teri knew that she wasn't the type to gush at her. She didn't need pity right now.

'As I said, it might be nothing, but Joe sent me to a consultant who suggested blood tests, an MRI and a CT scan just to see. I'm on some kind of relaxant and ordinary painkillers already for the aches I get and it could be natural ageing of my joints.' Teri tried to grin. 'Or, it may be the magic pills that I'm taking. They're good at keeping stray cancer cells in check but they can increase stiffness and pain in the joints, so I'm not panicking yet.

My consultant says it's all precautionary, but it has given me the shake-up I need about sorting out the girls. I can't become ill again without them supporting each other.'

Mary was at the cupboard finding glasses and pouring two drinks. 'It might be early for wine but there's nothing wrong with a mid-morning sherry at times like this.'

She handed Teri a glass and took a sip of her own. 'Right. So, what are you going to do and can I help?'

'I have a plan of sorts, and it might sound mad at first.'

'Try me.'

'I've promised myself a trip to Egypt for years. Something has always got in the way. First of all, I thought of inviting the girls along; although they haven't got my interest in Egyptology, it would be family time together.

Then I had a bolder plan; why not head for Egypt on my own and leave Cleo in charge of Alex for the whole time that I'm gone? What do you think?'

It was Mary's turn to pace the kitchen. 'I'm stunned. How long would you be away?'

'Two months or so to give me time to see all the sights and to give the girls a real chance to become close. I'm going to get an open ticket so I can book my return at any time.'

'It might work, or it might be a disaster. If it doesn't work out, we'll have Alex here so you can travel. That's no bother, truly. Don't worry about her.'

'You mustn't let Alex or Cleo know *that's* a possibility. I want the two of them to be thrown together and it'll be sink or swim for their relationship.' Teri knew her solution sounded rash but she hadn't got a better one and she hadn't time to make one. She'd already booked her flight and first hotel in Cairo for next month before she could back out.

Mary stood behind her and she felt a comforting squeeze on her shoulders. 'I can see why you needed a bit of time with Cleo to persuade her to go with that.'

'She agreed more quickly than I dared hope, if I'm honest. This weekend it's time to persuade Alex to stay with Cleo. I haven't wanted to mention it while she's so peaky.'

'I'm sure Alex will be fine, eventually. It's all bravado with her. Underneath her 'couldn't care less' attitude over her big sister, I'm certain Alex would love her to be nicer and have time for her. No Teri, it's not such a crazy idea at all.' Mary poured more coffee and Teri felt her mood lighten, this was all she needed. It felt wonderful to hear someone else say that this might work out.

'In fact, the more I get used to it, it's inspired thinking and the Egypt trip is just what you need. Tell me about that!' Mary smiled.

They drank coffee and enjoyed another scone while Teri described what she wanted to see and do. Mary looked enthralled but, as Teri was going to leave, she noticed her friend's face cloud over.

'What about these tests, though? Do you want me to go with you? Have you a date?'

'They're all done, one last week and one yesterday. You know I'd rather get these things over with on my own. The CT scan was quick and even the MRI was nothing; an injection, a walk around the shops for a couple of hours for the radioactivity to kick in and then lying very still while my bones were viewed from all directions. The results will be ready in a few weeks – or whenever I want them.'

'What's that supposed to mean for goodness sake?' Mary pushed her hair back from her face revealing heavy frown lines.

'Mary, these results aren't going to stop my trip. I won't agree to any treatment until I'm back. I've decided that I will only make an appointment to go over my results when I'm ready to hear them.'

'But it could be good news!'

'And it could be bad; I'll just wait until I've completed my trip and I'm ready to hear the outcome.' Teri was leaving Mary's feeling better than when she'd arrived, but she could sense that Mary was concerned.

Mary gave Teri an extra tight hug at the door and was about to say something when Teri distracted her with the dress hanging in the hallway.

'You'd *have* to be seventeen to get away with that shade of orange wouldn't you?'

'It's too hard to keep up with their fashion ideas,' said Mary. 'I'll take it up to the twins' room and promise I won't try it on!' They both laughed; Mary didn't look her age and was by no means plump but the dress was a slim size eight and might stretch over a thigh.

As the front door closed, Teri searched for her car keys in her bag and noticed that she had a phone message. Sinking into the driver's seat, she opened the text.

'Hi Mum. Italy tomorrow for rest and recuperation before I take up my teen care duties. Hope you've booked your trip. Love you lots. Xxx'

Marvellous. She'd got one daughter on side. Now she just had to break the news gently to Alex.

7

Cleo had never slept so badly. Troubled dreams meant that she was already wide awake when the alarm went off on Saturday morning, the first day of half term. She hadn't phoned Dan back but she couldn't stop thinking about him. What could she say to him when she was jetting off on holiday with another man?

She'd been dreaming about Alex too. Alex had been handing Cleo her phone to call Dan and when she woke up, she remembered the shocked look in Alex's eyes as she took her iPhone last weekend. Maybe she had been a bit harsh, but it seemed like her sister needed to grow up a bit.

As she showered, she thought about Heather's advice when they'd talked it all through, yet again, on the phone last night.

'You have no choice but to leave all this Dan and family stuff behind you for the week, Cleo. Go and recharge your batteries. This trip was already planned and you weren't to know Dan would reappear. It will show you how things are with Neil and you can sort everything else out when you get back.'

So that's what she intended to do. She wasn't going to burden Neil with any of her troubles; they didn't know each other well enough yet. She knew nothing about his family. She couldn't tell him about Dan but maybe she would tell him about the Alex situation when they got back. It would affect him if their relationship became more serious.

The airport was just a fifteen-minute drive away. Cleo got there promptly and looked around departures trying to spot Neil. The small airport was packed with families taking off for half term and long queues weaved up and down the baggage area for early flights to Majorca, Tenerife and Benidorm.

There were just a few people at the Bergamo desk, one or two business types and a middle aged couple who were speaking Italian. The queue was moving quickly and she didn't know whether to join it or wait.

Turning back towards the revolving doors, she saw Neil coming into the airport, smiling and helping an older woman through the doors with her case. He was wearing a white open-necked shirt and jeans under a beige linen jacket that skimmed his frame; he liked good tailoring. His dark blonde hair had been cut shorter, it suited his fine features. He carried his brown leather holdall and the woman's larger suitcase through into departures with ease.

The woman was thanking him effusively as Cleo went towards them.

'No problem, enjoy your journey.' Neil said. Catching Cleo's eye, he opened his arms wide and met her with a grin and a hug.

Cleo could see the older women shoot her an envious look before she moved on. She had to admit, he was a handsome, charming man and all hers for this holiday. She couldn't let a chance meeting with Dan spoil her chance of getting to know Neil better. Dan had been so unfair last weekend.

'A whole week away, it'll be wonderful,' she said linking arms with Neil and hoping she was right.

'Yes, let's get rid of these cases and relax in the bar.'

'Neil, it's 6.30 a.m. not p.m.' Cleo smiled at him

thinking he was jesting.

'You're not at school now, Miss Moon; we're celebrating our holiday and buck's fizz or a Bellini will be quite in order.'

Neil had left his credit card in his case, so Cleo settled their bar bill before they walked to the gate for their flight.

'Really, Neil, you are careless with your money,' she said. He'd lost his wallet when they met skiing and he'd needed his friends to bail him out then.

Neil was an expert skier, having spent a year in his teens as an instructor and he spoke fluent Italian. With his tan, his good looks and his speed on skis, Cleo had been bowled over; both literally by Neil as they both skied towards the café at the end of a red run and emotionally when she looked into laughing eyes as he picked her up.

They were chatting over a hot chocolate and had made a date for that evening when some of his friends joined them. One of them had told her that her date would be courtesy of him because Neil had lost his wallet.

'OK, OK, you don't need to lecture me, Cleo I'm not one of your naughty Year 10s!'

'Sorry, Neil, I know you're not.' He could make her feel like a stick-in-the-mud at times, was she really such a school marm?

'Anyway', he was smiling again,' let's get on the plane and drink a toast, to a fantastic trip.'

They arrived in Bergamo and walked through the newer area towards the Funicular, an old-fashioned cable rail that would take them to the medieval part of the city. It was late afternoon when they got there and the old cobbled streets, bathed in the last rays of sunshine, had a magical charm about them.

'Let's get rid of this baggage and take a walk around the old city wall.' suggested Neil.

'Sounds great to me, we can look for somewhere to eat,

maybe book it for later on our way back.' Cleo agreed.

Their hotel was just off the Piazza Vecchia. They found the old building and started climbing the steep steps leading to the entrance. Inside seemed cool after leaving the sunlight, it had a historic feel to it, dark with splendid paintings and ornate furniture.

'This is just perfect!' Cleo's eyes feasted on the sombre beauty around her. It didn't matter that the elderly gentleman on reception seemed to be looking at them with a dour expression, he was perfect for the building and its decor.

Cleo stood by as Neil spoke to the old chap, he loved showing off his ability to speak the language and whatever it was that he said, caused the chap to laugh. Neil seemed pleased that his charm had worked. *He does like to be liked,* mused Cleo. *Now, why am I thinking of that as a negative?*

Their room was spacious and high-ceilinged with a view of the bustling town from the little terrace. Cleo quickly freshened up, pulled a comb through her hair and added her holiday lipstick. Neil came behind her and picked up the elegant gold tube. He squinted to read 'insouciance' written in the circle on the base, translating he said,

'In Italy, it's 'Spensierato' I like that idea.'

'Know all,' she teased.

'*Sei cosi bella,* you are so lovely,' They kissed. Cleo lifted her arms round his neck and he murmured more in Italian while leading her towards the bed. Cleo sank onto the pillows; her holiday was getting better and their walk around the city would have to wait until morning.

They lay on the tousled sheets entwined in each other's arms and listened to the laughter and voices outside until it grew really dark.

'I'm starving,' announced Cleo sitting up and looking

admiringly at Neil's taught body. Their lovemaking had been a surprise. Neil had been a little rushed but he was passionate and they had lots of time over the next few days. It'll get better she told herself.

'Let's eat then, the chap at the desk recommended Dell Angelo's just around the corner. We'll shower and go.'

They shared the shower, quickly changed and Cleo was just about to pick up her handbag when Neil announced that his bank card wasn't in his luggage after all.

'Hell, Cleo, you will think I'm an idiot. Don't nag me; I must have forgotten to transfer it to this wallet. I have a hundred or so euros but you'll have to help me out with *your* card and we can settle up when we get home.'

Neil seemed upset, what could she say? She didn't want to ruin the holiday but she did feel annoyed. He *was* bloody careless about money.'

From Bergamo, they headed off for Bellagio, 'the pearl of Lake Como.' Their room was sumptuous; she adored the chaise longue at the end of their bed and thought about finding one for her apartment when she got home.

Neil used it as a deposit for all of his discarded clothes and she was itching to put his things away, but she stopped herself. She wasn't going to tidy up after any man even if it meant her OCD tendencies were offended by his used shirts and socks reclining on such beauty.

By the outdoor pool, she could feast on a panoramic view of the lake and surrounding countryside. Looking out on picture-postcard perfection was pure joy. They could feast on breakfast too which was plentiful but, for the rest of the stay, Cleo's card was hard hit.

She hired a car for them to drive right around the lake and their days were full. At night they ate nearby or in one of the hotels restaurants and listened to live music in the terrazzo bar before heading for their own room and a nightcap.

Several persistent niggles chattered around in Cleo's

head. Did Neil drink a lot, or did she drink very little? She had always liked a drink, but working her way well down a bottle of brandy wasn't her idea of fun after a busy day. It made less time for lovemaking and it was making lovemaking less fun that was for sure.

At bedtime, by the time she had cleansed and toned, she was greeted by snores, tiny muffled snores but they were definitely snores, irritating snores. Had Dan Collingwood morphed into a snorer? she wondered, and then felt annoyed with herself. She was comparing Neil with Dan more and more and it was doing her no good.

Their last day and night was to be spent in Milan. Cleo was looking forward to the shops and to buying herself, her mum and Heather a treat.

On the train, Neil suggested that Cleo should go shopping and he would sight-see on his own because he had very little cash left.

'Great idea!' she agreed feeling a rush of relief that she could enjoy her shopping without feeling guilty about leaving Neil out.

'We can meet back at the hotel when you have finished your spree.' suggested Neil

'Fine by me, about six?'

'OK.'

Cleo found a wonderful leather glove store in the main shopping arcade. Leather gloves of every hue, so soft and finely tailored and some really intricate designs. She spent a happy hour choosing a black pair with a pattern of silver studs on the back for herself, a rich beige with cashmere lining for Mum and a cut out design in Heather's favourite chocolate brown.

The tote bags were expensive, she couldn't work out whether Prada and other designs were cheaper here than in the UK or not; should she treat herself? I *should* have a lovely reminder of the trip where I decided to remain single, she thought. She used briefcase size tote bags for work and she spotted one in a dark purple shade that would work with lots of outfits. It took ten minutes of further deliberation before she convinced herself.

Leaving the shop with a large carrier bag meant for swinging and feeling content at being shopped out, she was about to return to the hotel when she spotted a small corner shop selling wooden trinkets. The animal jigsaw in the window was just perfect for Archie.

As she took one of the jigsaws to the counter, her eye caught a wooden sign.

'What does that mean?' she asked,

The girl shrugged, 'Non lo so.'

She was almost sure, so she bought it.

All spent up? Neil was showered and lying on the bed.

'Yes, I got quite a few things. '

'Show me,' he smiled.

He admired the bag and gloves and asked why she had bought a sign saying 'al giardino', 'to the garden,' when she didn't even have a garden.

'Mum'll love it for her garden room.' Neil wasn't listening; he was too busy pulling a bag from under the bed.

'I got something new too.' He took out a black jacket of the softest leather and threw it on the bed. It must have cost a fair amount.

'Wow, very nice. I thought you weren't shopping?'

'I had some very good luck today which meant I could shop and I can treat you to a special night out.'

'Did you find your card?' That would be a treat *and* a relief.

'No, I told you it's not lost, it's at home.' His smile slipped and she hoped he wasn't going to go into one of his moods. 'I had some spare time and a few spare euros so I had a flutter on some Italian fillies at San Siro and ... I won!' His smile was back again.

'That was lucky, how much?'

'Ah now, that is for me to know not you, but enough to take us out on the town for our last night.'

Cleo wasn't going to argue with that. She changed into a dress, strappy heels and, in case it turned chilly, she carried a fine lilac grey wrap in her new tote bag.

Neil was delighted she was carrying a bag big enough to hold his camera and his wallet because they spoiled the line of his jacket. Cleo had to bite her lip to stop herself from commenting that she felt like his pack horse. He was taking her out, she must try to enjoy the evening.

They had the most delicious seafood and linguine pasta and a bottle of Frascati that was so moreish that they ordered another. Neil didn't seem to be affected but Cleo felt her third large glass go to her head and was ready for her bed.

'Let's get to bed now, Neil, shall we?' She was tired and slightly drunk.

'Not now Cleo. Tonight we are going to try our luck at the casino. I'm having a lucky day.'

'Casino?' Cleo had never been to one in her life.

'Casino ... The most exciting place in the world when you're feeling lucky.' Neil looked animated as he led her out of the restaurant towards the Piazza Diaz.

I must shake off this sleepiness and enjoy our last night decided Cleo.

An hour later and Cleo was bored and confused. Neil had given her chips and she had won twice as many back but she didn't know how or why.

'Can we go soon, Neil?'

'Not now, I'm winning on this, look.' Neil indicated to his increasing pile of chips.

'Sorry, but I'm tired and we're flying tomorrow.'

Neil waved over one of the staff, said something in Italian and handed him several euros.

'This chap is going to call a taxi to pick you up and take you back to the hotel. You have a good night's sleep, I'll just be a while longer.' Already Neil's eyes were back on the roulette table.

What a great ending to our 'getting to know each other' trip thought Cleo. Well, I think I know enough by now.

Next morning, Cleo was showered, packed and ready to go for an early breakfast but Neil still wasn't back. He was cutting it fine; their shuttle to the airport was in an hour. What an idiot. She wasn't sure whether to worry about him or not but something told her that Neil would always take care of Neil.

He'll be in a real rush when he comes in, she thought. Should she help him with his packing? She decided that she may as well make a start and started folding his clothes that were strewn around the room and laying them in neat piles on the bed.

She started to empty the drawers by his bed and, in his sock drawer, she found a card case. Should she look? She couldn't help herself. There were three cards inside, Master, Visa, American Express and all in Neil's name. She put them back and closed the drawer feeling livid. Hadn't she been the fool! She wasn't going to make a scene here, but their relationship was over as soon as they touched UK soil.

Cleo went to the breakfast room on her own for coffee, fruit and toast but a solid lump in her throat stopped her from eating much. He had lied. Bare faced lies! A tear trickled down her cheek, but it wasn't because of Neil, it was the fact that she was worth more. She was rubbish with men.

When Neil returned, with minutes to spare and excuses tripping from his deceiving tongue about a card game, she was really calm. She could see that it surprised Neil. He had been expecting some sort of a row, but he didn't know much, she thought. People only row when they care. She didn't care if she never saw him again. She *was* worried about her bank account and what he still owed her though.

8

Cleo left her case in the hallway, kicked off her shoes and bundled up the mail nestling behind the door before she made her way into her living area. Sighing with relief, she flopped onto the sofa and looked around. The living space was light, airy, cool, quiet, empty and hers; she loved this apartment.

Kettle on, tea and look through the mail? Lie down for an hour on her own crisp, cream sheets and have the whole bed to herself? Unload her case and get the washing machine going? Ah, the freedom to choose, the freedom of not having to consider Neil's views and catch that petulant look on his face. She shuddered at the thought of him and went to lie on her bed.

Her thoughts were on overdrive. It was too quiet and she needed someone to talk things over with or someone who would distract her; stop her from ruminating over what to do about Neil and about her next few weeks with Alex. She also needed something to take her mind off Dan and how he had left her feeling unsettled.

It was a bank holiday so the chances were that Heather would be home; she'd send her a text to see if she was about. The reply came straight back and Cleo grabbed her car keys and a handful of sweets from her sugar-rush bowl and headed for Heather's.

She took real pleasure in driving round there with her

two-seater BMW's roof down, giving her hair and her mind a vigorous blast of refreshing air.

Walking round to the back of the house, friends and tradesman's entrance, she waved at Heather through the kitchen window.

'Come in and tell me all about it,' Heather called over the din of Little Mix on the radio and the washer on spin cycle.

Cleo side-stepped a truck full of wooden bricks and a tricycle to get over the threshold and circumnavigated two large islands of laundry to reach a stool.

'It's a domestic blitz, I see. Should've brought my holiday laundry.'

'I have to attack every now and then so we all have something decent to wear,' said Heather, busily stacking cups in the dishwasher while Archie was adding his own toys into the bottom rack and taking out the dirty cutlery.

Crouching down to replace the spoons, Cleo felt soft warm arms around her neck and a sloppy kiss planted onto her cheek from Archie.

'Hiya Cloee!' He struggled with her name. She loved the feeling of his sticky hands still clinging to her; she adored this little fella.

'I can't believe how fast you are growing,' she gave him a squeeze, breathing in the delicious, biscuity smell of him.

'Me helping Mummy,' Archie's solemn grey eyes looked into hers, 'Me a big boy.'

'You're such a big boy, Archie. Now why don't we put the forks into this part here?'

'Posting.' Archie nodded.

Heather placed a cup of tea on the breakfast bar and patted the stool. 'Over here, Miss Moon and tell all.'

Cleo removed the sharp knives and put them on the top rack, leaving Archie engrossed in filling the cutlery compartment and then emptying it onto the floor. Perching opposite Heather, she smiled, 'What do you want to know?'

'Everything. Did you have a good time? Do you still like him? Was it romantic?

'Disastrous,' stated Cleo.

'Cleo! I don't like the sound of that. Have you gone off him?'

'Totally.'

'Not joking?' Heather's eyes brightened.

'Definitely, seriously not joking.'

'*Good*. I didn't think he was your type when you brought him here, but never mind that. Tell me, how did you go off him? Is he rubbish in bed? Don't dare miss anything out!'

Cleo rummaged in her bag, and brought out a tube of love hearts and the remains of a tube of wine gums to help the story telling along. She was going to enjoy off-loading as much as Heather would enjoy advising.

'The place was fantastic and there was loads to do but he was hard work at times. He could be moody and he was a bit ...well, odd with his cash.'

'In what way odd? In what way hard work? Give me details.'

'You know I paid for the holiday with my card when we booked online? Neil said he didn't have the right card with him at my house. I was fine with that but I haven't had his half yet.'

'That's a bit much.' Heather scooped up Archie, wiped his hands and face and gave him his beaker of juice.

'Bearing that in mind, when we got to the hotel, he asked if I would mind paying for meals on my card because he'd forgotten to pick his card up and he only had a few hundred euros in cash with him.'

'Convenient, eh?' Heather's eyebrows were raised.

'Exactly. When I said 'Again?' he looked puzzled and I had to remind him that I'd paid for the trip online. He got all huffy, "I didn't think you were exactly on the breadline and needing that straight away," and made *me* feel mean for mentioning it.'

'Weren't you furious? I'd be bloody annoyed!' Heather was in there, eyes flaring.

'No, not really, just wishing I wasn't there with him really. After that, I resigned myself to shelling out and felt mean keeping all the receipts together. Now, of course, I've got the headache of asking him for the holiday money and the spends and feel bad for having to do that.'

'He's the one who bummed a holiday out of you, and he hasn't known you five minutes.'

Wails from the garden had them both rushing to the door. Cleo picked Archie up from where he'd fallen over some toy bricks and gave him a cuddle.

'He's tired and ready for his afternoon nap. Give him to me and I'll go and lie him down,' Heather said, reaching into the fridge and bringing out a bottle of wine. 'Get that opened and pour us a drink.'

Cleo handed Archie over and, as she made her way to the stairs, Heather called over her shoulder, 'Give me five minutes and when I get down, I want to know about the bedroom antics, I hope that wasn't all left up to you, too.' Chuckling to herself, she disappeared upstairs.

Cleo poured them both a glass and took hers into the garden. She could hear giggles from upstairs; Archie was gorgeous. Heather was lucky to have him and to have a great man like Mark and her career.

Maybe this 'all out' focus on work had meant she'd missed out on the family scene. Until now, she had always thought it could wait for later. *Get over yourself*, she tried to stop her thoughts in their tracks. Could this be her biological clock coming to life? No good getting broody while she was single.

Neil wasn't for her, she realised that. Now Dan, her thoughts drifted as they had all holiday, he made her feel different. Her romance with Dan was long over, so she may as well concentrate on working her way to a headship and being a doting aunt to Archie.

Taking a seat, she breathed in the freshness of the grass and felt the English dampness from the wooden bench. There had been an early morning shower but now the sun had come out and was trying hard to dry the grass, the bench and warm her skin. She was feeling better already just being with Heather and Archie.

When Heather came back downstairs, Cleo finished her holiday tale with the events of the final evening. They both agreed it was time to call it a day with Neil.

'We visited the most beautiful places but I was with the wrong person. Look at the snaps I took; the scenery is breath taking.'

Heather looked through the pictures on Cleo's digital camera and chuckled, 'You both look so happy; the camera certainly can lie.'

Cleo was staying to say hi to Mark when he came in from playing rugby. The door opened and Cleo heard Mark call,

'Set an extra place, Heather. Look who played for our team today.'

In stepped Dan. He hugged Heather and then stooped to pick up Archie. 'Hello big fella!' he swung a giggling Archie up into the air.

Cleo's heart flipped as his eyes met hers and he smiled before saying, 'Hi Cleo.'

'Fancy meeting you here,' she responded and then felt a blush flooding her cheeks. What a daft thing to come out with. Why was she so tongue-tied around Dan of all people?

'It's great to see you,' he said, 'are you eating here tonight? I hear the chef is greatly improved.' He smiled over at Heather who threw the dishcloth at him.

'No, I'm just leaving. I've...I've lots to do before work

tomorrow.' Cleo busied herself bringing out her presents for Heather and Archie and a bottle of Chianti for Mark. She was just about to leave when Heather insisted that she stay for dinner.

'You'll have nothing in. Nothing as good as my chilli, at any rate,' Heather said.

'OK, if you're sure there's enough.' She didn't need any more persuading.

It was almost like old times as they all laughed at some of the things they'd got up to. She enjoyed Heather's chilli and rice and, after one last cuddle with Archie and a kiss on her cheek from Dan, she took her leave because she really did have to unpack and prepare for school.

She'd had a lovely evening and kept churning over Dan's words, 'I'll see you soon, Cleo. Let's meet up again', until she pulled into her parking space outside her apartment.

As she got out of her car, she could see that her living room lights were on. Surely she hadn't put any lights on earlier that day? Cleo hurried upstairs and, as she unlocked the door, she could hear a sports commentary droning out from the television. She walked in to find Neil lounging on her sofa.

'What on earth are you doing here?' Her heart was pounding.

'That's a warm welcome, I must say.' Neil beamed his hundred-watt smile and it irritated her. 'I got home from the airport and found I'd had a massive water leak. Nothing I could do as it's a bank holiday and I can't live there until it's fixed.'

'So you came *here*?'

'I thought you wouldn't mind me staying a day or two. I can work just as easily from here. I've brought my stuff.'

'How did you get in?'

'I thought you would be at home and doing your laundry. You said you were going to do that.' Neil sounded aggrieved. 'Luckily, I still had your spare key from when I stayed a few weeks ago. Must've forgotten to leave it. Where have you been?'

'Out. I called in to see Heather and Mark and I ended up staying for dinner.' Why was she having to explain herself?

'I tried phoning.'

'I must've missed your call.' Cleo felt a bit guilty, she had seen his name come up onto her mobile screen when she was talking to Heather but had kept her phone on silent and hadn't called him back.

'Cleo, if you have already eaten, that's OK. Don't bother with much for me; a sandwich or a pizza with a beer will do.'

Cleo walked over to her kitchen. A pizza and beer will do, will it? She had loads to do before work tomorrow and here she was running after Neil. She was too drained to argue tonight. She had to finish this, but how?

9

Cleo closed the door and breathed a sigh of relief as she left for work early next morning. She had been able to get ready and have breakfast on her own, thank God. Neil had stayed slumbering away and showed no signs of being awake as she showered and crept around gathering the things she needed for school. She felt unsettled at leaving him in her apartment for the day when she wasn't there, but it couldn't be helped.

Neil slipped out of Cleo's mind completely as she thought of what she had to do before school started. She'd pop in to see the boss to find out what notices she had to read out at the ten-minute staff briefing, she'd listen to phone messages and make sure any staff absences were covered by members of staff who had a non-contact time and then she'd go along to the entrance to welcome staff in after their break and to ask them to look at her absence cover sheet.

She parked near the entrance, a perk of being one of the first in the car park, and met Jim cleaning the glass of a display cabinet in the school foyer.

'Did you have a good break, Cleo?'

'Great thanks Jim.' If only he knew, 'What about you?'

'It was fine until last night when we had vandals around the back. Graffiti all over the back wall, it'll take the cleaners hours to put it right.'

'It's time the kids were back at school then to keep them busy. Although it's not likely to have been any of our own, is it?'

'Looks like it was someone who knows Gracie Grieves and it isn't complimentary so I've sprayed over the writing until we can get it cleaned off.'

'Thanks Jim, that's thoughtful of you.' Gracie Grieves was a bright, mouthy girl in Year 11. She was always in the thick of things but no one deserved having crude remarks about them sprayed in a public place. She'd ask the Head of Year 11 to follow it up to see if Gracie knew who it might be.

Cleo saw the boss park his car and come into school. He came straight to her office with his coat on and car keys in his hand. The door was open, as it usually was.

'I have no special announcements for staff briefing, Cleo. Just remind them all to keep a check on uniform, especially trainers. I'm going to be out for most of today, but I'd like you to come back to my office at three to chat about your TeMPS project. I'll see you then.'

Cleo nodded, but he was off down the corridor. And a very good morning to you too, she thought.

It was a busy day at Tyneview High and Cleo didn't have a moment to spare until three o'clock. She had cleared her diary from then until the end of the day for the TeMPS meeting. It would be exciting to move on from the planning to the creating stage. Cleo had a timeline drawn up and she was sure Tef would approve.

Twenty minutes later, Cleo left Tef's office with her head pounding and tears pricking at the back of her eyes. Incredible, even for him! He'd sat there with that soapy-faced 'yes' man from financial services and had calmly popped all of her bubbles as if they were nothing! At the same time, his look had admonished her, warning her to be professional or pay the consequence. She had stated her case calmly but she got nowhere. It seemed like her project was off. But it wasn't just a project, it was more to her; it was so much more.

The school bell was due to go at any moment and then she was out of here for the day, enough was enough. She packed her bag, turned off her computer, closed the door to her office and reached the main reception desk just before the closure bell. As she signed out of school, Ann, one of the women from reception called over.

'Hi Cleo, are you off to a meeting somewhere?'

'Not today, I'm going home,' she said with a determined lift of her chin.

'Good for you,' Ann said as she watched Cleo head for her car to be first out of the car park for once.

'Something's happened to upset Cleo,' Ann told Jim, as he called into the office. It's not like her to do an early shoot off.'

Jim cast a look towards Mr Telford's office. Teflon Telford, that slippery sod, would be behind it.

Cleo was pulling her car out of the car park when the first pupils to leave trickled by. Where would she go? Neil was at her apartment and she didn't fancy facing him so early. Without thinking, she headed for Newcastle's quayside.

The Head had liked her idea of the TeMPs, he had officially said that in front of the governors. It would fit in with the new buzz-word of community coherence and he could offer places, at a price of course, to other schools in the nearby authorities.

She had presented her plan and budget to governors with his blessing and they had even been able to cost the whole new build due to a generous donation. Now, at the eleventh hour, he had changed his mind; the governors would be swayed to back him. Damn the man.

It was a great idea. It was needed! They lost a few young students every year because they wouldn't attend mainstream classes when they were too far gone and then didn't have the right crèche facilities to return to their studies once the babies were born. Other local high schools had submitted similar numbers so on those figures she had projected that each year there would be a small group of pregnant students and a second group of young mums with babies in need of tuition. The unit made more sense than home schooling and it gave the young people support and in a great environment for both them and their babies.

Before she knew it, she was parked by the Quay. The sun was shining, not even a wisp of fog on the Tyne today, so she sat at an outdoor table and ordered a latte with an extra shot. You could almost be on holiday, well some folk over by the bridge seemed to be.

The giant eye that was the moving Millennium Bridge of the Tyne was blinking and a group of tourists, cameras clicking, followed its progress. The 'eye' of the Tyne closed, making a footbridge across the river from Newcastle to Gateshead. On impulse, Cleo decided that, after her coffee, she'd walk over to the Southbank, wander around the Baltic art gallery and try to lose herself in an exhibition; the old flour mill always had something for her to love or hate.

She cradled her cup and sipped. Bloody Tef! Ditching her project... Fiddling with his stapler, avoiding her eyes, as he explained that an after-school sports programme would help the wider community and their large 'community cohesion' donation could be used for that instead of the TeMPS unit.

'Yeah right! There'll be far more photo opportunities and local news coverage with community sports than with pregnant students, too.' Had she really said that to him? She'd just managed to leave his office before she really lost it. Oh, to staple those well-manicured hands to his desk.

Cleo was reaching into her bag, to leave a tip for the waitress who seemed almost as harassed as she felt, when her phone rang. Seeing the photo that lit up on the screen, her heart leapt.

'Hi, Mum. Are you OK?'

'Of course I am, darling. Quite au fait with this mobile lark now. I need to be sure you can keep in touch with me while I travel; just emergencies of course. I might be up to texting you back and video chatting soon. Now, how was your holiday and what are you up to?'

'It's lovely to hear your voice, I'm having a coffee in town to cheer myself up.' Oh no, she shouldn't have said that.

'Why do you need cheering up sweetheart? Is it that man of yours being a pain?'

'He's not mine and yes he is but that's not what's upsetting me.'

'You're *upset*. Why?'

'Oh please don't be sympathetic or I'll blub.' The familiar voice did it: she missed her and she hadn't even gone off yet. Cleo's sobs, held back since that meeting, poured out as she filled Mum in on her shitty news.

She was aware of some of the tourists giving her odd looks as she strode across the bridge, probably ruining their photos but, at that moment, she didn't care. After crossing the Tyne, she stood in the entrance to the Baltic gallery venting out her anger and frustration and knowing that Mum would understand.

'It's not just the work I've put into it, Mum; it's something I'd be truly proud of. Especially after you having me...look at what I made you miss out on.'

'Hey, stop that this minute; I missed nothing my angel. Now you must dry your eyes and look at your plan again and go back in a few days and ask him to reconsider.'

'He won't.'

'He might darling. If you make sure your planning is

sound and you don't lose your rag but give him good reasons to go ahead.'

'I suppose you're right in that I should try again but I don't think I can keep my cool with him, Mum. He's devious and doesn't like to be crossed.

'Look Cleo, the flower moon is full tonight so you must harness its strength. It gave you your wish, to persuade the governors at the meeting when it was new, so be thankful and trust that your project *will* happen but you may need to help things along yourself, darling.'

'Mum, you're mad and I miss you already...'

'I'm hearing crackling, is that breaking up? Take care, Cl ...'

She'd gone. Cleo smiled, her mum had some loopy ideas. Politely asking Teflon to reconsider was more crazy than wishing on the moon. Well, did she have anything better to try?

Teri clutched the phone, long after it was silent. Her daughter was hurting and that ate into the mother in her, but she could sort this out. She was seething and she felt that she may have inadvertently made a blunder herself.

She scrolled to her solicitor's number and dialled. He was out, but his secretary assured Teri that he would call and up-date her on her charity donations as soon as he returned to the office.

Sports had its place, Teri was aware of that, but that wasn't what she had chosen to support when she'd made her donation to Tyneview. She didn't want Cleo to know it, but she had a great deal invested in the baby unit too and she was not going to rely entirely on the flower moon to sort this out.

10

Cleo called at her local supermarket to get something easy for dinner. What would Neil want? Would he have been shopping? After being on holiday, she had nothing in the fridge but couldn't face a big shop. Better get a readymade salad for two and a micro meal.

As she put her key in the lock, Cleo could smell frying and as she opened the door thick smoke escaped into the hallway. Her smoke alarm was beeping away and Neil was wafting a towel at the ceiling as if that would stop it.

'Hi Cleo, thought I'd treat you to a mixed grill but your grill isn't the same as mine and it's overheating or something.'

Cleo looked at charred steak and blackened sausages, Neil must've raided her freezer to find the meat, and a dozen oven chips in a bag - leftover from goodness knows when. He had opened a tin of peas and sweetcorn to complete the feast.

'There aren't many chips,' she said.

He had opened a window and the noise had stopped but the acrid smoke was choking them both.

Cleo fixed a smile on her face, retreated to her bedroom and closed the door to keep the smell out of her clothes. Oh hell, how could she stand another night with him? She shuddered at the thought of the burnt food as she changed into jeans and a fleece top. She'd have to say something.

Cleo walked back into the kitchen area, 'Look, Neil. Can I give the grill a miss? I've got some work to do and I'll make do with a salad or something later on. I really want to get my work out of the way first.'

'Oh, I've looked forward to seeing you all day and thought you'd like someone to spoil you. Can't work wait till later?'

Cleo felt uncomfortable; her awful day wasn't Neil's fault. 'OK, but I'll have salad with mine; you have the chips seeing as there's only a few.' Cleo sat at the end of the breakfast bar.

'I thought we'd have it at your dining table.' Neil smiled at Cleo and proudly led the way to the dining area. Her best glasses were out and he had opened a bottle of her expensive Rioja.

'Wow, Neil. This is OTT for a workday. I usually keep it simple and I don't often drink on work nights.'

'This will be a great change for you then and you can get used to the special treatment while I'm here.'

I don't want to get used to it and I don't want to get used to you either, she thought.

Cleo toyed with the cremated steak, ate the salad she had bought in and had a glass of wine before heading for her office.

The tiny box room was only big enough for her desk and a bookcase and when she opened the door, she gave a gasp. There was a suitcase by the door and a second laptop and piles of files on her desk.

'Neil?'

He came behind Cleo and gave her a hug, 'Hope you don't mind, I brought some more clothes and my work over. I wonder whether you could make some wardrobe room for me?'

Cleo turned and faced Neil and his dashing smile. It just wasn't working any more. 'Neil, just how long is this work on your place going to take?'

'Why? You aren't fed up with me already are you?'

Cleo said nothing.

'You know, I do believe you are, Cleo. I thought we had something... that you'd help me out in my hour of need. Come on darling, lighten up! Be pleasant to your old boyfriend, eh?'

'You are *not* my old boyfriend, Neil. We've only just met, really. We are just sort of dating. This is all a bit much.'

'Sorry I didn't realise you felt like that. I suppose you want to chuck me out with nowhere to go?'

'No Neil. I... I just don't want us to be living together. In fact, I was thinking of us cooling it a bit because...well I think we are a bit *too* different.'

'What do you mean? We had a great time on holiday, didn't we?'

'No. No we didn't, Neil. *You* had a great time. You enjoyed the holiday on my money and you haven't paid me back yet. You enjoyed the casino and left me to get back to the hotel on my own. You think of *you*.'

'Ha, that's rich coming from you Cleo.'

She could see his demeanour had changed and he looked daggers at her.

'Just listen to yourself. You think of you *all* the time. You don't give a thought for others. You wanted to leave the casino - why should I? Your office has some of my stuff in it and you want to call the whole relationship off. That's perfectly OK with me. I'm happy to do that, but really... I mean... doing it when you know I'm homeless for a week or two.'

'A week or two? You said a day or two.'

'The water damage, it's worse than I thought. I've had to pay out a lot of cash today so I was hoping to wait till the end of the month to pay you back. Do you want me to raid my long term savings? If you insist, I will.'

Cleo couldn't stop her resentment from spilling out. 'I

had to raid *my* savings for the holiday. Don't you think you should too? And, Neil, I know you had three credit cards with you in Italy.'

There was a long silence. Neil seemed to be unsure of his next move for once.

'What shall we do now then?' he had calmed down again.

'You should go.' Cleo was glad she'd said it at last.

'I can't. Not without somewhere else to go.'

'Haven't you got other friends to put you up? Or a B and B near your house?'

'I *need* to be able to work, Cleo. You have an empty apartment. Come on, have a heart!'

Cleo wasn't sure whether she was being mean or not. What would she do, if she was in Neil's situation? 'What about making an insurance claim?'

'If this was covered in my policy do you think I'd be here begging?' He looked such a crestfallen little boy. Not appealing, but not someone she could kick out.

'OK. You can have my spare room for now. Take your suitcase and dump it in that room. Take your laptop and files too; you can use the dining table to work from. I need my office.'

'Thanks, Cleo.' He came to hug her but she backed away.

'Not now Neil, I'd prefer it if we were just friends. Tomorrow, why don't you make your meals and I'll make my own? We'll flat share till you are ready to go back home. Let's *try* to be friends. I'm sorry, but I don't want us to be any more than that.' Cleo studied Neil's face; she wasn't sure how that had gone down.

Neil smiled, but it didn't reach his eyes and they stared coldly at her. 'You'll regret it and end up a sad old spinster, Cleo. I'm rather a good catch you know and you need someone to liven up your life.'

'Let's beg to differ on that,' Cleo took in a calming

breath before adding, 'I will live with my great loss if you can just keep out of my hair. When I'm at work, I work long hours and, when I get back here, I need space to think, relax and work some more. I'm sorry if you think I'm selfish, maybe I am.'

Neil moved his stuff out of the office and Cleo closed the door. What a nightmare! She turned her laptop on but couldn't face logging on to her work. She cleared her emails and surfed one or two favourite shopping sites.

It was almost bedtime when she ventured out to make a drink. Neil was in the spare room and she could hear that he was watching a film on his laptop.

Damn and blast, the kitchen was a disaster area of pans and washing up. Her crystal glasses were laying in tepid water with the grill pan. She was tempted to leave it for Neil to tidy up but the thought of drinking her morning coffee looking at that was too much. She was ready for something to chew on but her sugar-rush bowl was missing from the bench. He must be munching on her sweets as he watched the film.

Cleo rolled up her sleeves and spent half an hour putting the kitchen to rights before making a drink. She decided on a hot chocolate.

'Cleo, is that the kettle I hear?'

Cleo paused. *Sorry, Neil... can't hear you.* She swiftly took her mug, turned off the light and escaped to her own bedroom.

The apartment sharing struggled on uncomfortably. On Thursday night, Neil sent Cleo a text to say he was staying elsewhere for a couple of nights, house-sitting for a friend. She didn't care what he was doing, she had time to herself.

After cleaning the apartment of Neil debris, empty mugs, apple cores, sweet papers and waste bins full of crumpled sheets of paper, Cleo appreciated getting her own space back.

She prepared for an important meeting with Tef. He had emailed her to say he wanted to discuss the TeMPS project again on Friday. She wanted to be ready for that and had even turned down her night out with Heather.

With no Neil to disturb her, she had finished her work by seven thirty.

She rang Heather. 'I've finished my work, do you fancy coming over here for a while? It's blissful just being on my own...no guest. That doesn't include you of course.'

Heather arrived with chocolate bars for herself and a mix-up of Cleo's favourite sweets to munch on as they watched *Gone Girl*.

Her first words were, 'Guess what I heard today!'

'Here we go. I can't possibly guess what you heard, I give up already.' Smiling at her friend's excited face, Cleo waited for a snippet of gossip.

'Dan told Mark that he'd tried giving you a call this week.' Heather looked at Cleo with glee.

'But, he didn't, he hasn't.' Cleo frowned.

'He did, but he didn't get you. Neil answered your phone. Dan thought you might want to meet for a drink before he leaves for Australia. Anyway, Neil told him that *he* was living here and your week was all booked up.'

Cleo shook her head feeling confused. 'I thought that Dan was really annoyed about Italy. I know he was OK when we met at your house but...'

'Apparently he thought that he hadn't heard you out properly but then Neil put his oar in. He answered *your* mobile. You must have left it lying around.'

'Yes, I don't carry it around when I'm home. Why would I?'

'Looks like you'll have to. I sent a text to Dan to let him know that you are definitely no longer an item with Neil and that you are having him here out of the goodness of your heart. Was that OK?'

'Thanks, Heather. Will he believe that?' Cleo scrolled

through her phone. There was no call from Dan logged. It must have been erased by Neil, the sneaky so-and-so.

'Maybe you should call him,' Heather suggested.

Cleo knew that she just couldn't do that, not when she still had Neil at her apartment.

'I wouldn't know what to say. I'll leave it up to Dan,' she said. 'I've decided to go to Dunleith for the weekend, maybe he'll be there.'

11

On Friday morning, Cleo was up early. She showered, dressed and had her weekend case packed for Dunleith before going into the kitchen to make her morning coffee. The unwashed mug in the sink caught her attention at the same time as she heard snoring coming from the spare room. So Neil had come back after all. What had happened to his house sitting plan? He must've come in really late, after Heather left.

Cleo decided to leave straight away and grab a coffee from the drive-in on the way to Tyneview. She was still livid with him for messing with her phone and didn't want to row about it before work. In fact, it could all wait until after the weekend because she was off to Dunleith to finalise arrangements for 'sistergate' with Mum and Alex. Maybe she would run into Dan... have a chance to explain. She closed her apartment door at 6.30. That was a record, even for her.

Cleo was on tenterhooks before her meeting with the boss at lunchtime.

'Come on in, Cleo. Take a seat.' The financial slimeball was there again. Cleo sat in the seat that Tef had indicated and tried to keep her face blank. She had no idea what this meeting was about and didn't want to give her feelings away like last time.

'You'll be glad to know that we've taken into account what you've done and we've been reconsidering our options, Cleo.'

What did that mean?

'And... Mr. Gordon and I feel we were a little...a little too hasty.'

'Yes. Too hasty, Miss Moon,' nodded the 'yes' man.

'What are you reconsidering? Do you mean you're willing to forgo community sports and look at the TeMPS plan again?' Cleo could hardly curb her excitement.

'More than that, Cleo. We'll definitely look elsewhere for funds for our sports plan. I've told financial services and the deputies that TeMPS can't be discarded. We are backing you all the way with this. I want you to go ahead and run through your plans with Mr. Gordon now and we'll get the ball rolling, get this up and running ASAP!'

Was she hearing right?

'Now Mr. Gordon, if you'll kindly leave here and go with Miss Moon, I have the rest of the school to run.' Tef stood by the door and they were dismissed.

Cleo beamed, 'Follow me, Mr. Gordon and I'll show you the plans in detail.' You can practice saying 'yes' to me now. She didn't say *that* out loud.

At four o'clock she sent a text to Neil to say she was away until Sunday and turned her phone onto silent. For someone who excelled in communication at work, she wasn't doing brilliantly with the Neil situation. She was never very good at facing difficult personal situations. Right now, she just wanted to play Bruce Springsteen all the way home and tell Mum that she'd been right after all about giving Teflon Telford a chance.

Cleo plugged her iPod into the music system, opened a bag of sweets and, as music surrounded her, she was off and carefree. At least she would be if she could enjoy chewing her wine gums and stop chewing over today's events. What *had* made Tef do such an about turn? It seemed too good to be true. Whatever it was, she was on her way to making things up to Mum. Teen mothers in this area would have a real chance to stay in education.

As she headed towards Dunleith, her thoughts turned to Dan and his call. Was he really willing to forget Neil and Italy and meet up with her? Would he take notice of what Mark told him about Neil? He was going back to Australia and she did want to see him again. Was it his call or hers?

She was five miles off the village when a red mini travelling south flashed her. She was sure it was Mary Collingwood's car but Mary didn't drive fast. That meant, damn it, it would be Dan at the wheel and, by the looks of it, he was headed out of Dunleith. No chance of bumping into him over the weekend then.

12

Teri and Alex were out in the garden. Teri was weeding one of the flower beds and Alex was sprawled on the grass beside her telling her about the two week trip to France that the twins were going on in August and how the EllaBellas has assured her that the Collingwoods would ask her along too, if only Teri would agree.

'We're not discussing this, Alex. I've explained that I really want you with Cleo while I'm away. I wouldn't feel happy leaving if you two weren't together and looking out for one another,' Teri stopped weeding and looked out onto her garden.

Just gazing at the warm array of colours calmed her, her plants were flourishing in this milder weather and a heady mix of vanilla and cinnamon from the purple and white heliotropes filled the air with a home-baking smell.

'She hates me!' The conversation stopped right there as Cleo rounded the corner.

'Mum, great to see you! You're always working at something; you should get Alex to help you.' She walked over to where Teri was kneeling and dropped a kiss on her head.

Alex sat up and greeted Cleo with an angry glare, 'I *do* help. I do loads of stuff that you never did, so shut up.'

Cleo ignored her. 'I'll just take my case inside, Mum.'

Teri had brewed a pot of tea by the time Cleo came

downstairs carrying two parcels.

'Here you are Mum, open this first,' she said with a grin. Teri, tucked the parcels under her arm, carried the tray outside and put it beside Alex.

'We'll pour the tea after we've opened these.' She took the second package and handed it over to Alex, 'Here, this must be for you, darling. Really Cleo, it was kind of you to think of us. Did you have a lovely time?'

Cleo circled past Pharos who was sunning himself on the doorstep and joined them on the lawn.

'It was interesting, Mum. Lake Como was absolutely stunning but, I mentioned on the phone that Neil wasn't always the best of company.'

'I had so hoped that he might be your Mr Right.'

'No, he isn't. He's *Mr not-even-ok*, so we're going our separate ways.' She glared at Alex who was taking a great interest in this latest failed relationship. 'Now go on and open your present.'

Teri unwrapped the chunky wooden sign saying 'to the garden' in Italian and laughed in delight. Cleo could be so thoughtful, 'This is a great companion for our French sign. How lovely Cleo, thank you.'

She wondered what Cleo had chosen for Alex, 'What have you got, sweetheart?'

As Alex unwrapped beautiful beige leather gloves with three buttons at the opening that were clearly not meant for her, Teri noticed Cleo's discomfort. Too late, she realised what had happened. Cleo had bought her both gifts and had left Alex out. She should have twigged before handing Alex the packet.

Alex looked as if she guessed as much too; her face was guarded as if trying not to show any emotion.

Time to avoid another fall out, 'Very chic, Poppet. You'll be able to wear that colour with anything,' she assured her.

'They... they're rather sophisticated for me, Mum. I'm

sure they'd suit you better.' Alex looked steadily across at Cleo who was embarrassed.

'Oh no,' she said, 'Sorry, you've got the wrong packet, Alex. Hang on. She disappeared back upstairs and came back into the garden with a different package.

'Wow! thanks, Cleo.' Alex smiled in genuine surprise at the black leather gloves with a triangle of studs decorating the back of each glove and red lining.

'These gloves are yours too, Mum,' she explained and Teri was relieved that the tricky moment had passed. Maybe they would enjoy a lovely family evening.

Next morning, Teri sat in her studio above the garage waiting for the girls to walk over from the house. She felt closest to Mac in here. Their studio was large and airy with panoramic views of the countryside right to the coastline and she could see as far as Alnmouth. Mac's architect's equipment still lay on a table at the far end, dusted but unused for seventeen years. She rather hoped that Alex might follow in his footsteps.

Teri's design and sewing area was at this end with the mini kitchen and communal table in the middle. The windows at this side out onto their paved courtyard linked the studio and the garage, which had once been an old barn, to the main house.

Mac had designed the house to be built on the foundations of three farm workers cottages. He had used the original stone and timber in his design and had made High Rigg a contemporary house that blended with its surroundings as though it had been there forever. They'd loved it, loved building it. Oh Mac, I miss you just as much now, she thought. How I wish you could tell me if I am doing the right thing.

Teri had arranged all of her papers and financial affairs in order and had updated her will to make sure that there would be no misunderstandings if something should happen to her on this trip or afterwards.

After the 'misunderstanding' about her donation to Tyneview, it was a relief to know her affairs were in order. She'd been meaning to do all of this during that last ghastly illness and it had all seemed too complicated but, once she'd enlisted the help of her lovely solicitor, Mr. G. Moore, it had been painless and such a weight off her mind.

She wanted to go over the finances with both girls present and then file her papers away in the studio safe. Some of her personal papers and her jewellery were stored in the lid of the moondream jar in the garden room, but they weren't details that she needed to discuss yet. The compartments in the lid and base of that jar were hard to open up and probably the safest place in the house.

She watched Pharos, his silver coat glinting as it was caught in a pool of sunlight, saunter across the yard towards the studio door followed by Cleo. She had seemed happy when she'd arrived yesterday and it had been thrilling to hear her school news over dinner. Teri was relieved to know that Cleo's enthusiasm about her TeMPS project had not diminished and it was all going ahead.

Ever since she'd heard of Cleo's idea, she'd worked with George Moore, her solicitor, to become a benefactor of the school but to keep her identity secret. The pregnant schoolgirls unit was her 'baby' too but Cleo didn't know that. If Cleo knew that she was using family money, it might put too much pressure on her. Besides, the girls weren't exactly in the know as to how much she had made during her designer heyday in the eighties.

After the utter treachery of Mr. Telford, who had been only too happy to receive half a million for the project, she had worried that she'd messed up and her hard earned money was going to be spent on something else. Her solicitor had assured her that the use of her donation was watertight and had let Mr Telford and his financial manager, know this very forcefully. It had been a bumpy few days, but now all was sorted.

Cleo had walked into the village and brought back the papers. Thank goodness she was walking over in old jeans that Pharos couldn't cover in cat hair or claw at. She smiled to see Alex, her baby, at the back door in a hooded onesie and Uggs looking as if she'd just rolled out of bed. At ten o'clock on a Saturday, she had!

Both girls appeared together at the top of the stairs with Pharos weaving around their feet. He plaintively called his human sounding 'Maam' and sat by the fridge in the tiny kitchen area of the studio. Teri poured him a dash of milk topped with water into his saucer. She'd read that cats could be lactose intolerant so didn't give him a lot of dairy nowadays. She must remember to tell her cat sitter, Betty from next door, about that.

After Pharos was settled, Teri resumed her business-like attitude by indicating seats and sitting herself at the top of the table. It didn't take long to explain who her solicitor was, where her papers were kept and to outline the allowance she was paying monthly into Cleo's bank for keeping Alex in the manner to which she was accustomed.

'That's too much,' argued Cleo.

'You're clearly not used to what your sister can eat in a week or how much she might like to 'borrow' from next week's allowance,' explained Teri.

Alex looked embarrassed, as if she didn't know whether to frown and deny this or ignore it.

Teri gave her a hug and said, 'Most teenagers need to learn to budget and don't start off too successfully, darling.'

'I always managed on mine at that age, Mum.'

Cleo was right but it didn't help matters right now.

'You were never like *most* teenagers, Cleo,' Alex answered, regaining her cool before Teri explained what her own personal allowance would be.

'But Mum, that's the same as when you're here and you've just said that it's never enough. You've heard that *she...* that Cleo won't let me borrow. What am I supposed to do?'

'Budget dear sis. Spend wisely.'

Teri knew she'd have to interrupt before another war of words made her even more nervous about leaving the two of them together.

'Let's say no more about allowances. We've just about covered everything except for valuables and the safe. I've got some personal valuables in the moondream jar as you know and I'll just show you how to lock the safe.' As she showed them the combination, Teri noticed that Alex was looking out of the window and heard Cleo say, 'Are you listening to Mum, Alex?'

Teri stifled a grin; she couldn't help noticing that Cleo could sound just like a schoolteacher when she talked to Alex. Hopefully, they'd mesh together because they had to. No good having misgivings now.

'I'm perfectly aware of what Mum is doing, but I'm looking at Pam waving up at us, actually. I'm just wondering what she wants.'

Teri crossed the room to the window to get a view of Pam, Betty's daughter, who was beckoning one of them to come down to her.

'I'll go and see what she wants, save your legs,' said Alex. She smiled at Teri as she headed downstairs and towards the fence adjoining their property to Betty's.

As they both watched her progress, Teri said, 'Cleo, I'm ever so grateful that you're doing this but it'll be hard for Alex, so please don't...'

'Don't *what,* Mum?' Cleo interrupted,' Don't expect her to pull her weight, don't ask her to do anything, don't expect her to keep to her allowance? You're far too soft and, if you trust me, as you keep saying you do, you'll have to just let me do things my own way.'

'OK. OK, I was just hoping you'd go a bit easy on her.'

'Let's hope she goes easy on me too.'

'Shush... She's coming back up.'

'Bad news,' Alex said, her eyes huge and round. 'Betty's slipped and broken her hip on the back patio. She's going to be laid up for quite a while and she'll have to stay with Pam until she's mobile again.'

'Oh dear, poor Betty,' Teri groaned. 'She said that patio was slippery and needed to be hosed down. She was hoping that one of her grandsons would do it now the weather is a bit warmer.'

'Why was she waving to tell us that?' asked Cleo.

'Because she's a neighbour and Pam knows that we care about her mother, Cleo.' What a question! Teri couldn't help thinking that Cleo could be exasperating at times.

'*And* because she wanted us to know that Betty can't look after Pharos while you're away,' said Alex. Her eyes were glinting with mischief as Teri looked from Alex to Cleo whose expression was sheer alarm.

'What will happen to him now?' asked Cleo.

Teri was trying to find the right soothing words when Alex blurted out,

'What the hell do you think will happen? Mum can't just cancel. He's old so he can't go into a cattery for that length of time. *We'll* have to take Pharos with us.' Alex picked up Pharos and cradled him.

Teri cringed as both sets of green eyes looked at Cleo, not a friendly expression between them.

'Poor Pharos uprooted like me, at least we'll have each other to comfort,' soothed Alex.

'Look girls let's go across to the house and think all of this through.' Teri was playing for time. She didn't want to cancel her plans but she wasn't sure that Cleo could cope with all of this after all. She had a stressful job and her city apartment wasn't intended for a teen and a cat as well as the resident ex-boyfriend who seemed to be there all of the time nowadays.

'You go across and start on the lunch, Mum. I'm going to be starving soon. Cleo and I will just practice this unlocking and locking of the safe and sort out how we'll look after this old man.' Alex was still cradling Pharos and looking at Cleo.

Teri glanced at Cleo who nodded to her.

'Right. I'll get that joint of pork in the oven and prep the veg, then. You'll lock up and be over soon?'

Both girls nodded and she was struck by how alike their expressions were. Guarded, giving nothing away.

Teri went downstairs and crossed over the courtyard to the house half relieved that she wasn't part to the discussion that they were obviously going to have and half wishing she was there to act as a buffer. This is why I'm leaving them, so they can sort things out together, so they can rely on one another. She lit the oven and rummaged for the right roasting tin. If they can make a start with a decision like this, I'll know it's going to be OK to leave them together.

Maybe Cleo should stay here and commute to work? That would be perfect, but no, it was a hundred mile round trip and she liked to be at work by seven. Cleo would see nothing of Alex either if all that driving was added to her day. Maybe she should just ask Mary to have Alex. It was all too hard to arrange.

The kitchen door was open and Pharos came back first. 'Hi, Pharos, what have my two girls decided to do with you?' Teri picked Pharos up and carried him, in his favourite position looking over her shoulder, to sit beside her on the bench by the back door. 'Oh, Pharos, it's becoming very complicated.' Teri bent over the cat and scratched under his chin setting up a loud purr. 'Just to get away would've been so good. To know that the girls loved one another and could rely on one another would be all I could ever wish for but maybe it's not meant to be,' she whispered into his fur.

Both felt a jolt of surprise as a tear rolled down her cheek and mingled with his fur. Pharos leapt onto her lap and stretched to nudge her face. Hugging him to her chest, she released a river of held back emotion and he let her soak his majestic, silver spotted coat until he looked more bedraggled than he had ever done in his entire seventeen years.

Teri washed her face, put some makeup on and had the Sunday roast well underway when the girls came over. Alex went upstairs to change and shower and Cleo took a bottle of pinot out of the fridge.

'Would you like a glass before lunch, Mum?' A calm, pleasant request, Teri was relieved that she seemed happy considering the time she'd spent in the studio with Alex.

'It's a bit early for me.'

'It's just after twelve. And you've got something to celebrate.'

'Have I?'

'Yes. Landing me with an ungrateful cat and with Alex for weeks on end.'

Cleo's smile told Teri that she was OK about it all. She had said ungrateful about the cat but not Alex, that was a start. Oh yes, she was ready to celebrate now.

'Better pour me a large one before you change your mind.'

Alex came downstairs just in time for lunch and she was smiling too. They had a laidback family meal that Teri really savoured, because such an event was rare.

It was late afternoon when Cleo gathered her things together to head back to Newcastle. As she hugged Teri goodbye, she added, 'Not long before you start your adventure, Mum. I'm proud of you for going after what you want, at your age.'

'At my age! I'm not quite fifty yet, I'll have you know I'm in my prime.' Teri grinned and gave Cleo a push towards the door. She waved until the little sports car was out of sight.

The sky, streaked with pink, promised a fair day tomorrow and a pale waning gibbous moon shone over High Rigg. At my age indeed, she hugged her excited feelings to her chest. Yes, I'm finally doing something just for me and I'm loosening you two from my apron strings.

Closing the door, she grinned to herself, she never wore an apron but those two had strings wrapped tightly around her heart.

Teri's thoughts were interrupted by Alex calling from upstairs.

'Is she gone?'

'She is my darling. Did you want to say goodbye?'

'No I did not!' Alex leaned over the banister, 'She was up here giving orders again before she left. Mum, is she actually serious? Do you believe it when she says I can take two cases max? Is she an airline or something? No clutter in her precious apartment. I hope you appreciate what it takes for me to keep my mouth zipped when she spouts off.'

MEAD MOON

13

Teri gave a final wave to the girls and walked through to departures. She had done it. For the first time, since she was seventeen and found out she was pregnant with Cleo, Teri only had herself to think about. Weird! Scary. She felt weightless, not sure who she was when she was adrift from her usual ties. After this short breakfast flight from Newcastle to Heathrow, she would be boarding a flight straight through to Cairo.

As she sauntered through the departures lounge at Heathrow, Teri was without a care in the world, well hardly a care. She still felt slightly guilty about leaving Pharos and Alex with Cleo even though she thought it was for a good cause in the long term. They'd pull together. Was she sure or trying to convince herself?

There was the health niggle too. She'd been told she could ring for an appointment to receive her MRI and other test results after two weeks and she hadn't done that last week. No excuse for that, she had thought long and hard and decided to wait until she returned from her trip. That way, the source of her bone pain remained unknown to her, it didn't become a huge dark cloud threatening her future.

Teri had to spend a couple of hours between flights in the departures area. A nail bar quiet so, instead of going for a coffee and watching the clock, she decided to treat her hands to a makeover with the lovely gel nails they offered.

'Are you going somewhere exciting?' asked the pretty young girl who looked about Alex's age.

'Yes, I'm off to explore Egypt.' Teri was happy to tell the nail technician all the details of her trip, she could talk about the wonders of Egypt forever.

As she was paying for her treatment, the gel varnish had dried instantly, so she could reach into her purse, when her phone rang. One of the girls already? Only a handful of people had her mobile number. She glanced at her phone's display and the name illuminated on the screen was that of her consultant, Mr Amonkar. She left her phone ringing; she certainly didn't want to take that call.

Once she boarded the plane for Cairo, Teri settled into her seat and took out the e-reader that she had been given by Cleo for Christmas. Alex had helped her to load it with some new novels and a few of her favourite books on Egypt, but she still packed several more. For Teri, her hard copies of reference books, annotated over years of reading; were irreplaceable.

Teri noticed that her neighbour had a tattered copy of a guide to Cairo that she hadn't seen before. She tried to get a better view of the title and he caught her looking. She'd better say something.

'Sorry for looking over your shoulder. I just can't resist travel guides on Egypt and I haven't seen that one before.'

Warm brown eyes under heavy black brows appraised her. He was a good-looking man, she guessed he was slightly older than Cleo. Would Cleo have liked him?

'I've had this for a while and it was second hand. I don't know if it will still be in print. Would you like to look through it? I'm going to read this complementary paper first.' He handed the book to her.

Teri couldn't resist, 'Thanks, I'll just make a note of the title and authors and I might be able find it on my e-book later.' She quickly became engrossed in the photographs of treasures to be seen in the museum of Cairo.

The drinks trolley came around and she asked for champagne. Her neighbour chose a can of beer.

'Is this a celebration for you?' he asked nodding at the champagne.

'Yes, in a way, but I do love champagne anyway.'

He seemed really friendly and pleasant to talk to. Teri handed him his book back. 'Thanks for lending me your guide. It just makes me want to get there and see everything. Have you been to Egypt before?'

'Yes, I'm there a lot. I'm doing a stint as a guide for an English company. Have you heard of 'Travel4Adventure'? They do tours, for solo travellers mainly. I'm picking up my group tomorrow and we'll explore Cairo together before they move on to other destinations.'

'That sounds like a wonderful job. I'm not a 'joiner in', I love just wandering around on my own, but it must be good to have an experienced guide at hand.'

'I'm not *that* experienced as a guide and I'm not that great at organisation but I like meeting new people and I know the sights of Egypt quite well, so the company put up with me.

I'm an archaeologist... taking a 'sort of sabbatical' and I'm doing the guide stuff to fund my own travels later in the year. There are so many places that I need to see. What about you?' He gazed at Teri with interest.

'What about me? Well, the place I've always wanted to visit since I was at school is Egypt. I'm just amazed that it's happening at last.'

'That's some wait.'

Teri laughed at his incredulous expression, 'I know,

I'm ancient. A late starter in travelling.'

'Oh no, sorry, I didn't mean to be rude. It just seems like a long time to realise your dream.'

'I know exactly what you mean. I'm from a different generation and things got in the way of my dreams but now it's 'my' time. Oh that sounds much more grandiose than I meant,' she smiled.

Those bubbles and the altitude must be having a giddy effect. Here she was chatting about dreams to a complete stranger. A handsome stranger with dark curly hair tied back into a thick ponytail and a stubbled face. On second thoughts, he wouldn't be Cleo's type at all.

'Shall we have another drink to celebrate your dream?' he buzzed for their hostess and they sat back in a comfortable silence.

'I'm Greg, by the way.' He clinked his can towards her glass.

'Teri, Teri Moon.' She smiled and took a sip of delicious crisp, cool bubbles.

'Unusual name. Mine's Greg Smith. Very ordinary.'

'I had a very ordinary name too, Greg, until I changed it.' Had she really said that? Told a total stranger one of her best kept secrets.

'Through marriage?' he asked.

'No, I didn't change my name when I married. I changed it much earlier to escape a previous life.' Now she really *had* said it.

'I'm guessing that's an interesting tale, Teri Moon. We have plenty of time so, if you don't mind, you can tell me exactly why you did such a thing.'

Teri looked into his eager eyes and was happy with his readiness to chat to her on their journey and thought, why not?

'I suppose I should start from where I started life. I was Margaret Donaldson; pretty ordinary eh? I was the only child of Liz and Bobby Donaldson and we lived in Elswick, on the outskirts of Newcastle. My mother had me when she was in her late thirties and you'd have thought she'd be thrilled to have a little girl later in life. She was happy enough but her one aim was for me to excel. I had to succeed, to be perfect at everything that Mother wanted me to do. Dad didn't have a look in; he worked hard, provided for the family and I knew that *he* loved me whatever I did but, my mother, she was different. I had to be perfectly behaved, always clean and tidy, always top of the class or else she'd be so annoyed and let down and we knew it.

It was lucky that I was fairly easy going because I accepted that Mother was just like that and I did my level best to be the daughter she wanted. I was someone who kept Liz Donaldson happy.

Passing for grammar school was the first time that my mother had been really delighted with me and I made sure that I never slipped behind with my studies. When I think of that girl now, it seems like someone else.' Teri was lost in her own thoughts of working hard and trying to please until she caught Greg's glance and realised that he was waiting for her to carry on.

'You were going to explain how Margaret became Teri,' he reminded her.

'Oh yes. Well, when Margaret got to her teens there were rows.' It was much easier to talk about Margaret as another person. She thought of her as that, someone from her past. 'The usual teen rows about going out and staying with friends, but her dad often took a stand and, as long as Margaret continued to do well at school, her mother allowed her some freedom.

Friends weren't often invited to her home though. If they did, Liz would hover around and ask questions. She constantly compared the other girls, in a critical way, to her wonderful Margaret and they felt uncomfortable going there. Margaret ended up in sixth form with one or two good friends who understood her home life was difficult and didn't expect invitations back to her house.'

'You shouldn't do that, you know. You're talking about *yourself*, what made you what you are today. Don't discount yourself.' His eyes were young, but Teri could sense that he'd known hard times; he understood.

'It's less painful that way, but I agree. I should remember that Margaret's bloody awful upbringing made me what I am now. Her...sorry... *My* parents never knew if I was seeing a boy or not because I didn't chat to my mother like the other girls did with theirs and it wasn't until I had been seeing Ralph Fenwick for almost six months that I mentioned it to my mother at all.

I knew it might be OK because Ralph was the head teacher's son and just the sort of boy that my mother wanted me to mix with. He was polite and, when he called for me, oh how my mother gushed and preened.

Ralph was really good fun and a real character when he was away from his own strict parents and out of sight of mine, but my mother didn't know that. We understood, we glimpsed one another's oppressive home background and loved getting out and going to other friends' houses. We were both determined to leave home and applying for Oxford was our main escape route.

We knew that if we didn't get in to one of the 'prestigious' colleges there, the parents would expect us to opt for Newcastle, 'a fine red brick university,' and we would both be living at home for years. We worked hard and were the only two from our grammar school to be accepted by Oxford that year.

My mother was ecstatic and my dad went along with it. They had saved since I was born for this; their daughter was going to read History at Oxford.'

'Did you change your name when you got to Oxford?' Teri shook her head, couldn't look at Greg. This was the most painful part of Margaret's story, of her story.

'I didn't get there; it all went wrong for Margaret...for me, when I found out I was pregnant.

My mother went ballistic and made me go to a home out in the country to have the baby – and this was the early eighties, in the days when far more families accepted having babies when you weren't married.

My mother wasn't accepting at all. She wanted nobody to know and Ralph's dad, my head teacher, was only too happy to contribute towards the nursing home and keep his son right away from the gossip. Dad said nothing, not to me anyway, and Ralph and I had no say in the matter and so I was bundled off.

My withdrawal from school was explained briefly to staff and friends. I had apparently panicked about A levels and didn't want to finish my course. I was going to do a secretarial course instead.

I heard my Mother telling Dad that two of the staff who knew I had potential thought this was foolish and went to the Head to offer to talk to me, but they were told to concentrate on their other students, those with staying power.

Dad asked Mum if they could look after my baby and give me a chance but she cut him off, saying there was no way that would happen.

One morning they told me to pack a few things and I was dropped at a nursing home, but I didn't stay. I couldn't. I'd been given cash to pay the matron of the home, but I only got as far as the entrance before I did an about turn.'

'How did you manage that?' Greg seemed intrigued.

She remembered it all so clearly.

'They drove me to a handsome stone house that was totally hidden from the road by thick trees and high walls.

The driveway was long and ended in a curved vehicle-turning circle outside, with wide steps up to double doors. I had expected doom and gloom and bars across the windows but it looked just like a country house; dull and out of the way. Dad got my case out and I stood there shuffling my feet on the gravel as he went to help Mum out.

That's when she went off it again. The weeping and wailing grated on my nerves and Dad didn't appease her with his usual patting and whispers of 'come on' and 'there, there, don't get upset'. His silence didn't seem to be helping. I went around to hug her and Mum sniffed and turned her head away.

I said, 'Look Dad, you just go and I'll go in there myself. You and Mum have seen the place anyway and going in there is going to make her even worse. They're expecting me, so let's just say goodbye from here.'

Dad came over, gave me a long hug, told me not to worry and everything would be sorted out. He then handed me the envelope of cash to give to the staff and as I walked towards Mum, she put her hand out to stop me approaching.

I climbed the first steps and composed myself to wave them off. As the car disappeared from view, I turned towards the door. I was facing months of incarceration and then I would have a tussle to keep my baby. I was about to open the door, feeling despondent at what lay ahead, when a waft of cooking, it was like boiled cabbage, made me retch.

That jolted me into action. I fled back down the steps and darted into some shrubbery to the side of the house, thinking I might be sick on the steps. The morning sickness was getting better but certain smells were lethal.

A retch or two and a few breaths of air later, I returned to my suitcase just as a taxi was pulling up. A heavily pregnant girl got out and the driver helped her to the doors.

One door opened and swallowed her up and the driver came down the steps and noticed me. I hadn't moved from my case.

'It must be all over for you then, love?' he questioned looking at me and my case. 'Are you wanting to go to the station?'

'Yes.' It was out before I could think and I jumped into the back of the cab and was off. The cab driver chatted about the number of times he had done this run and then the train station appeared.

'Where are you off to now then? Are you on the two o'clock to Manchester? You have ten minutes to get it from platform two.'

I nodded at him and gave him two notes. 'Two pounds and keep the change, thanks.'

I bought a single to Manchester and stood at platform two. I got aboard thinking, what have I done?

I found a seat and sank into it. As the train moved away, I realised that, for the first time in months, I felt light. *I felt alive.* I didn't feel full of guilt and blame and regret. It was similar to how I felt today, getting on board this plane.

I got off at Manchester and found lodgings, found friends and changed my name so that my parents couldn't track me down. If they found me, they'd make me give baby up. I sent a letter to say I was fine but wouldn't embarrass them by keeping in touch and that was the last they heard from me for a very long time.'

'And your chosen name was Teresa Moon,' Greg said.

'Oh no, not Teresa,' Teri shook her head and smiled at Greg. 'I was seventeen, very fanciful and I was mad about all things Egyptian. I wanted to read Ancient history at Oxford, remember.

On my first night in Manchester, I changed into Neferteri Moon. Neferteri after the Egyptian queen and Moon because it was a full moon that night and I needed to quickly think up a surname to get digs.'

'So you are Teri because the name Neferteri is beautiful, but a bit of a mouthful?' Greg still sounded interested; she hadn't bored him too much with her meanderings.

'Yes, that's right, and now you're the only other living person to know the history of my change of name.'

'I'm honoured. I really am. You're a very interesting companion, Neferteri. Did you know that Neferteri means beautiful companion?' he asked.

Teri nodded and felt her cheeks flush. She hadn't known the meaning when she chose it for herself.

They sat in silence for a while, each with their own thoughts.

Teri looked at Greg who had fallen asleep. That would pass some of the journey away. Teri thought she'd never relax enough to sleep, but she dozed off and her old nightmare came back to taunt her.

She was leaning over the sink in the cold, dark bathroom feeling sick, splashing cold water on her face. A rapid banging on the bathroom door gave rise to a different lurching feeling of sickness. She rested her cold, clammy brow on the bathroom wall in utter despair. Her mum, must she face her?

'Margaret! Margaret! Come out of there now. I need a word with you.'

Wearily she opened the bathroom door, wiping her face with the towel she had been clutching to her mouth to stifle the noise of her retching. She met the dark, raging face of her mother. With a halo of curlers and a pink candlewick dressing gown hugged around her, she looked comical; Margaret felt only terror.

'I knew it. I just knew you would have to go and do something like this to let down the family. You're pregnant aren't you? You stupid, stupid little fool!' The words are spat out.

She said nothing, it was best to say nothing when her mother was in full flow; it would pass sooner if she stayed silent. This was Dad's strategy and she tried to adopt it. The urge to say something was strong, but her mother was past listening.

'Say something!'

'What on earth is going on?' Dad appeared on the landing rubbing his eyes and looking dazed.

Feeling cornered and ready to throw up again, she rushed back to bed and burrowed under the blankets. Muffled sounds, raised voices, and then the weight of someone on the side of the bed. Dad drew the covers back from her face.

'Is it true, Margaret love?' he whispered.

Opening her eyes to meet his, she wondered if he was for her, or for her mother.

'Yes,' relief and fear swept through her. Would Dad make it all right?

She saw him drop his head and let the covers fall over her and felt his weight leave the bed. The door closed. Silence. No one could put things right. She was left alone; she had a reprieve, but for how long?

Teri woke up with a start and felt ice cold. It had been years since she'd dreamed of that. She'd been Margaret then, another life ago and her girls knew nothing about it. She really should just tell them, but her parents' rejection was still raw. They were better off not knowing how her parents had reacted. Cleo felt bad enough about her start in life without knowing her grandparents did not want her.

Just seventeen, she had been a mere babe like Alex, and she had never forgotten that hurt. Shivering, she buzzed for a blanket.

Greg woke when their food was about to be served and

they were both starving enough to tackle the airline's meal. As they gamely tried to drink the coffee, rather thick and bitter, Teri asked Greg why he was taking a break from archaeology. He didn't answer for a while and she was starting to wonder if he had heard her. Eventually, he looked at her and, from his expression, she could guess that he'd gone back to a painful place.

'You've been honest with me, so I should be open with you in return. I was married, my wife was an archaeologist too and we went on digs together. I'm not ready to do any without her just yet.'

'I can understand that. It's hard to carry on the same way when you're on your own. How long have you been apart? Is it permanent?'

Greg's face was ashen as his gaze met hers. 'Oh, it's permanent all right, Teri. Laura was killed. A helicopter crash, coming out to meet me. She'd just had confirmation that she was pregnant. I didn't find that out until later. I've lost her and our future.'

They sat in silence for a long time. Teri was remembering the horror of finding out that a lorry had smashed into Mac's car when they had so much to look forward to.

'I do understand, Greg,' she explained, 'I lost my husband when I was about your age.'

The remainder of the flight flew by as they regaled each other with stories of Laura and Mac and found they were recalling happy times.

14

Cleo sat in front of the TV, her eyes were looking towards the screen but she wasn't following the recording of *Endeavour*. Her mind was racing over the day's events while thinking about how she'd survive the next day... and the day after that. She was sitting here on her own, yet she wasn't happy in her own company, with Alex in the spare room and her office being taken over by Neil.

She'd had it out with him about misleading Dan on the phone and deleting his number but she couldn't forgive him. She never did get to see Dan before his flight back to Australia and just hoped that the Newcastle vacancy would come up soon and she would get a chance to see him and talk things over.

Before that, she wanted Neil out. Now that Alex was here, he was camping out in her office and had brought in a hideous blow-up bed in a brown cover that took up most of the floor space. He'd assured her it was only a matter of days now so she'd just have to be patient. Patience! The very word irritated the hell out of Cleo.

She walked across to her bowl on the kitchen counter and, as she took a handful of gummy jellies, she tried to close her eyes to the dimly lit kitchen area. Disaster area more like, she firmly turned her back on it all and perched on the sofa, annoyed that she was unable to ignore the mess.

Cleo delighted in chewing furiously on several jellies at a time. Open plan living was fine when she was on her own but from the sofa she could see the dishes and debris from their dinner and the dining table still needed to be cleared. Her idea of having a welcome dinner for Alex had been met with a lukewarm reception from both Neil and Alex and she'd prepared and cooked on her own, while they both busied themselves with an iPad and laptop.

After dinner, Alex had left the table and said she would just go and settle into her room and Neil had excused himself with work to do. No offers of help with the clearing up. Cleo had left the table too and now she couldn't relax while she was looking at that aftermath and worrying about how they'd all fit in.

A god almighty terrible smell wafted across the room. Where had that come from? She got up to follow it to her bedroom; the door was ajar. It was definitely coming from her room. She put on the light.

'Oh for heaven's sake! What have you done?' Her piercing cry brought Neil and Alex rushing from their rooms.

Pharos had clawed a latrine for himself in the centre of her duvet. He was now curled up sleeping peacefully in a wicker basket on top of her clean washing.

'I thought he was with you. You said you'd look after him, Alex!' Cleo shouted. 'Don't laugh, it's not a bit funny'

Alex dashed across to the basket and picked the old boy up,

'Poor Pharos, you're not used to being a city cat. Come on and I'll show you your new litter box.' She sailed out of the room controlling her grin but Cleo could read her delighted look of pure mischief.

'Gross.' Neil just shrugged and went back to the office.

Cleo loved that white cover, she loved her goose down duvet too but a closer inspection showed that both were beyond rescue. She had given up her apartment, they were all unappreciative and now her bed, the only sanctuary she had left, had been defiled. She really wanted to cry or throw something.

Swallowing back hot tears of self-pity, she formed a plan of action. It started with turning off the TV and looking through her iPod to find the playlist that she used when she was running. As *Echo Beach* blasted out of the speakers, she grabbed a big bin bag and set about binning, cleaning and putting her apartment straight.

Alex was now sitting on the sofa, cradling Pharos as Cleo put glasses and plates away and sang along to *Don't stop me now*. As Cleo paused to pour herself a well-deserved glass of wine into one of the sparkling clean glasses, Alex said,

'You're just like Mum when you do housework, nothing gets in your way.'

'Am I?' Cleo felt unaccountably pleased to be compared to her mum. 'It's a shame you're not and can't join in'

'I would have but you didn't ask and I am a guest,' Alex had a deadpan expression.

'Are you joking?'

'No, why would I? *You* have no sense of humour.'

Cleo walked over to the sofa and sat by her. 'Look, Alex, I want you to feel at home here and don't want you to feel you have to be treated like a guest.'

Alex broke up laughing, 'Fooled you! And Cleo I'd *never* feel at home here in a million years. It's too, too... you.'

Cleo left her and escaped into her bedroom. She closed the door firmly; what a little madam but she just wouldn't rise to it.

She took a spare duvet and cover from the high shelf of her wardrobe, polyester from student days - no goose down then, and pulled down a panel of quilting that her mum had made her when she first moved into her apartment. It didn't really match Cleo's style and she'd put it out of the way. She thought that it would be ideal as bedding for Pharos. She took it through and handed it to Alex.

'Here you can use this as a bed for Pharos and make sure that he knows about that litter tray in your room too.'

Alex was looking at her in dismay. 'Cleo, you must be joking. You're not going to use that piece of art that Mum made for you for the cat's bed?'

'He needs somewhere to sleep.' Cleo was puzzled. Alex usually thought nothing was too good for the Egyptian prince.

'Mum spent *months* making that and you haven't even appreciated it.'

Cleo was unsure whether this was another wind-up. Their mum was always in her studio making patchwork and tapestry stuff and Pharos had slept on many of her quilts. She'd thought it might make him feel more settled and leave her bedding alone.

Alex spread the panel on the table. It might have made a half-counterpane for the bottom of Cleo's bed but she wouldn't think of using it as a wall hanging like Mum sometimes did.

'Look at it. Mum made it all in shades of cream and grey because *you* like boring colours but she made it a story about you too. She used Dad's ties for some of it and it took her ages, you ungrateful doylem!'

Dad's ties? Cleo studied it more carefully than she had when she was given it. She wasn't the biggest fan of Mum's craft stuff but she had to admit it was intricate.

Alex jabbed her finger at part of the panel.

'Look at the baby cradle with an embroidered C –that's you. Look here, at the scroll and the cap –that's your degree. Look at the M scrolled around an apple; that's McAplin for Dad. See all the new and full moons around the border and the Moondream jar here? Just look at the details and then step back and look at it all from a distance.'

Cleo stepped back wondering what she should be looking for. Then she saw it, it leapt out at her and took her by surprise. 'My God, It's the approach to home. It's a landscape of High Rigg and the road leading to it.'

'And *you've* only just realised?' asked Alex.

The incredulous look on Alex's face told Cleo that it was too late to pretend otherwise. She could see it all now, but she'd never bothered before. She had unwrapped it, thanked Mum and then pushed it away when she got home. Cleo felt ashamed. It was a beautiful personal panel of her life and she'd pushed it to the back of a shelf.

'You were meant to have this for your wall, Cleo. Mum *is* talented you know. Her work, like this, was sought after in the eighties.

This deserved criticism on top of the events of the day caught up with Cleo and she felt tearful.

'Hey chill, don't cry about it now. Mum and I know just what you're like and how you need things spelling out at times.' With that Alex left with Pharos over her shoulder.

Cleo, clutching the panel, retreated to her room to have a good cry. Perhaps Alex was right, perhaps she did need some things to be spelled out.

Sunday wasn't as bad as Cleo had anticipated. Alex and Cleo went over to Heather and Mark's for dinner and Neil went out for the day. Alex chatted and laughed with Heather much more easily than she did with Cleo and they were both entertained by Archie.

Afterwards, Cleo drove by the school and filled Alex in on how the school ran and what she thought Alex's new teachers were like.

The school had agreed to take Alex for the last few

weeks of term. She had to complete some work set by her own school but she could go into Art, English and Drama lessons because their syllabus was similar and she would probably benefit from different viewpoints and from mixing with the students.

Alex seemed subdued after they got back. She retreated to her room and Cleo could hear that she was on the phone to the EllaBellas for ages.

When it went quiet, Cleo knocked at her door and to ask if there was anything she needed or wanted to know before school next day. Alex opened the door and Cleo could see that her eyes were reddened and she looked miserable.

'The school is OK Alex, you'll be fine.' Cleo wished that she felt as sure as she sounded.

'Cleo, I don't want to travel with you. Could I go by the metro train? I don't really want the kids to see *me*, a 'newbie', arrive with the deputy.'

Cleo could understand that and she tried to ignore the fact that Alex was scratching at the door edge and flaking the paintwork as she talked. The kids at school would find out they were related soon enough with their surnames being the same. There weren't that many 'Moons.'

'Good idea. I go really early anyway so you could leave after me and walk to the metro station if you want. And Alex, at school I'll be Miss Moon to you.'

Alex put her tongue out and grinned before closing the door.

Cleo picked up the flakes of paint and started to get ready for the next day. Would it all go smoothly at Tyneview? She hoped so.

15

Alex woke early and heard Cleo in the kitchen but she didn't get up. She felt nervous about going into a new school but she knew she was more than capable of holding her own. It was just such an embarrassment being related to Cleo. She'd had a brainwave about that before she fell asleep last night. She heard a gentle tap and Cleo saying she was off.

'OK see you later.' *Unfortunately*, she added silently. Actually, Cleo hadn't been that bad last night. She'd even looked sorry about offering her mum's quilting to Pharos.

As Alex lay in bed deciding whether it was time for her to get up, she heard Neil moving about. God, she'd forgotten about him. He was a real taker and she was amazed that Cleo hadn't shown him the door. He was in the kitchen, and then on the phone.

'No, Marianne, that's impossible. I can't do that. I'm homeless. This is a temporary address and the landlady that I'm lodging with is an old bag.' Then he went off into another language, too fast for Alex to understand. What was he talking about?

She got up to go to the bathroom and, as she passed Cleo's room, she saw Neil lounging back on Cleo's bed with a plate of toast in one hand and the house phone in the other.

'My God, you gave me a fright!' his hand jumped and

the toast slipped onto the duvet when he saw her.

'I live here as much as you do, Neil.' She was about to add 'with the old bag' but she didn't. It was unfair to Cleo and she didn't want Neil to know she'd heard him on the phone.

She felt like supporting her big sis, for once.

'Why haven't you gone with Cleo?' he asked.

'That's for me to know - and get off her bed! She wouldn't like your toast crumbs all over it.' Alex left him moaning about his back and the blow-up mattress.

Catching the metro was fine. It was easier and quicker than the bus she took to get to her own school from Dunleith. A few kids from Tyneview got on at the next stop and were eyeing her up. You would with any new girl. When she reached school, she headed straight for the office. She asked for the head of Admin who had enrolled her at the school. Ann came out to chat to her.

'I think it would be better for my sister, and for me, if I used my middle name while I'm here. I'm Alex McAplin Moon but while I'm here I'd like to be known as McAplin. Can you do that?'

'That shouldn't be a problem, Alex. Leave it with me and I'll see that your name change is passed to your tutor.'

'Thanks. It may save Miss Moon from being embarrassed – and me!' she grinned and checked her school planner to see where her tutor group met. Phew, as Alex McAplin the day would be easier.

Gracie Grieves had been sent to the office to pick up the new girl.

'Gracie this is Alex. Take her to the sixth form block and show her round,' said Ann.

Gracie looked Alex up, down and back up for good measure. Alex pretended not to notice and tried not to show she was swallowing hard. Stand firm, look chilled.

'A new lass, the lads are ganna love you. Stick with me

and I'll point out the dickheads.'

'Thanks. I'd like that.' Alex breathed a sigh of relief.

Gracie Grieves was tall, muscular and had jet black hair backcombed into a nest of a ponytail that made her tower above Alex. She talked like they did on 'Geordie Shore'. The EllaBellas would be gobsmacked by her.

'Are you Scottish then?' Gracie frowned down at her.

'No, but I live... lived on the Northumbrian border so we can sound a bit like that.'

'As long as you're not posh.' Gracie's smile showed big white teeth. 'Ha'way - that means come on - I'll take you to meet the rest.'

'I can understand you, I'm not daft,' Alex grinned back. 'Ha'way then, let's go.'

Gracie and her gang befriended Alex and she went for lunch with them. They weren't actually having lunch, they were going to the local precinct for a 'c and c', ciggies and chips, but she was glad to tag along. She caught sight of Cleo looking out of her window as she was walking down the drive and felt a thrill of rebellion. Big sis certainly wouldn't like her hanging round the shops.

Alex just listened at first and didn't believe half the things the girls said they got up to. When she joined in, she found herself telling them about Edinburgh, with a little embellishment about how many times she'd been to The Nest. The night of the hospital drama gained her a bit of credit, she could tell.

She felt a bit guilty about using Ella's hellish time to impress them, but she knew that Ella would understand when she described the crowd she had to fit in with.

A group of boys sidled up to join them. Gracie nudged her.

'Told you they'd be round you like flies around a cowpat. Anyone new. Just watch the gobby one with the stupid hair.'

The gobby one, they called him Ty, kept looking at Gracie as they all joked and argued with one another loudly enough to get dirty looks from shoppers trying to get past them. Alex was relieved when it was time to head back to school.

'See you tomorrow, Alex. I'm not gannin in this afternoon.' Gracie was walking away from the group.

'What are going to do?' Alex called after her.

'Fryin' other fish. Can't say.' What did that mean? Alex felt puzzled as she walked back into Tyneview. Ah, that was half the day over.

The Art department was fantastic; much better equipped than her own school's cosy but ancient art block. Mr. Rutherford was really laid back. He introduced her to the others, asked Lee to show her around the studios and then left her to her own devices.

She would be able to work with the group and get on with her portfolio of work over the next few weeks. They all knew each other well and there where 'in' jokes that she didn't pick up on but they were open and showed her where things were and she thought she'd fit in better here than in her tutor group.

Lee walked out of school with her and they discussed the differences in their Art syllabuses because Alex was studying under a different exam board.

'I live in Victoria Crescent; whereabouts are you headed?' Lee asked as they reached the main road.

'I'm taking the metro,' Alex started to explain just as Gracie caught up with them.

'Hi, I came back looking for you to make sure you get on the right metro. Ha'way there's one due in five minutes.' Gracie looked down at Lee. 'She's a toony, not a posh piece like you,' she said, grabbing Alex by the shoulder to hurry her off.

'Bye, Lee!' Alex smiled and hurried off.

'Bye, Lee!' Gracie parodied her and then grinned and stuck up two fingers as they walked off.

Alex had to say something. As they approached the station she said, 'There was no need for that, Gracie.'

'For what?'

'The two fingers, at Lee. I like her.'

'Ah that. It just makes the posh bitches a bit nervous of me and that's how I like it. It's just a reminder that they don't take the piss out of me, not ever.'

'I think it's uncalled for.'

'Bloody Hell, it's a good job that I've decided I like you or you'd know what was uncalled for. Look here's the train.'

Alex walked towards Mariner's Wharf, Cleo's block of apartments, thinking about Gracie. She liked her but she was mouthy and seemed defensive about lots of things. Questions were answered with 'What's it to you?' or 'Never you mind' but she was nosey about Alex. She grinned as she thought of how she'd used Gracie's own answers to avoid saying where she lived or why she was there. She definitely didn't want Gracie knowing that she had anything to do with Cleo.

They'd travelled home without giving anything away but Gracie had still called out that she'd see her in the morning. She'd couldn't wait to give the EllaBellas a ring and tell them about Gracie and Lee and her day when she got in.

Alex unlocked the door of the flat and, as she pushed the door open, Pharos jumped onto her shoulder from a bookcase by the door.

'Hello lovely boy!' he loved a shoulder carry.

'Hello' a small voice piped up from the sofa. Alex looked over to see a blonde haired boy with a face covered in orange ice lolly and sticky hands that were being wiped on a grey cushion.

He turned back to the TV and was watching 'Charlie and Lola' on CBeebies.

She gently put Pharos onto the floor and he strolled towards the kitchen.

'In a moment greedy, I'm just going to say hello to this other lovely boy.' She was rewarded with a head turned from the TV and a grin.

'I'm Alex. How did you get here?' she asked, sitting down on the sofa and away from melted lolly.

'I'm Josh. Daddy's just in his office.' Daddy? Bloody hell, Neil you're full of surprises.

Neil came out of the office. 'Hi Alex. I see you've met Josh. His mum has had to leave him with me. A bit of an emergency.'

His hair was ruffled and harassed. Not the usual suave Neil at all. 'Have you any idea what time Cleo will be back?' he asked.

'It'll be late. She has a meeting and said she'd bring in a Chinese supper at about seven. I think she meant for just the two of us, though.'

'Ah OK. Look Alex, I *must* go to see a client. Would you mind if I left Josh with you for an hour or two? It would be very difficult to take him.'

Josh was looking at her with solemn grey eyes; what could she say? She couldn't refuse in his hearing.

'All right but *you* must be back before Cleo comes home to do the explaining.'

'You're a star, I will. Josh, Daddy's going out and you must be really good for Alex.'

Josh nodded and went back to watching Cbeebies.

Alex followed Neil to the door. 'Is he sleeping over?'

'Unfortunately, he has to. His mum has gone off for a week, maybe two,' whispered Neil.

'That long?'

'*Exactly*. What can I do?' he hissed. 'Alex, do you think you could put him in the bath and ready for bed before Cleo gets home? He's never a bother. His bag with pyjamas and clothes is in the office. I'm going to go and get some groceries after this five o'clock meeting and I'll be back before seven. It would be best if Josh was in bed before Cleo got home and then I would have a chance to explain.'

'Make sure you're back.'

The door closed. Alex thought of how Cleo would take this news and actually felt sorry for Neil.

She looked at little Josh; poor kid it wasn't his fault. She had done quite a bit of kiddie sitting in Dunleith so she didn't mind keeping Josh occupied. She'd make him something to eat and pop him in the bath so that he'd look like a little cherub by the time Cleo got home.

16

Cleo stifled a yawn. The senior management meeting had gone on for ages and she really wanted to get back and find out why Alex had chummed up with Gracie Grieves of all people. She liked Gracie but she could be the centre of trouble and often got into fights or slanging matches with other girls. She hoped that Neil would be out so that she could chat to Alex and they could enjoy their Chinese takeaway in peace. Should she get extra in case he was there and hadn't eaten? Bloody Neil, he'd better get himself sorted soon.

'Cleo, Cleo?' she brought her attention back to the table and felt Telford's eyes on her. 'We're waiting for an update on your teen mothers' project.' Cleo was on instant alert. Yes, she couldn't wait to tell the others how well it was going and how everything was on schedule.

It was after seven when Cleo pulled up beside the apartment. She looked around for Neil's car. Not there, she felt a surge of relief that she could get home and relax. To her surprise, she had found that having Alex to stay wasn't half as irritating as having Neil around.

She walked in to a tidy apartment with the table set for two.

'Hi Alex,' she called. Alex came out of the office with

her finger on her lips. Cleo automatically lowered her voice.

'What are you doing in the office?' she asked.

'Sit down and I'll pour you a drink and tell you.' Alex sat her on the sofa. There were damp patches on it.

'Has that cat been peeing on my sofa?'

'Certainly not!' Alex indignant.' It met with a different accident and I'll tell you, if you don't overreact and you have a drink first.'

Anxiety raised its familiar head; so much for a relaxing meal.

'What about the food?' Cleo indicated to the cartons on the bench. 'Can you put it in the oven with the heat on low if we're not eating right way?'

Alex slipped into the kitchen area to turn the oven on and deal with the take away and she sat there waiting,

'Come on, Alex. There's something you're not saying and I'd rather know.'

Alex brought her a very large chilled white. She sipped. It was one of her very good Pinots.

'Well,' started Alex. She was kneeling on the floor in front of her and Cleo looked over Alex's shoulder at a small green figure under the coffee table.

'Does that dinosaur belong to the cat?'

'No. *That's* what I need to tell you. It's Neil again and, typically, he's not here to do his own explaining even though he promised that he would be back.'

'What now?'

Just then, the office door opened and a small figure in superman pyjamas stood there.

'Hi Alex. I could smell Chinese and thought Daddy might be back.' Cleo was speechless as she stared at the boy and then at Alex.

'Cleo, this is Josh, who I'm trying to tell you about.'

Neil arrived just as supper was being served. He looked sheepish and was all apologies for being delayed at his meeting but he took a huge portion of their supper. It was a good thing that she'd played safe and bought extra.

Cleo found that she'd lost her appetite anyway and watched Alex and Neil tucking in to the Szechuan chicken that she usually loved. Josh sat beside his daddy eating fried rice and yawning. What the hell was she going to do? She'd have to have it out with Neil but not in front of his son or her sister.

Eventually, Neil lifted up a very sleepy Josh and carried him into the office.

Cleo grabbed Alex and ushered her into the kitchen area to whisper, 'Alex, when Neil comes back in here, I'm going to take him down to the car for a private word or two. I don't want to wake up Josh. Is it OK if you stay here while we're gone?'

Alex nodded, she was still munching her way through her third bowl of food and the odd prawn cracker.

Neil came out of the office and shut the door quietly. He turned to look at Cleo and seemed subdued for once. 'Cleo, now he's asleep, let me explain...'

'Stop right there, Neil. Get your jacket because I want to talk to you privately. We'll have to sit in my car seeing as my whole apartment has been taken over.' She strode to the door and Neil had little choice but to follow her.

'What the hell is going on in your life and why is it happening in *my* home? Answer me without any lies or excuses.' Cleo knew she was shouting instead of talking but felt like physically shaking this man who had got her into such a mess.

'Cleo, calm down. This isn't making anything better. I can explain but please hear me out.'

'Don't dare to tell me to stay calm. Don't dare to say another word unless it is to say goodbye!'

'Don't be mean. I didn't intend to put you in a spot. I'll move on as soon as I can.'

'When?'

'It's complicated. First of all, I haven't been completely honest. I'll come clean and tell you that I rented part of a house and I got behind with the rent so I was asked to leave. The locks were changed while we were in Italy so I had to move in with you. I was a bit cowardly and I didn't tell you the truth because...because I owe you money already and you'd realise that I couldn't pay you either.'

'Why? How can you owe so much when you're working?'

'I do have a house but Marianne, that's Josh's mum, lives there and I help her with the mortgage and bills.'

'Are you *married*?'

'Technically, but we don't live together.'

'Then this Marianne is your *wife*. You have a wife and child that you didn't tell me about, Neil. That's so unfair of you.'

'I liked you and I wanted us to have a chance at a relationship, Cleo.'

'By lying? You are so dishonest!'

'I'm not, Cleo. I do have feelings for you'.

'Oh yes, a fine way to show it. Get Cleo to pay for the holiday, forget to mention a family, a little boy. Pretend you've mislaid your credit cards and sponge from Cleo. That holiday really finished things for me, Neil.'

Neil looked surly, 'So you've said but, for the whole flight home, you didn't say.'

'I didn't say! Look at what *you* haven't said. I just want us to call it a day and for you to take Josh and yourself back to wherever you can go.'

'I'm sorry you feel that way. I've got nowhere until I get some money from clients; it's a question of cash flow. I now have the added worry of Josh because Marianne is away for two weeks.'

'Two weeks! How could she leave a little boy with a complete waster like you?'

'Steady on, I'm his father and he loves being with me. She knows he'll be fine. She had to go because her father's ill, seriously ill, and he lives in the Netherlands.'

'Why couldn't Josh go with her?'

'More complications.'

'I'm listening.'

'Marianne is Dutch; her father lives in Delft. She couldn't take Josh because she couldn't find his passport.

That was my fault. You see, I was worried she'd move back over there one day and I'd never get to see him so I destroyed his passport months ago. I couldn't foresee all this!

She didn't know about the passport so she couldn't sort out a new one in time. I've signed the forms for a replacement so he can join her as soon as possible. She wasn't at all happy about leaving him with me.'

'I wonder why.' Cleo felt some compassion for the little boy left with an unreliable parent and for his mother, who must've been pulled between seeing her father and leaving her son.

She reached her hand down the side pocket of her door, pulled out some wine gums and started chewing. What choice did she have in all of this? One last try. 'Neil, is there *anybody*? Anyone you could go to?'

'If there was, I wouldn't land all this on you Cleo. Sorry. We won't be any bother and I'll try to get somewhere when some money comes into the business at the end of the month. Just a week. Two at the most. Please?'

Cleo took a deep breath, she'd run out of steam, 'I'll say yes but I want it to be as soon as you can. I want you to pay back what you owe me and then I want my life back.'

Neil rewarded her with one of his endearing dimpled

grins. How had they ever worked on attracting her to this shallow, selfish man?

'You and Josh had better have my room. You can't share that narrow camp bed with him. I suppose I'll have to take that.'

'Thanks, Cleo, that's more than generous.'

'You go and sort it out. There's clean bedding in the airing cupboard. I'm just going to sit here awhile.' She shrugged off Neil's hug and he got out of the car.

As she watched him walk back towards the building, Cleo pressed the button that rolled back the roof of her car and then she reclined back to look at the darkening sky.

She relished the silence; a moment of calm. She closed her eyes and tried to forget the day she'd had and the night she was going to have on that camp bed.

Cleo shivered, feeling icy cold and looked at her watch. She must've dozed off; it was after eleven. The dark velvet of the sky was lit by the bright crescent of the Mead moon but the city lights were hiding the stars that were out there too. Glancing up at the windows of her apartment, she noticed that the hallway lamp was the only other light shining. Her guests were all bedded down so at least she could go back up there without facing anyone else.

17

At the end of another hectic week, Alex woke to the now familiar sounds of Cleo making coffee in the kitchen. She guessed it must be six in the morning. She was surprised at how she had felt sympathy for Cleo over the past two weeks. Her big sis had to sleep in her office, work long hours and then come home to a houseful of lodgers. It couldn't be fun for her.

They'd Skyped Mum last night and had chatted about how things were going without a mention of Josh's arrival and the bedlam that reigned in the apartment. Cleo had even stroked Pharos as Alex had held him up to the screen to purr at Mum.

Mum had looked tanned and happy and wanted to talk about what they were up to much more than her travels. That was Mum.

Alex had another hour before she needed to get up and was about to turn over when her door opened and Josh came in clutching one of his dinosaurs. She groaned and put her head under the duvet.

'You there, Alex?' Josh peered under the duvet.

'Yes, I'm here. What made you get up so early?'

'It's not dark and Daddy has gone to work,' Alex sat up and helped Josh onto her bed.

'No, it's far too early for Daddy to be at work. Is he in the bathroom?'

'Mm...mm' Josh shook his head frowning at Alex. 'Daddy is at work. He told me to go back to sleep but I couldn't.'

'You stay here with your dino and I'll just check.'

She checked the bathroom and then knocked on Cleo's bedroom door. No sound. She peeped inside. Empty. No Neil. She checked the wardrobe for clothes and breathed a sigh of relief. His clothes were there so he hadn't scarpered off. His watch and phone weren't on the bedside cabinet but there was a note propped up there.

Sorry Ladies, I have an urgent trip and didn't want to wake you. I'll be back tomorrow. It's Friday, so Alex, maybe you could stay off school for one day and look after Josh? It is important or I wouldn't ask. Love Neil x

The cheek of that man. It was an ultimatum not a request. She took the note into the office to show Cleo, just as she was packing her work bag and about to set off.

'Have you seen Neil?'

'This morning?' Cleo looked puzzled.

'Take a look at this.'

As Cleo read the note, Josh wandered in.

'Shall we have brekkie, Alex?'

'Good idea, Josh. Why don't you watch Peppa Pig while I make it?'

Cleo hadn't said a word but Alex could see that her sister's mind was working overtime thinking of something, a solution.

She wouldn't mind taking a day off to look after Josh but Cleo wouldn't be happy about her missing school and she was due to have a history tutorial about an assignment she'd completed. That was at eleven and she didn't want to miss it. She had Art all afternoon too and loved that Friday session.

Cleo was on the phone. 'Heather, I know how you always have loads to do on your day off but can I ask you a huge favour?'

As Cleo's face relaxed, Alex knew that Heather had stepped in and was going to help out. Cleo was filling Heather in on the latest development as Alex made breakfast for Josh and herself.

'Tell Heather that I can stay here until ten. I'll miss my tutor group and go in for my history tutorial,' Alex called.

After the call, Cleo came into the kitchen and gave her a hug as she poured milk on Josh's rice crispies. Alex almost spilled the carton. Wow, that was a first!

'Thanks for all you've done Alex. This isn't your mess but I do appreciate you helping out. Heather is coming over with Archie as soon as they're ready.'

'No problem.' She felt as thrilled as she did whenever she made Mum proud.

As she was leaving the apartment, Cleo called, 'But, Alex, don't you let him have that cereal bowl near my grey sofa or carpet!'

Now that was more like her sister, always a 'but'. She was still smiling though, as she sat Josh up at the breakfast bar and tied a tea towel around his neck.

Alex was glad to leave Josh with Heather and catch the metro to school. Dinosaurs and dishes weren't a great way to start the day. She was surprised to see Gracie get on at her stop.

'Hey, Gracie, over here! Looks like we're both late.'

Gracie gave her a watery smile and said, 'Don't talk about being late.'

'I didn't think you'd be so bothered.' Alex knew that Gracie skipped school a lot. She was often looking after her younger brothers and going off when she had 'other fish to fry', whatever that meant.

'It depends on what sort of late,' Gracie muttered.

Alex guessed what she meant straight away. 'Do you mean late, as in period?'

'Very late. I need to do a test. Don't you tell another

soul, Alex, 'cos nobody else knows.'

'I won't, of course I won't. Do you want me to come to the chemist with you?'

'Would you? I've been saving dinner and smoke money to get a kit.'

They got off the metro a stop early and walked to the large chemist further away from school. Alex still had plenty of time before her history tutorial.

'Does the dad know?' asked Alex.

'Don't be daft. It might be nothing and I'd have made a fool of meself for nowt,' laughed Gracie. Her bravado was back. 'I bet you're dying to know who it is.'

'Is it anybody I know?'

'Aye. I'll tell you but mind that you keep *this* to yourself ... It's Ty.'

'Tyrone? Bloody Hell! You're always arguing and rude to each other.'

'You know nowt. That's just how me and him go on Alex. We've been courting since primary school, not like this of course. We've been proper serious for over a year but he goes off and has his daft flings every now and then.'

'Other girls?'

'Aye. I find out and scare them off and they soon dump him. Me and him were always meant for each other but I didn't want this, not before A levels and a job and a flat.'

'What'll you do?'

'I'd never get rid. If that's what you mean. That's not for me, not when it's Ty's. Anyway we'd better be sure first.'

They'd reached the chemist and Gracie looked uncomfortable. 'Will you ask, Alex? I'm more well known round the shops than you. Them at the counter might start some gossip.'

Alex shook her hair out of its loose bun and borrowed some of Gracie's juicy tube gloss to try to look a bit older before they approached the counter.

'Excuse me, can you give me a pregnancy test, please?'
'Any particular sort?'

Alex felt confused; what could the woman mean? 'The most reliable sort, but not too expensive please.' Alex knew that they only had fifteen pounds.

'They are all reliable after two weeks and this one is nine pounds ninety nine. Some others have two tests for fifteen pounds.'

'Oh no, one will suffice,' Alex said.

Gracie was giggling behind her.

'Thank you so much. No, I don't have my loyalty card with me this morning.' Phew she was glad to get out of there.

Gracie broke into peals of laughter as they got to the door.

'What's so funny?' Alex felt confused. She'd done this for Gracie and now it was a huge joke.

'You! "One will suffice." You sounded so bloody la-di-da'

Alex saw the funny side and they both laughed as they walked back in the direction of school. Alex kept the test in her bag; Gracie hadn't a schoolbag with her as usual.

'We'll do it at lunchtime but out of school over at the cafe, shall we?' Gracie suggested.

Alex agreed and they hurried into the building because it was now almost eleven and she had to meet her history tutor for her one to one.

Alex waited by the gates for Gracie but she didn't appear. Her tutorial had gone well and she wanted a quick lunch before going to the Art studios for an afternoon of painting.

Ty came up as she was standing there. 'Gracie said to tell you she's not in school. She had an argument with Batesy about being late into school and walked out. She's a moody cow at the moment. She's meeting me over at my place and she says the plan can wait until Monday.'

'Oh, right. Tell her that's fine,' Alex said. She was about to go back through the gates when Ty caught her arm.

He asked, 'Do you know what plan she meant because I don't and she wouldn't tell me?'

'Sorry Ty, if Gracie doesn't want you in on this, I don't either. Just tell her I'll see her on Monday.'

'She asked me to give you her mobile number.'

Ty handed her a slip of paper; Alex took it and hurried off before she gave anything away and went to meet Lee at their Art session.

In the studio, as they gathered together the materials they needed for the afternoon, a couple of the girls were talking about the Karate sessions they'd signed up for. There were four 'taster' sessions after school starting tonight for lower 6th form only and Lee was going to give it a go.

'It's useful to be able to defend yourself around here, well anywhere really. You should come with us, Alex.'

'I haven't any gym stuff with me or I would. I used to love gymnastics.'

'That's no excuse, it's in bare feet and those white suits are provided for the taster course. Go and sign up at afternoon break.'

Alex thought about it and decided it might be fun. She found the notice board near reception and signed her name. There would be fourteen of them attending four till five. She checked no one was about and asked for Ann at reception.

'Hi, Alex, how's it going?'

'Great thanks. I'm going to go to Karate tonight so I'll be here until five. Can you let Cleo know? Tell her I don't want a lift but I'll be home late.'

'Are you still incognito? Nobody twigged?' Ann asked.

'Not yet, I'd hate anyone to find out we're related,' she

shuddered.

Ann winked, 'It's safe with me, Alex.'

They were sorting out a pile of freshly laundered karate suits in the changing rooms and tying white belts around the baggy outfits, when a deep Scottish voice yelled through the changing room door,

'Come out as soon as you have your *gis* on, we only have an hour.'

Alex hurriedly tied her hair in a pony tail and followed Lee into the gym.

Their instructor, a tall powerful looking man, was standing waiting for them. Alex noticed his black belt and then, as he introduced himself, she studied his face. It was familiar. Where had she seen him before?

His eyes looked over her as she stood in line and there was no recognition there. They hadn't met then, but there was *something*, even the voice.

He had set them off on a paired exercise and was visiting each pair to watch them more closely when it hit her. *Oh damn and blast!* Her face must have changed because Lee was asking her if she was alright.

'I didn't hurt you, did I Alex?'

'Of course not, I'm OK.'

'Less talking girls and keep moving,' the instructor said as he passed them.

Alex gathered her scattered thoughts together and concentrated. No way was she going to attract extra attention. She *did* know him but, thankfully, he didn't recognise *her*.

The last time they'd met she had been off her face, hysterical and he'd saved her friend's life. The club doorman from Edinburgh was here in Tyneview and teaching her karate.

18

Teri stretched out in the shade under a grass umbrella and looked out over silver sands to a turquoise sea. That heady mix of sun and sea lingered on her skin and she was sure that the climate was soothing her aching joints; this was a healing holiday. The Red Sea was an unbelievable shade and underneath it was another world; a glorious variety of multi-coloured fish, coral and plants. She had started to explore the tip of this existence just by snorkelling yards from the shore. She felt like one of the Cousteaus from one of those wonderful old documentaries when she followed Greg underwater, using hand signals to point fish and plants out to one another.

Greg. She hadn't dreamed of meeting a fellow traveller, a true friend to share her exploration of Egypt and its treasures. He had invited her to join his party to tour the pyramids and the Cairo museum and she had enjoyed being part of the large party who wanted to see as much of Egypt as possible in a few days.

When the party left to go on to a Nile cruise, Teri stayed on in Cairo for a few more days and revisited the museum several times; there was so much to see there.

The special room that contained several mummified Pharaohs fascinated her. She was drawn back to it time and time again. Lying there was Ramses II, who she'd read so much about and his hair was as fair as her own, she'd never imagined that. Many moons ago, she'd renamed herself after his favourite wife and she hoped he didn't find her visits too intrusive.

After Cairo, she visited Sinai on her own and climbed, with a party of noisy Italians, up the mount. They started at midnight when it was cool and it had taken five hours to reach the summit. She got up to the top just before dawn to witness the most spectacular sunrise of her life.

The Egyptian gods had taken a giant golden egg and broken its yolk all over the darkened sky to herald the start of day. Cameras had clicked all around her but she just feasted her eyes on it; no picture could capture that magic. She had the urge to create, to make a tapestry with those jewelled colours. That scene was etched in her memory ready for when she got home.

Teri decided to take a beach break at Hurghada before the trip to Luxor and all its wonders. She was going to meet up with Greg again to explore Luxor and the Valley of the Kings. She checked into a luxury hotel, enjoyed the air-conditioning and the chance to Skype her girls and had been delighted at how they both seemed to be comfortable in one another's company. Even Pharos seemed to be settled; it seemed like her plan was working.

Greg had surprised her. He'd asked if she'd mind him joining her on the beach break and had arrived at Makadi Bay a couple of days ago. They'd had fun and relaxed and were very easy in each other's company but now Teri felt rather confused. They'd held hands walking along the beach last night and she knew they were getting fond of one another. Maybe too fond?

He'd told her he was forty, that was nine years her junior, was it such a gap? That was the main thing stopping her from succumbing to a holiday romance. That and the fact that Greg was the first man she'd looked at in that way since Mac. It must be the spell of Egypt.

Greg's shadow stood in the way of the sun. He threw an ice cold lolly that landed on her midriff.

'Greg!' she shrieked. He sat on the end of her lounger. Tall, tanned, long hair ruffled by the sea, who could resist him? He was thoughtful and caring too.

'Teri, you've lain there long enough. When you finish that ice lolly, we should go for a dip then a siesta.'

'What do you mean, a siesta? Teri sat up.

'A short sleep in the cool air conditioned rooms that we've got. What did you think I meant?'

Teri turned pink and it wasn't the sun. She held his gaze. 'It was the 'we' I was questioning,' she said.

Greg's brown eyes were reading hers. 'Teri, there's no one I'd rather siesta with than you and I think you know that.'

She was lost for words. He'd placed the beach ball firmly on her patch of sand.

Becoming lovers developed as naturally as their friendship. Teri and Greg walked back to the hotel and, when the lift reached her floor, instead of getting out on her own, she took Greg's hand and they walked to her room together.

She led him to the wet room and they showered off the sand and salt of the beach together. They shared their first kiss. Warm and tender at first and then more demanding as they shared their hunger for each other. She pulled slightly away but wanted more, so much more.

'It's been such a long time,' she said as he wrapped her in a towel and carried her over to the bed.

'Let's just take lots of time now and make sure it's worth it.' His kisses teased her neck and moved along her throat and down her body. She arched her back as he kissed the scar just below her bikini line, Teri raised her head and looked up and Greg smiled, 'You just lie there and relax. We have all afternoon to siesta.'

Teri lay watching Greg as he slept. Such long dark lashes and a very kissable mouth. She loved the smell of him. Underneath the shower gel fragrance, he still smelt of sun and warmth and Greg. Enjoying her newly awakened sexuality, making love, after seventeen years had taken her by surprise. It had been exquisite and healing. Healing for them both. Greg confessed that he hadn't made love since losing his wife.

It couldn't last, she knew that; he deserved a family and she had her own girls to go back to but this was more than a holiday romance. Her sensual side had been reborn and they had limited time in Egypt, so they would make the most of this hiatus in their lives.

THUNDER MOON

19

Even though it was Saturday, Cleo was up early. She had to complete the timetable for the next academic year before the end of term and they were approaching the final week. Staff appreciated having their timetable before they broke up for summer but it wasn't easy to finish it with all the interruptions she had at work and at home.

Camping out in the office wasn't comfortable and she was ready to have yet another moving out discussion with Neil whenever he next reappeared. Yesterday, she had considered ringing social services about Josh. Neil wasn't caring for him properly if he could just up and leave him. He was being unfair on her and on her sister too; Josh was an easy going kiddie but he wasn't their responsibility.

She could hear Josh in the bedroom, talking away to his dinosaur collection. She'd stop for a coffee in a few minutes and fix him some breakfast. She would just finish the timetabling Year 9 English first.

Success! Cleo saved her work and stretched; sorting out Year 9 had taken her longer than she thought. All was quiet in the apartment; had Josh gone back to sleep? She left her office to check on him.

'Ah, there you are Josh. Good morning sweetie.' He was lying on his tummy in the living area drawing dinosaurs on a sketch pad that Alex had given him. Pharos stretched out beside him trying to flick a felt tip under the sofa but, on seeing Cleo, he yawned and strolled purposefully towards his food bowl.

Josh grinned up at Cleo, 'I'm not a sweetie, I'm a superman, silly. Look at my steg'saurus.' He proudly waved a green and purple drawing at her. Cleo crouched down to look and succeeded in ignoring the open felt tips lying all over her rug... well almost.

'That's really good, Josh. Where did you get the felt tips from? You usually use your wax crayons.'

'Alex says I can use them, but just if I'm careful,' he explained.

'Oh, is she awake then?' Alex didn't usually surface until after nine on Saturdays.

'No, not yet but I *am* being careful.'

Cleo noticed that he had dragged Alex's bag into the living area and had opened her felt tip case. She picked up the loose felt tips.

'Let's put these back until Alex wakes up and you can ask her if she minds. Anyway, you and Pharos and I are going to have breakfast.'

'Sc'ambled eggs?' his hopeful grin won her over.

'Pharos would prefer a smelly fish pouch but yes, we've got time for that today.'

As Cleo put the felt tip case bag into Alex's bag, she caught sight of a half open bag. Josh must have looked into it when he was searching for the pens.

She was just about to close the bag when she caught sight of the pregnancy test carton. Oh please no, what the hell had Alex been up to? A pregnancy test! She'd only been with her for two weeks so it had to be before then. She hadn't mentioned a boy back in Dunleith. That night in Edinburgh maybe? The silly girl.

Josh had gone back to his drawing; shouldn't she make breakfast and calm down before she talked to Alex? Better still, wait for Alex to come to her in her own time. She stood up but her feet wouldn't move towards the kitchen. She had to talk to Alex now, even though her common sense was shrieking bad idea, wrong move.

'Alex! Wake up, you and I need to talk.' She was drawing the curtains as Alex rubbed hair eyes and yawned.

'Hey Cleo, calm yourself. What's the matter now?

Alex looked about twelve with her hair tied back from her face in a plait for bed. She was sitting up and looking crossly at Cleo.

'This is what's wrong, Alex. Why do you need this?' Cleo sat down and her hands trembled as she put the chemist's bag onto the bed beside her.

Alex grabbed the bag, 'What the hell are you doing, going through my things?' she blustered.

'I wasn't. It was Josh who opened it, he...'

'Oh, yes, blame someone else. You have no right to go through my things.'

'I didn't!'

Alex glared at her, 'Please get out of my room and give me *some* privacy. I'm seventeen and don't need to explain anything to you. You're out of order to even suggest what you're suggesting.'

Was Alex right? Maybe she hadn't handled that in the calmest way. She could hear Josh shouting about breakfast.

'Look Alex, whatever's happened, we can sort it out. I'm sorry to confront you with it but I just know that Mum would expect me to help you.'

'Cleo, sod off. Get out and leave me alone.' Alex buried herself under the duvet.

So much for counselling skills. It seemed they were impossible to apply when the problem involved your own family. All Cleo could do was leave the room and wait until Alex was ready to talk.

Half an hour later, Alex made sure that Cleo heard her

leave the apartment by banging the door after her. Josh had eaten all of his breakfast but Cleo hadn't been able to touch hers. She should have handled the situation much better than that.

She blinked back tears as she cleared their plates. She was worried, she was tired and she was stuck here until Neil showed up. She really needed to get back to her timetable but Josh needed to go out and get some exercise and fresh air. It wasn't fair on him to be cooped up all day.

'Hey Josh, why don't we get ourselves washed and dressed and then go on the metro to Tynemouth beach?'

'Yay! Shall we take our cossies?'

'No, it's still quite cold but we'll take wellingtons to splash in the water.' Cleo felt almost cheered. She could do with a Northern sea breeze to clear her thoughts.

Cleo enjoyed their splash time as much as Josh and as they made their way back to the metro station, the smell of Longsands Fish Kitchen beckoned.

'Shall we have a chippy lunch, Josh?'

'Could I have the chippy but not the fishy please, Cleo?'

'What about a sausage with the chips?' she suggested.

'Cool.' He looked up at her and grinned. She matched his grin thinking he'd picked that superlative up from Alex.

'Let's just go to the hole in the wall and get some cash. It's on the way to the chippy.'

Cleo was aware of the queue forming behind her as she looked in puzzlement at the bank's screen. It wasn't going to pay out. She tried again and asked for her current account balance. Minus?... Minus!... She tried again. There had to be an error. She had this month's salary in there and her emergency overdraft was for a thousand pounds.

'Are you going to be all day love?' a gruff voice enquired. She ignored the remark, tried one more time and her card was eaten up. She felt her cheeks flushing as she took Josh's hand and walked away empty handed, trying to avoid the looks from the growing queue. Just wait until she called the bank. They had some explaining to do.

'Sorry, sweetheart. It looks like we're going to have to share a bag of chips and then have a proper meal at home,' explained Cleo.

'It's OK, those holes are mean. They do that to Daddy too, you know.'

I bet they do, thought Cleo.

As they ate their shared chips, Cleo couldn't get rid of the fiery anxious feeling in her chest that was like indigestion but worse. It was as if her body knew what her brain was scared to admit. What if the balance was real? What if someone had cleared her account? She could have been cloned in an internet fraud or it could have been someone in the flat, Alex or Neil?

Straight away she ruled out her sister. Alex may be in trouble but she was honest. Alex even replaced her jelly sweets when she ate them, but Neil...Neil had shown he was untrustworthy several times. Let's face it, he'd taken financial liberties since day one. Surely even Neil wouldn't be so dishonest as to deliberately steal from her?

She'd have to go online to her bank when she got back and sort all this out. Please let it be a banking error. Please!

'Hi there, you two!' Neil was making coffee when they got home. 'Sorry about leaving you with Josh but I had an emergency to sort out. Would you like a coffee?'

Josh had run to hug his dad and Cleo stood weighing up the situation. Should she say something now, and risk jumping to conclusions as she had with Alex this morning or should she look online at her bank account first?

'No, no coffee for me. You've held my work up

enough today. I need to go back to my office,' she said and excused herself.

As she logged on, she could hear Josh talking to Neil.

'We jumped the waves and then I nearly had a sausage but the hole wouldn't give Cleo any money so we had to share chips. That was OK, though.'

She stared at her accounts on screen, Savings account - zilch, Holiday account - zilch,

Current account - minus £3520. Cleo felt sick. She went into her holiday account and saw that the whole lot had been withdrawn last week. She clicked on savings and saw that £4500 had dwindled in chunks of five hundred or a thousand pounds at weekly intervals, until it reached zero. This had been going on all month. Why, oh why, hadn't she checked?

The door opened behind her. 'Oh shit, Cleo. I meant to have the money back before you found out. I've been in a bit of trouble you see.'

Cleo slowly swivelled her chair towards the door. She looked at Neil, incredulous at what was coming from his mouth. Ice cold rage froze her to her chair. A good thing too because she really wanted to wipe that stupid vacant look from his face. 'Explain.' The calm request belied her rage.

'You *must* realise by now that I have a bit of a gambling problem, Cleo, love.'

Love? Love! Cleo's head pounded. She would strangle him if she could move.

Neil carried on, 'I... I just can't help it and sometimes I'm near to winning and clearing my debts but just need a bit more.'

'A bit more of my money, of my savings? Mine, not yours!'

'Yes, I know. I shouldn't have taken advantage, but I'll pay you back and that's a promise.'

'Promise? A promise from you is pointless, less than

useless.' Her voice was raised and Josh came to the door.

'Are you two arguing?' he asked.

Oh no, poor Josh, she couldn't let him see this!

'No darling. Look, why don't you go and watch some TV?' she found the CBeebies channel and gave him some juice and then went back to find Neil. He was in her bedroom packing a holdall.

'Running away?'

'No. Well, yes I *am* going away but I'm not running Cleo. I'll be back. I need to come back for Josh, don't I? Please, don't do anything rash like calling the police, I'll sort it all out, honestly.'

'*Honestly? Promise*? You have to be joking Neil!' Cleo barred the doorway. Her hands were on her hips but she was longing to throw something heavy at him. An alarming thought struck her,

'Neil, is that it? Is that all you've borrowed? Is there anything else I should know?'

'Why don't you sit down?' he suggested.

Cleo sat on the edge of the bed. Was there more to this nightmare?

'I'll come clean. I've pawned your Gucci watch. You never wear it and it's just at the brokers on the West Road. You can get it back. And... I may as well tell you that I've got a credit card. It's in your name and up to its limit, I'm afraid.' He had the good grace to wince as he revealed this.

'Oh, my God.' Cleo felt such a trembling rage that she almost forgot Josh was sitting in the next room watching Peppa Pig.

'I'm calling the police, Neil,' she managed to say calmly. 'You're a crook.' It sounded old fashioned and she almost giggled with nerves but it was true; he was a trickster and a crook.

Neil continued flinging things into the holdall.

'You can't make a getaway when you have your son sitting here, Neil, don't be silly.'

'Watch me,' he answered and made for the door.

'Neil, don't be stupid. You have to face the music sometime.'

The front door closed. Had he really just walked, gone and left her, his victim, with his son to look after? Cleo didn't know what to do next. She picked up the phone to call the police but then decided to call Alex first.

'Yes? Have you finished snooping into my things now and stopped accusing me of things?' Alex asked.

Damn, she'd forgotten about that. This morning seemed so long ago.

'Alex, I'm sorry about that but *please* can you get home? Tears started and Cleo sobbed down the phone. 'Something horrible has happened.'

'Are you OK? Is Josh OK?'

'Yes we're here and all right but I've got myself into a right mess.'

'I'm coming now Cleo, don't cry, it can't be that bad.'

Alex thought it couldn't be that bad but it really was. Cleo put her head down onto her closed laptop and sobbed. She'd been an absolute fool.

'This is serious crime Cleo, so we must call the police.' Alex's reaction, after she'd listened carefully to the whole tale, encouraged Cleo to pick up the phone.

It had been difficult to discuss with Josh around but they'd made him a long overdue meal and then he'd fallen asleep watching Shrek. He'd had far too much TV today but Cleo knew that she wasn't thinking straight and was grateful that he loved it so much. Hell, he shouldn't even be their responsibility; she'd have to try to contact his Mum if Neil didn't return.

Cleo was relieved that Heather was coming around to help look after Josh and to see if he would like a sleep over with Archie before the police were called around. It seemed as though they didn't think a live-in fraudster was urgent but they'd try to fit a visit in later today. On top of that, Mum had sent a text to say she wanted to Skype them both later tonight, their time, so Cleo hoped that everything was sorted by then.

By nine that night, Cleo looked better, even though her head was pounding and she couldn't stop making frantic calculations in her head about how to pay her mortgage, the bills and still eat for the rest of the month. The police hadn't shown at all. She obviously wasn't a priority; she'd have to give them a call tomorrow. In a way, she was pleased that she didn't have to go through the whole sorry mess and admit, yet again, that she kept her passwords and bank details in a file in her desk. Who expected someone in their own home to be so devious?

Alex and Pharos were sitting on the sofa with Alex's iPad on the coffee table waiting for Mum's weekly Skype. Both girls had put make up on and agreed that Mum was going to hear that everything was rainbows and lollipops for the Moon sisters. It made no sense to worry someone on the other side of the world and she would be certain to cut short her trip.

'Cleo, here she is, she's coming through.'

Cleo rushed to the sofa and saw Mum as clear as day looking tanned and like a *Ten Years Younger* after shot.

'Hi girls!' Her green eyes sparkled against golden skin and her smile was as wide as Cleo remembered it. Tears stung her eyes as she joined Alex.

All three talked at once as there was such a lot to say and Cleo's spirits had lifted considerably when they were interrupted by the doorbell ringing. Cleo glanced at Alex who looked equally alarmed.

'Hang on Mum, you carry on talking to Cleo, I'll be back in a moment.'

Cleo kept the conversation going as, out of the corner of her eye, she glimpsed two police officers in the doorway. She heard their radios relaying information as she tried to swing the screen out of view of them.

'What's that sound, Cleo? The picture is out of focus, I can't see you?' Then Mum's puzzled voice rose in alarm, 'Is that a policeman in your room? What is going on?'

20

Alex sat up in bed watching a film on her iPad with Pharos draped around her neck and purring so loudly that she could hardly hear the dialogue. Her mind wasn't on the film but she couldn't sleep. The police had been very thorough with Cleo and she'd felt sorry for her when she had to confess that she'd allowed someone else to have access to her laptop and had kept all her passwords together in a file.

Alex didn't even feel pleased that her sister was such a dolt. She hated Neil for taking advantage of Cleo's kindness. She might be bossy but, lately, Alex had discovered that Cleo could be really kind and didn't deserve someone like Neil taking advantage of her.

Alex had called Mum back and explained that the police had knocked on the wrong address. She didn't like to lie, but Cleo didn't want Mum worrying while she was away and couldn't do anything about it. Mum had believed her anyway, so that was a relief.

Cleo was going through her computer files and paperwork to see what other mischief Neil may have been up to. They were giving Neil until tomorrow to collect Josh; he'd gone happily enough to Heather's with Archie but the poor little lad had been tossed from pillar to post over the last week. If Neil didn't return, they'd have no choice but to get in touch with social services to find his

Mum. All they knew about her was that she was somewhere in Delft.

With all this racing around in her head, Alex was nowhere near sleep even though it was almost twelve.

A hunting horn blasted out from her phone; she had a text.

'Phone when you can. Ella x'

Alex had been itching to phone the EllaBellas but wasn't sure whether Cleo would want them to know about her plight. Anyway, they must have news for her if they'd texted at this time. She moved Pharos from her neck and snuggled under the covers to make the call.

'Hi, Ella, of course I'm awake. What's up?'

'What's up? You tell us! *Your* Mum has been on to *our* Mum saying that there were police at your door and you two look guilty about something! She wanted to know if any of us knew anything. Your mum said that you couldn't lie for toffee and you were clearly spinning her a yarn about the police and that she could tell you couldn't wait to get her off the phone.

'*Our* mum asked us about it but drew a blank, so she had the bright idea of phoning Heather and Mark and testing the water there. Heather had to tell her whatever she knew, in case your mum flew straight home to find out for herself.

'So now *our* mum knows something that we don't know but she won't tell us. We've guessed it's about Neil.'

Ella managed to relay all that to her without drawing a breath. Oh God. How embarrassing for Cleo but at least she hadn't been the one who let this kitty out of the bag.

'Alex? Are you there? Don't leave us out of this one,' Ella pleaded.

She didn't need any more persuading to tell them the whole story. After she'd finished, it was Bella's turn take over the call.

'Dan flew back yesterday because that consultancy vacancy has come up and he's heard all about this from Heather and Mark too. He is furious, calling Neil some choice words and saying that Cleo has been too soft and that she's been played for being so kind. You'd think he still fancied her, Alex, truly you would.'

Alex came to Cleo's defence, 'There's nothing wrong with that. She can be lovely when you get to know her.'

'Oh God, Alex, you've changed your tune. But I'm glad if you can see some good in her.'

21

Cleo tussled with the sheets and watched the moon slip in and out of the clouds for hours; it was July's thunder moon, how bloody apt. She tried, but she didn't sleep; too much coffee while she was going through her laptop files and too much to worry about. She'd found the unpaid bills for a store card in her name that had reached its maximum. She worried about what else she might find out.

Why did Alex have a pregnancy test in her bag if she wasn't going to use it? She hadn't brought *that* up again but it preyed on her mind. She would have to trust that Alex would talk to her eventually, on her own terms.

How many more loans were there and would she be liable for the lot? She'd already resigned herself to using Mum's old Range Rover and selling her car to clear her bank debts.

She must suffer the embarrassment of talking to someone at the bank about her accounts on Monday and admitting how foolish she'd been. Both worries whirled relentlessly around and kept sleep at bay.

The phone ringing at six in the morning didn't disturb her, she was wide awake, but the unknown number did. Who would call at this time on a Sunday morning? She couldn't ignore it; it might be something to do with this sorry mess.

A female voice said, 'Hello, am I speaking to Cleo Moon?'

'Yes who is this?'

'Oh, thank goodness. How is Josh? I'm Marianne, his mum.'

So, she'd got in touch at last. 'How is he? He's confused of course, but he's ok. He's a very easy-going little boy but, now *both* his parents have disappeared, he must feel mixed up. How did you get my number? Are you going to come and collect him?'

'Can I speak to Josh, to reassure him? I got your number from Neil and he's told me his story; that's if there is any truth in it because he makes things up to suit himself.'

'What, exactly, has he told you?' Cleo asked.

'That he wasn't in lodgings but living with you, his girlfriend. I didn't know *that* before I left Josh with him. That he'd borrowed from you and you threw him out but you have room in your cold heart to keep Josh with you until I collect him. Don't worry, I'm not taken in by Neil's excuses. He'll have messed up big time and I can guess that he's trying to hide something.'

Cleo couldn't help herself, she had to ask, 'How *on earth* could you leave your little boy with Neil when you seem to know *just* what he's like?'

There was a long silence at the other end of the phone.

'I don't know what I was thinking. I certainly wasn't thinking straight and I didn't know what to do. You see, my father is critically ill; he had a heart attack and I needed to get home to see him and Josh didn't have a passport.

'After we broke up, Neil took Josh's passport and destroyed it. I was hunting all over for it and called Neil to ask if he'd seen it and he eventually owned up. I was desperate to catch my flight; that's why I told him that the responsibility for Josh was his, until my father was out of danger.'

'Neil did tell me that but I didn't know if it was true,' Cleo said. 'Are you still in the Netherlands?'

'Yes. My father's just out of hospital and needs nursing care. I'm trying to sort things out and his sister is coming to take over in a day or two but now Neil has left our son with people I don't know. He says you're a teacher so you must understand kids and be treating him kindly, I hope.'

More sobs down the phone made Cleo feel helpless. 'Shush, don't get upset; Josh is fine. As I said, he's a bit confused but fine and he is quite settled here. He hasn't been that phased about his dad going because he's been with my sister and me quite a lot over the past couple of weeks.' Cleo tried to soothe Marianne. *Maybe she'd been a bit hard on her at the beginning of the call*

'That's Neil. I should *never* have left Josh with him but I was in a panic and thought maybe it was a chance for him to show he could cope, like a proper father. But no, he's an idiot.'

'Look, Neil has left in a hurry because of more than a disagreement and I'm not sure *if* or *when* he'll be back, so how soon can you get home for Josh?'

'I'm trying to get a flight straight over and to get care in place for my father. Please, can he stay with you until I arrive? I have no one reliable over there and I've talked to him a couple of times on Neil's phone and he always says he's having fun.'

Cleo's mind was in turmoil. She needed time to think. No, she didn't really have to think this through.

'OK, Marianne. At the moment, Josh is sleeping over with a friend of mine who has a son of her own. I work, so Heather has offered to help with some day to day care. I'll give you her number so that you can chat to Josh now, but do be assured that he is in safe hands.'

'Oh, please, give me that number. I need to know that

he is not pining too much.'

Cleo gave Marianne the number and said, 'We'll both look after Josh but, in return, can you help in finding Neil? Any clues at all?'

'I'm sorry, he didn't tell me where he was and he changes his number all the time. I'd guess that, if he's in trouble, he'll have gone into hiding until he finds someone else who is willing to rescue him. His favourite place to retreat is Milan but who knows where he could be?'

'Thank you, I thought as much myself,' Cleo admitted.

'Don't be offended when I say rescue, I was the biggest fool. I married him and he went through my money like water; my father was furious and only now can I make my peace with my him. I'll be back as soon as I can - in a day, maybe two at most. I do keep my word. I've sorted out a new passport for Josh, so we can both return to my father's home. Thank you so much for this help.'

'Don't worry; we will make sure Josh is looked after.'

'Thank you. I'll call again soon.'

Cleo put the phone down. *She* had worries and Marianne had just as many by the sound of it. Now that she'd agreed to help out, she wouldn't be calling in social services.

Cleo lay back in bed feeling relieved; things were never black and white. She'd thought the mother was uncaring leaving Josh with Neil but she had a difficult choice to make. Marianne had more trust in Neil's parenting skills than Cleo could ever have, but then at times, Neil was very attentive to Josh. She would have hated to see that little boy being taken away to more strangers. His Dad was a louse but his mum seemed caring and she must be missing him so much.

Cleo's agitated mind gave up the fight with her exhausted body and she sank into oblivion.

Oblivion lasted all of an hour. The phone rang again dragging her from her much needed sleep but hearing Dan's voice jolted her wide awake.

'Hi, Cleo. Are you and Alex at High Rigg?'

'No. No, we're at my apartment. Why do you ask?'

'I'm out walking the dogs and I can see all the lights are on at High Rigg - there's someone moving about in there and, if it's not you, I'm going to investigate. I just wanted to check.'

'Dan, what are you talking about? Don't you go in there on your own!'

No good; he'd gone.

22

Cleo looked in the hallway cupboard; her key for High Rigg was not on its usual hook and, although he'd never been, Neil knew the address. Neil always had the lights blazing in her apartment and she was sure it was him at High Rigg. She called the police explaining that she thought Neil had taken her mother's key and that he could have gone to High Rigg.

She gently shook Alex awake and told her what was happening, as they pulled on clothes and put Pharos in his basket for the journey home.

Heather was up with Archie and Josh and had promised to keep Josh until she heard from them. She had already had a chat with Marianne and Josh was happy after hearing from his mum.

Within half an hour they were in the car and heading north. Before eight o'clock on a Sunday morning, the roads were empty and they were making good time. Alex tried Dan's number to tell him they were on their way but got no answer.

A coral dawn sky was breaking when Cleo pulled up at the house behind a police car - the only other car on the drive. As she got out and stretched herself awake, she looked up at the windows; all the lights were on but she couldn't see any figures in any of the rooms. Alex was out of the passenger seat and already running along the side of the house to the back door to use her key to get in.

They didn't need a key as Pete Laidlaw, their local bobby, was in the kitchen. Alex made tea while he updated them on the morning's events.

'It seems like young Dan Collingwood was walking the spaniels past here before he called for the Sunday papers. What he was doing out with them that early, I don't know; Mrs. Collingwood usually takes them out at around nine.

'Anyway, he sees the lights on and thinks that something is amiss. He phones you girls to check it's not you or your mum back early from her trip and, when it's not, he goes to the door.

'Nobody answers when he rings the bell so he goes round to the back and sees a fellow in your garden room and he's going through a lot of your papers. There's a mess of documents on the floor and the fellow is looking toward the main house, so he gets a shock when Dan bangs on the window. Brazen as brass, he comes to the garden room door and has the nerve to ask Dan what he's doing snooping round the back. He tries to bluff his way out of trouble by saying he's a friend of yours and has been invited to stay.

'Dan says he's phoned you and this chap gives him a sharp right hook and tries to run past. That sets the springers off and they are onto him, licks not bites, more's the pity, but they trip him up. Dan drags him back in and holds onto him while he phones the station.

'I race around, almost breaking the speed limit on my bike, and we get him into handcuffs. The chap is moaning and saying that he's in pain and needs a doctor because Dan has roughed him up. Dan says this is rubbish and *he's* a doctor and can see there's nothing wrong with him. Dan's lip is bleeding and he tells me that Neil threw a punch before Dan could get hold of him.

'I can't risk taking the perpetrator into custody without a medical check-up - procedures you know; and I can hardly ask Dr Collingwood when his son is involved, so I call an ambulance to take him to A and E and call in PC Johnson to go with him. I stay here to secure the building...can't abide hospitals meself and now... here you are!'

'So Neil is in casualty, but where is Dan?' Cleo asked.

'I take it you know the intruder...this Neil?' Sergeant Laidlaw answered her question with his own.

'Yes, he's wanted by Newcastle police for fraud and theft, Sergeant Laidlaw. He took Mum's key from my apartment. Now you must tell me, where is Dan?'

'Ah, I'll leave all that side to the city chaps and if they need me they'll find me. There's no damage as such, Cleo; so it's a clear up job you'll be needing to do and a check to see if anything is missing. The blighter said he'd taken nothing but I saw him drop a couple of things from his pockets before he left the house so I take it he's going to try to get away with as little as possible.'

'Dan? *Where* is he, Sergeant?' Cleo wasn't bothered about the house, she wanted to know that Dan was OK.

'Oh Dan? Ah yes, he took the dogs off home and was going to get cleaned up and come straight back here to give you girls a hand.

'I'll be on my way, I'll get in touch with the city team and we'll sort out the paperwork in the morning. No need to take up all our Sunday because our detainee is going nowhere.' The sergeant put his notebook away and bid them goodbye.

After he left, Alex and Cleo checked all the rooms; drawers had been turned out everywhere and valuable items were lined up on the beds ready to pick up. Downstairs was left tidy, except for the garden room. He'd emptied their moondream jar out and papers were spread out all over the floor.

Luckily, Cleo hadn't a key for Mum's studio at her apartment and the safe in there remained secure.

Cleo tried Dan's phone but there was still no answer, so they set about the painful task of replacing everything into drawers and cupboards

'Gosh, Alex your room looks tidier than usual,' Cleo said, as they set about putting things straight.

'Ha, bloody ha, you're so unfunny,' but Alex was grinning.

Once the upstairs was straight, they went downstairs and made more tea.

'Shall I risk the shops in the square and go and get some supplies?' asked Alex.

Their break in would be news of the day in Dunleith. There wouldn't be paparazzi but there would be Mrs. Weddell to contend with.

'Yes, you could do that. I'll just try Dan again.' He answered this time.

'Hi, Cleo. No, no damage, I'm fine. I was just about to drop by, to give you a hand. I'm bloody furious though, that sneaky bastard is trying to get time in hospital instead of the cells. I didn't touch him, as much as I would have liked to!'

Trying it on for leniency, that sums up Neil, thought Cleo.

'It would be lovely to see you, Dan. Alex and I are just going to buy some brunch before we sort the garden room out.'

'Why don't I buy some stuff on the way round and help you to eat it?'

'Great idea, see you soon.' Cleo walked into the kitchen with a smile on her face.

'You look happy, sis.'

'That's because I've heard from Dan and he's not

badly hurt.'

'I think you still feel *the love* for him,' Alex teased.

Cleo felt a blush and was going to say "rubbish" but she said nothing. She couldn't hide it- yes, she did feel *the love*.

Dan turned up, with a plaster over one brow and a grazed, fat lip, looking as sexy as ever, with the EllaBellas in tow.

'These two were woken up by Alex and had to come around. Chuck them out if you want to.' He looked pensive and Cleo knew why; old wounds. She'd never liked all the kids around them in the past.

Cleo thanked him and told them they were all welcome, purposely ignoring the surprised glances that the EllaBellas were giving each other. He helped Cleo with breakfast while the girls laid the table and got caught up on all the events from Alex.

As they sat down, Cleo sensed Dan looking at her and, as she returned his smile, she wondered whether he was thinking along the same lines as her. It was really nice, but seriously weird, to be sitting here having breakfast with their sisters after all this time.

When the Collingwoods left, Cleo and Alex agreed that they'd try to nap for a couple of hours. They were both shattered and they still had the garden room to put to rights before they returned to Mariner's Wharf and got ready for school next day.

Cleo slipped under the duvet in Mum's room because her bed wasn't made up and was just drifting off when her door opened. Alex stood there in her dressing gown.

'Cleo, can I come into Mum's bed with you? '

Cleo pulled the covers back. 'Come on then.'

They had never, ever bunked up before thought Cleo, as they snuggled under the duvet.

'I miss Mum,' Alex murmured.

'So do I, munchkin.' As she uttered one of Mum's pet names, Cleo wondered what she would have made of all this. She'd be happy, as long as they were safe and together; her girls, as she always proudly called them.

'What do you think Mum will say?' Cleo asked, but Alex was already asleep. As she stroked the hair from her sister's eyes, a protective jolt struck Cleo; she really liked having her baby sister around.

Alex's arrival had felt like the end of the world to Cleo and, until now, she had never been able to forgive her sister for ruining her life. It was not *her* arrival exactly; Mac's accident seemed like the end of the world to Cleo and, for years, she convinced herself it was Alex that had caused it. She'd told herself that from the beginning, otherwise she'd have to face all of the blame herself.

As Cleo lay back on Mum's bed, her self-centred teenage self, seemed long gone. She was such a different person now but it still made her cringe to think of her last evening with her dad. She remembered, but could hardly bare to recall, that night of the accident.

On that terrible day, Mac finished working in the studio and walked over to the house to chat to Cleo.

'I've phoned the hospital and your mum has to stay in there for a few more days because they need to keep an eye on her and the baby,' Mac explained.

Cleo felt slightly put out; the baby wasn't even here yet and was taking over all of their lives. This was the night of the lower sixth disco so she couldn't visit Mum. Mac would go and she hoped he would give her a lift, as planned, then go on to see Mum after that.

'Visiting is strictly seven until eight thirty tonight, so I can't drop you off, Cleo. Your mum is not well and I don't want to keep her waiting.'

'It's just half an hour! Mum won't mind.' Usually, she could wrap Mac around her little finger and Mum would want her to have a good time.

'No. Maybe Mum won't mind, but *I* will - and so should you, Cleo. You can take the bus to the disco for once or walk around to the Roberts' and ask for a ride with Heather.'

'I've put your favourite shepherd's pie in the oven ready for when you get home, I've gone to visit Mum every single night and I've done the washing. I have a life too, Dad! I can't walk all the way round to Heather's in heeled shoes and I can't wear my *school* coat, which is the only one I've got, for a night out. You're just mean!' Cleo stomped upstairs and waited. She loved Mac, he wasn't mean at all and was always a pushover when she wanted something.

Sure enough, five minutes later, he called up to her, 'Hey, Cleo grumpy pants, it is all organised. You've got a lift with Heather's dad and I'll drive you around to her house but get a move on. I don't want to keep your mum waiting and we need to leave *now*.'

Cleo smiled, he never let her down. She finished her makeup and dashed downstairs a few minutes later to find Mac pacing along the hall looking agitated.

'A minute or two won't matter,' she said. 'Come on!'

She knew that Mac wasn't really pleased with her by the way his jaw was set and because he didn't say she looked great. It was just a quick "take care" as he stopped outside Heather's house.

He was too busy rushing to Mum and that unborn baby who was changing everything. Well, she could be 'off' with him too. Cleo flicked her hair, didn't give him his usual hug and, with a brief 'thanks', she was out of the car.

Cleo got home from the party to find the shepherd's pie burnt dry in the oven and nobody home. The phone flashed to show several messages. Her heart pounded as she picked up the receiver; was Mum OK? She heard message after message as her mum got more and more concerned about Mac's whereabouts and then finally heard a call from someone else, asking her to call the hospital.

She hadn't even dialled the hospital number before Mary Collingwood had arrived at the door with her husband, Dr Collingwood. Their faces told her it was bad news.

Mac had been killed in a crash on his way to the hospital. It was one of those things - a truck had skidded and Mac was in its path.

Cleo knew differently; he had been there on that road because of that baby. That baby had put Mum in hospital. If it wasn't for that baby, her mum and dad would be here at home. She had to think that way, otherwise she would have to face the fact that he was there on that stretch of road, much later than he should have been, because of her.

Dad had gone. He was annoyed with her, and now, he always would be. They hadn't hugged goodbye and that broke her heart.

Silent tears ran down Cleo's face as she watched Alex sleeping. Alex didn't know that her big sister had made her father late and put him right in the path of that truck. Even Mum didn't know about her selfish behaviour that night. Facing up to her part in the events made Cleo feel dreadful but it was much fairer than placing the blame on her unborn sister. If she could face her own part in Mac's death, she could face anything.

23

Alex's phone woke them late in the afternoon. The loud blast of a hunting horn ensured that Alex never missed a message. A text let them know that there was a Mary Collingwood chicken casserole, still hot, sitting on their back doorstep.

They got up and ate it, enjoying the warm freshly made bread that had been left with it. After that, there was no more putting off the inevitable. They still had the garden room to put straight and the contents of the moonbeam jar were scattered into every corner, as Neil had frantically searched for something of value.

Cleo had looked into the room when she'd first got home and guessed that there had been nothing of value taken. She knew Mum kept most of her valuables in the studio safe and a few special things in the lid of the moondream jar. The studio was still locked and the lid of the jar hadn't been opened.

Alex picked up slips of wishes and daytrip tickets and a few old photos while Cleo picked up the ornate lid, knowing its contents were safe by the weight of it in her hands. She gently shook it; yes, Mum's things were still inside. There was a knack to opening the lid, rather like opening a giant bottle of pills. A push down and twist motion.

'Did Mum ever show you how to open this?' she asked Alex.

'No. Does the top open?' Alex stopped looking at one of the photos and sat back on her heels.

At least that was one thing that Mum hadn't shared with Alex, Cleo thought and then immediately felt guilty. It was such a habit to have a down on Alex that she sometimes did it automatically and now it just didn't feel clever any more.

'Here, I'll show you,' she said, trying to assuage her guilt. 'You grip it between your knees and then push down and twist.' It didn't work. '*You* hold it, Alex and I'll push then twist. It's hard to do it yourself.'

'Neil would never have guessed this hidey-hole,' Cleo said as she pushed and twisted and felt the lid twisting open.

Inside were Mum's saltwater pearls, Mac's gold Saint Christopher charm and both of their baby bangles. There was an envelope with certificates in it. A birth certificate for Alex, a death certificate for Mac, their parents' marriage certificate, and one or two other papers that belonged to past McAplin relatives. Cleo had her own certificates, one birth and one adoption. She'd asked Mum if she could keep them after renewing her passport a while ago.

As Cleo returned the certificates to their original folds to fit into the envelope, she noticed that Alex was staring at the empty jar, rolling it over on the floor and deep in thought.

'Did Mum say there were three compartments?'

'No, just the lid and the main part of the jar, why?'

Alex's eyes glistened with excitement, 'Look at the pattern on the rim of the lid and see how it's repeated at the base. The base feels heavy even now that the jar is empty and I think it might open as well.'

Cleo studied the base. Mum hadn't mentioned that, but

Alex, the bright spark, could be right.

'Maybe Mum didn't know,' she offered.

'Ok. While it's empty, let's try. You hold on to the main part of the jar and I'll try and do that push and twist thing with the base.'

Easily, more easily than the lid, the base opened to reveal another cavity. Out dropped a bottle green cotton bag; it was an old fashioned gym shoe bag gathered at the top with tape handles. Alex picked it up and Cleo read the yellow chain stitch embroidered initials, 'MD' on one side of the bag. Who was MD?

'I don't think this can be Mum's; maybe it's been here all the time,' she said, as Alex was opening the bag.

'We'll have to look to see who could have put it here and what's inside,' Alex said.

Cleo picked up an old exercise book, there were a few of them, with M Donaldson written on the front. Inside, she could see dated pages; it had been used as a diary. A spike of fear pierced through her. There was no mistaking Teri's beautiful cursive writing - the books belonging to 'M Donaldson' were something to do with Mum. Cleo dropped the book she was holding as if it was an unexploded bomb.

Hidden in the base, the girls found a birth certificate for Margaret Donaldson and a change of name certificate for Neferteri Moon, as well as the four exercise books that had been used as diaries.

The diaries started when Margaret Donaldson was sixteen and ended four years later. So Mum had changed her name. Why?

'She's never spoken about her family; just said she lost her parents before we were born. Why would she change her name?' asked Alex.

'We'll find out if we read the diaries,' Cleo said.

'Maybe we should ask her first,' Alex looked longingly at the books, 'but I bet she'll say no.'

'I deserve to know who I am,' Cleo said.

'And me.'

'We know who *you* are, Alex, with me it's different.'

'How's that?' Alex was looking at Cleo and waiting for an explanation.

The words stuck in Cleo's throat; the thing she had hated most about Alex. 'Mac is your biological father but he's not mine,' Cleo admitted.

'He's *not*? I didn't know that. This family is full of bloody secrets. I know the grownups weren't married when you were born but I thought you were their 'happy accident' as Mum calls you.'

'The accident part is right, I'm not sure of the 'happy' but it wasn't for you, or anyone else, to know about my father.'

'Why not? Why the secrets?'

'Mum didn't speak of her past much and I suppose she preferred to think we were full sisters. Mac adopted me, I've got the papers, so we are, sort of.'

'You were so lucky to know him,' sighed Alex.

'You were even more lucky to have him as your real father. You are Mac's flesh and blood.' There, Cleo had said it, the fact that had given her so much grief. She felt lighter and maybe it didn't matter so much. She *had* been lucky because she had been chosen by the best dad ever.

'Alex, I'm not proud of this but I have always felt really envious that you were part of Mac and Mum while I had a father who didn't want me. You know, it really doesn't matter anymore because I wouldn't have changed having Mac as my dad for the world.'

Alex came over and draped herself over the arm of Cleo's chair to give her a hug. 'You're as deep as Dunleith ell at times, Cleo. Come on, let's just read the first book and see if we can find out why Mum changed her name,' Alex persuaded. 'All of this was over thirty years ago and if she hasn't told us yet, we need to find out a bit about our family history for ourselves.'

They read the first book and there it all unfolded. Mum falling in love with Ralph - her biological father, she couldn't ever say *real* - their romance being frowned upon by Ralph's father, who was their headmaster, and being a secret from Mum's own parents because her mother was so strict.

They read about the awful realisation that she was pregnant, too frightened to tell her parents and Ralph, too frightened to support her or tell his father. They learnt about her fear of being sent away, the dreadful reaction of her mother when she found out. They just couldn't stop reading.

Tomorrow I have to go to the home in the country to hide away until the baby is born and then adopted. R's parents are helping to pay for this and both parents have agreed that we are never to see one another again. Is he as broken by this as me? I think not. R is going to go to Oxford; nothing has changed for him. I have lost him, I've lost my place at Oxford and I'll lose my baby. Well little one, until I have to give you up, I'll love you more than my parents have loved me.

'You'd never dream that Mum had such a hard time.' Tears coursed down Alex's cheeks.

'I did know a bit, but she never really elaborated. She just said that teen pregnancies shouldn't ruin girls' life chances and she'd fought for hers but not everyone could. That's why the TeMPs unit for the school is so important to me. It's something that I have to do because of Mum fighting to keep me.'

They read on and discovered how Margaret had bolted from the maternity home, took a new name in case her parents found her, and made a new life for herself in Manchester. She'd shared a house with students and here was the first mention of a new friend, Angus McAplin.

They read two more books together; reading silently and nodding at each other when they were ready to turn a page. When they came to the end, Alex sat back and looked at Cleo.

'This was your start in life so it's bound to be more of a shock, Cleo, but I've got to admit that it's all such news to me and I'm bloody shocked too. It's like we're reading about other people in here.' She stared at the faded maroon exercise book that she'd been hugging to her chest and then looked back at Cleo, waiting for a reaction. Since they'd got to the end of this one, Cleo had said nothing.

'Is that it? Is that the last one? It doesn't carry on past then?' asked Cleo, looking around the floor for another exercise book.

'No... Mum's either kept them elsewhere or she stopped writing after this one.'

'I can remember bits of this; I'm sure they're real. I can remember being with Dad when I was small and calling him Mac long before I called him Dad.

I remember missing him and crying when we went away, I think it was to London for a while and I remember us all being together again. As this comes back to me, there's something else I've remembered about being young and it's not here. It happened after this last book ends and I need to check with Mum if it was real of not.'

'What is it?'

Cleo rubbed her hands across her eyes. Were the images she was seeing her imagination or a memory?' she couldn't be sure.

'I was young, about three or four, not school age, and we had been living away, in London I think. We had packed up and were going to see Mac so I was really happy. We had cases and we took the train but Mum said we had to make a stop somewhere else, first of all.

'We went to a house and a woman answered the door to us. She looked at us in a horrified way and then she was bloody horrible to Mum, saying, "You're not wanted back here, get away, you and your brat".'

She shouted, "How dare you come dirtying my doorstep" and awful things like that. I remember looking at my shoes because they were clean and we hadn't been in any dirt. Mum took my hand and, as we turned to go, the lady yelled at her.' Cleo covered her face with her hands.

'Go on Cleo, tell me what she said. I know you remember,' Alex urged.

'It killed him, you going missing like that. You destroyed him.' That's what she yelled.

We returned to the station to get our second train and Mum was upset. I asked her why we had to see that naughty lady and she said, "It wasn't to see *her* my darling, the person I wanted you to meet isn't there anymore".'

'I asked her,"Did you kill someone, Mummy?" and she hugged me. "Of course not and she is a very naughty lady to say those things," she said.'

Cleo had forgotten about the incident in the excitement of getting onto another train to see Mac and she'd never mentioned it to Mum after that day.

'Who was that, Alex? It must have been family.'

'I'd guess it'd be Mum's mother and she'd be blaming her for killing her dad,' said Alex.

'Aren't you a regular sleuth?' Cleo hit back, but she was smiling. 'Yes, after reading those diaries, I'm sure you're right. We must have gone to Mum's old home, her mother was still angry; her dad had died and so she knew she had nothing left there.'

'Then she came to Dunleith, well to Berwick station and you and Mac and Mum lived happily ever after, until I spoiled things.'

Cleo looked at Alex and tried to read her expression. She was calm and didn't seem upset.

'Be honest, that *is* what you think, Cleo. Fortunately, I know better than to blame myself for being born. You didn't ruin Mum's life by being born and I didn't ruin yours. We were both babies. It's funny how, in all of this, you don't ever blame Mum for being pregnant with you but you blame her for my appearance. What about the sainted Mac, our father, wasn't he involved in my arrival too?'

Cleo put her head in her hands. Alex was right, and over the years she had allowed herself to develop the most screwed up take on things. Until now, she'd never been willing to deal with losing Mac and any of her mixed emotions.

Alex gave Cleo a hug and she didn't shrug her off but leant into her. Her little sister made a lot of sense. Changing her views meant accepting she'd been wrong all these years but her feelings had shifted and there was no going back to her old way of crooked thinking. She felt a rush of tears of regret and relief as she cried and admitted to Alex that she'd been wrong, totally wrong in the way she'd looked at Mac's death and Alex's birth. She admitted that she'd felt jealous but hadn't known why.

She told Alex about her guilty feelings over Mac's accident and their lack of a proper goodbye and how responsible she felt.

Alex wasn't horrified by this confession at all, she said, 'Mum and I often have words and we both know it's nothing. Look at how *we* weren't speaking this weekend until you called me about Neil. Families can't make every day be as perfect as if it's their last. You should forget what makes you sad about Dad and just remember the best times, Cleo.'

Alex was young but, Cleo had to admit, she spoke sense at times.

Cleo noticed it was dusk already, too exhausted to pack up and drive home, she suggested that they should stay another night and make a really early start to travel into school the next morning.

'OK. Shall we bunk up together in Mum's room tonight?' asked Alex. 'It sort of makes her closer.'

Cleo nodded and as they went upstairs, she realised that she didn't feel guilty and she didn't resent her little sister, in fact she admired her and she felt responsible for her. No, it was more than that, she had opened her heart and let herself love her.

24

They were up, packed, had put a protesting Pharos into his crate and were intending to be on the road by seven the next morning when Sergeant Laidlaw called.

'It is my sad duty to inform you that your burglar managed to remove himself from the infirmary and from the grasp of PC Johnson yesterday evening and we can't find a trace of him. I've informed the city police and they said they'll take over the search.'

'How the hell did-?'

'He's a very devious man, Miss Moon.' The Sergeant interrupted her query and seemed embarrassed when he admitted, 'PC Johnson was hoodwinked into letting him go to relieve himself on his own and he scarpered out of a window.'

'Oh never mind, he's gone again and that's it.' Cleo felt exasperated. 'I'd better have all the locks changed. Now, excuse me Sergeant, but we're going to be really late for school.'

Once on the A1, it was a straight road through to Newcastle but, as they got nearer the city, it was congested with commuters who liked the Northumbrian countryside yet needed to work in the city.

'You'll have to drop me off before we reach school; I

don't want anyone to see us going in together.' Alex reminded Cleo.

'So you still don't want anyone to know who your big sis is? Cleo was smiling, she might have felt the same if she was in Alex's shoes.

'I'll have to choose my time that's all. It's not the easiest thing in the world when your sister is a bigwig in school.'

'I'm a bigwig am I?'

'You know what I mean. They do all like you though.' Alex conceded.

Cleo felt like she'd won the lottery. 'Great,' she said 'but remember you don't go to school to like your teacher; you go to learn.'

They both burst into laughter; that was one of Mum's stock phrases they'd heard *so* many times.

Cleo phoned Dan to tell him the latest. He had known that Neil wasn't really hurt so wasn't at all surprised that he'd given young PC Johnson the slip at the hospital. He was annoyed though and offered to sort out a locksmith for High Rigg and to bring the new keys over to her next day. Cleo was both grateful and glad to have another chance to see him. They talked about how he had to leave for Australia straight after this week's meeting but promised each other that they would meet up when he came back, later in the summer.

Cleo knew that Alex was listening intently because the phone had been on speaker but she said nothing about this new friendship between Dan and Cleo.

Ten miles into the journey, after listening to the traffic update, Alex declared,

'I've been waiting for you to ask but you haven't.'

'Asked what?' Cleo was puzzled.

'I'm not pregnant and that test you found wasn't even for me.'

'Glad to hear it.' Cleo replied. Glad? That was an understatement, Cleo didn't want Mum coming back to that news and it was a sweet relief that Alex wouldn't be one of the first students in her new unit.

'I'm keeping the test for a friend and I have to respect their privacy' explained Alex.

'Quite right. I'm sure that Gracie will appreciate that.'

'I didn't say...'

'No, but come on Alex, I can guess... and you must tell Gracie, or whoever your friend is, that whatever the result, she can always come and chat to me.'

'Gracie really likes you so she knows that. She has a hard time at home.'

'Don't you think I know that? She's a great student but can't always get to school. Life hasn't been easy for Gracie Grieves.'

They drove on for a while and Cleo's mind was starting to wander away from Gracie over to thoughts of Dan and how they were becoming good friends when Alex piped up.

'I couldn't be pregnant. I've never done it... you know.'

Bloody hell, thought Cleo, how was this kind of chat harder when it was a sister not a pupil? She'd better tread carefully.

'That's a good thing Alex, because it's best to be in a loving relationship.'

'Had you? Do you think at seventeen I *should* have had a serious boyfriend? Weren't you with Dan at my age?' Alex was in full flow.

Cleo thought hard; did she really want to discuss herself or Dan with her little sis? Yes, why not? It was about time her family were more open with one another.

'When I got together with Dan, I was a little bit older than you. I'd liked him for ages, it was first love and I believed that we'd stay together forever. We both did. It didn't work out that way but he was the right person for me at that time. You *will* know when you meet the right person for your first time, Alex.'

'I haven't yet but I *do* really fancy someone,' Alex confided.

Oh, ring the bells of Dunleith tower, not Ty or his gang. Cleo mentally crossed her fingers. 'Someone from Tyneview?' she asked, hoping her light tone masked her anxiety.

'You're trying to sound not bothered, like Mum does, and you are.' Alex was grinning at her. 'No, he's not a Tyneview student, and I'm saying no more for now. It's a secret romance,' she sighed, folding her arms and looking out of her passenger window.

Cleo racked her brains for who this crush could be and a minute or two passed before Alex turned back to her and she caught that familiar mischievous look.

'I'm just thinking, if Dan seemed *so* right then, he might be right for you now. You both seemed very friendly to one another in that last call.'

'It was just a phone call, Alex,' but Cleo couldn't help smiling.

They turned into the apartment car park, took Pharos upstairs, had a quick change into school wear and Cleo dropped Alex off at the end of the road before nipping into her parking space at dead on eight fifty. It was unheard of for her to arrive as the morning bell was ringing but luckily, she had no new staff absences to cover so perhaps her day was going to start smoothly.

25

Alex was walking down the road when the school bell rang and she heard a familiar voice calling her.

'Alex, wait for me!'

It was Gracie and a fragrant cloud of vanilla and sugar. She was eating mini doughnuts fresh from Greggs' bakery. Offering the bag to Alex, she asked, 'What were you doing in Miss Moon's car?'

'Oh? I was late and so was she it seems. She offered me a lift'. There, that was wasn't a lie.

'She's kind like that. Daft place to drop you off, though. She should've taken you to the door.' Phew, that was lucky. Alex was relieved that Gracie didn't question her further.

'Have you brought my kit?' Gracie asked.

Blast, she had been racing around and forgot it. 'I've left it at home. Sorry, Gracie, like I said, I was late and in a rush.'

'Right. Well I canna wait any longer so, you and me, we'll take off at lunchtime and go to yours to do the test. You don't have any important classes straight after lunch do you?'

No, she didn't but, she didn't really want Gracie around at the apartment. Then again, Cleo didn't do family photo displays so it wasn't as if Gracie could play 'Through the Keyhole' and have any idea of who lived there.

'Righto, Gracie. I'll meet you at the gates at twelve fifteen.'

After morning classes, Alex hurried to meet Gracie. It was a sunny day but, as she approached she noticed Gracie looked shivery with hunched shoulders and a grey tinge to her olive complexion. Gracie Grieves seemed scared for once, so she linked arms with her but said nothing as they set off for the metro station. What *could* she say? It'll be alright, don't worry. This was a big deal and both of them knew it.

Gracie spoke up first.

'I'm not speaking to Ty, yet again. He's got his eye on that Stella Watkins and I'm just not in the mood to fight anyone off right now.'

'Does he know you're late?'

'No and I don't think I'm going to let on even if I am pregnant. I'll have enough to worry about telling me mam without having to worry over him. I'm not going to let on about the father to anybody so don't you dare say a word.'

'I wouldn't.'

'It's funny, I've only known you for five minutes but I trust you, Alex. I feel like I've found a proper mate in you.'

'You've been great to me too.' Alex smiled and linked arms a little tighter.

Once they got on the metro, Alex found herself telling Gracie that her own Mum had been pregnant in her teens.

'It wasn't with me it was with C... with my older sister.'

'The one you're staying with now?'

'Yes.'

'Will she be in when we get to yours?'

'No she'll be at work.' Please don't ask what she does prayed Alex.

'Good. I'm not in a mood for politeness today Alex,' said Gracie.

The train, almost empty, whizzed through the stops and they got off near the apartment.

'So, how did your Mam cope?'

'She had no support from the dad and her parents were all for adoption so she went off on her own and made a life for herself, somehow. She was very brave. Still is.'

'What do you mean, still is?' Gracie was curious.

'She had ovarian cancer and got over that, she had me and my sister to contend with as a single parent and we didn't get along until recently and she's travelling around Egypt on her own. I reckon that's bloody brave for someone who's nearly fifty.'

'She sounds mega-mazing. My mum got pregnant with me and then the rest came along; that's why she'll hate it if I go down the same road. She thinks we've all stifled her. She's always thinking "what if?" Well that won't be me. I'll be like your mum and make *my* life work.'

Alex watched Gracie's steps slow down as they approached Mariner's Wharf apartment block.

'This is dead posh and leafy around here, Alex. You didn't say. Your sister must have a bloody good job.'

Alex felt the heat in her cheeks as she fumbled to find her key, 'Come on, let's get inside and get this test done.'

Alex popped into her room to get the chemist's bag and returned to the living area to find Gracie looking around with her mouth open.

'It's like in a film. You're so bloody lucky! I didn't think people really had all this.' Gracie pointed to the pale rugs and wooden floors. 'Even the bloody cat matches!' The fur throw that was Pharos was draped along the top of the grey sofa observing them with his shrewd gooseberry gaze.

Alex glanced at her watch, 'Come on, get into the loo and do your test - we need to get back for my two thirty class.' She didn't want Gracie looking round too closely even though there was nothing to give the game away.

It seemed an age before Gracie reappeared holding the result in her hand. She looked surprisingly calm when she said, 'Congratulate me – it's positive.'

Alex grabbed the stick to double check. 'Oh, Gracie! I was sort of hoping that you'd got it wrong.'

'No, I knew. I bet that I'm well on too. I'll have to see the doctor soon. Do you mind if I sit down for a minute? I'm feeling a bit odd.'

'Lie down on the sofa and I'll make coffee and toast. You haven't had anything since those doughnuts.' Gracie kicked off her boots, sank into the sofa and Alex busied herself in the kitchen area.

'What the hell?' Alex heard Gracie cry and she rushed to the sofa.

'Are you alright?'

'Me? Yes, *I'm* alright but how the hell is *this* here? You've been nicking haven't you?'

Alex saw Gracie was holding the Montblanc pen that Cleo used for work. *C Moon* was inscribed on the side, so it was no use denying it belonged to Cleo.

Bloody Pharos! He loved to play with a pen and then tuck it under a cushion. Gracie looked appalled. Did she want Gracie to think she was a thief or did she have to own up to who her big sister was?

'Alex, this just isn't on; I mean not to Miss Moon.' Gracie was sitting up, glaring at Alex and the colour was back in her cheeks.

'Hold on, it's not what you think, Gracie. Honestly it's not.'

'Explain then, because this pen is going back to school with me, Alex McAplin'

'I can't explain.' Alex couldn't meet Gracie's eyes. 'Look, have your toast and then we'll go and you take the bloody pen back to school.'

Gracie's eyes filled with angry tears. 'I don't want your toast, not now. You know, I thought you *were* somebody, Alex. I liked you. You have all this,' she waved her arms around the apartment, 'and you nick a pen that Miss Moon got from her dad for her sixteenth birthday.

'She told us one day in class when we were chucking pens about. She said that she had kept this pen since she was at school. No one else in Tyneview would do that, not to Miss Moon.' Gracie swung back her ponytail, picked up her bag and headed for the door.

Alex couldn't let Gracie think that about her, 'Wait!'

She turned, and Alex saw that the Gracie Grieves' glower was on full beam. 'This had better be good, Alex.'

'There's no easy way to say this but, you see, this apartment... it's hers, Gracie. That's why the pen is here. Miss Moon, she's my sister.'

'*No way*? You're having me on. Really? You lucky sod! Why haven't you said?' Gracie sank back down on the sofa.

'I was a bit embarrassed.'

'Embarrassed? She's mint! Oh my god, this is Miss Moon's; no wonder it's so cool. She won't mind me being here will she?' Gracie looked anxious.

'No she won't mind but, look Gracie, I'd rather not everybody knew.'

'You keep my secret and I'll keep yours, but you're mad. Why be hiding the fact that your sister is Miss Moon? You could have done a hell of a lot worse.'

On the way back to school, Gracie never stopped talking about the wonderful Miss Moon.

'To think *she* was that unplanned bairn of years ago that you were telling me about and now she's starting up the TeMPS unit. I'm going to tell Miss Moon about my bairn the minute I see her and make sure I get a place in the unit when it's ready.

Imagine, Alex... Miss Moon had that start in life and got to where she is so there's nothing that this kid of mine can't do.' Gracie had a big grin and seemed happier than she had been for a while.

Alex was glad to get back to her class for a rest from hearing about Miss Moon. She sat by Lee for Art and decided she'd really had enough of secrets.

She tried Lee first. 'Lee, I've been meaning to mention, you know Miss Moon the deputy? She's my sister. That's how I got a temporary place here.'

'Cool,' answered Lee as she carried on sorting through scraps of material for her collage. 'I wish I had an older sister instead of younger brothers. Alex, I was wondering, do you want to call into Cob and Cookies for a snack then look in the library for ideas for this new project after school tomorrow?'

'Yes, that'll be great,' Alex answered.

So that was it? No big deal. The big reveal had been all in her head.

26

Cleo closed her laptop and shredded the papers that she had dealt with after school. She had finally got to the bottom of her in-tray and was ready for home. It had been a hell of a day. The early start, Neil's escape, the late arrival at school, Teflon commandeering her lunch hour because he wanted a TeMPS update and then no time to call the banks and credit companies to sort out her financial mess. Thank goodness that Dan was sorting out the locksmith at High Rigg.

Now, she had to make her way home where Heather would be dropping off Josh. What a great friend she'd been this weekend, just taking over and not making a fuss.

Cleo popped into the ladies and saw dark mascara smudges under her eyes. What a mess! She tried wiping them off and realised they weren't runaway make up, those dark shadows belonged to her. She really needed a good night's rest. She picked up her bags to head for home and had just reached the foyer when she heard,

'Miss, have you got a minute?'

For a moment her heart sank, but she could never say no to a student. Turning, she saw Gracie Grieves with eyes as tired and dark as her own.

'Gracie, what's troubling you?'

Gracie's face crumpled. My God, Gracie Grieves was crying! She dropped her bags and stepped towards her,

'Hey, come on now, it can't be so bad.'

'It is Miss, it is!'

'Let's go into my office and see what can be done.' Cleo's tiredness had gone, she picked up her bags, unlocked her office door and took Gracie inside. Cleo Moon never shirked anyone else's problems; she just wished she could be as good at sorting out her own.

An hour later, Cleo dropped Gracie off at her own house then headed for home. It was almost six o'clock and she'd have to apologise to Heather, sort out Josh's stuff and get him to bed then order yet another takeout before thinking about sleep.

She stopped in the car park of her apartment and took a pack of jelly snakes from the glove compartment. She chewed through three, she really didn't want to go in; it was all so draining.

Mum was going to Skype tonight too. Heather had forewarned Cleo that Mum knew about some of the things Neil had got up to but she'd have to explain about the break in and the weekend they'd had. They weren't going to mention reading the diaries in the moondream jar. All of that could wait until she came home.

Bloody hell, her life was an absolute car crash. Immediately she checked that thought; how could she say that? She hadn't died like Mac, she was here and she could do this. She fiercely wiped the tears from her cheeks, no time for self- pity, she had lots to do.

Cleo opened the door expecting chaos and was met with the delicious smell of Italian cooking. Garlic and cheese wafted her way. Josh was already back here in his pjs on the sofa cuddling Pharos and reading a book. The TV was off and George Ezra filled the room with his melodic voice.

Alex popped her head from her room with a smile. 'Hi.

I'm making us an economical lasagne instead of the usual Monday takeout, because we're broke. Heather left Josh at five and dashed straight off but she says that Archie's child minder can have him tomorrow morning, if we drop him off *and* his Mum's flying into Newcastle airport at one.

'I'm just finishing an assignment; so dinner is at seven and there are olives to snack on and wine in the fridge.'

Without thinking, Cleo dropped her bags, gave Alex a bear hug and said, 'You're an angel,' before kissing the top of her head.

'And Dan must think you're a damsel in distress,' Alex answered.

'Dan and Mark came around just before Heather with a locksmith mate they know from playing rugby. We've got new locks and keys for here as well as High Rigg and we don't have to pay.' She pointed to the bunches of keys by the sweet bowl. 'The locksmith said that Dan had settled the bill.'

Cleo felt relieved to have one worry removed from her shoulders but she'd *have* to pay Dan, she was responsible for all this. She was disappointed that she'd missed seeing him.

A glass of wine and two readings of '*Hairy Maclary from Donaldson's Dairy*' with Josh and she noticed that the tense throb at her temple had disappeared. Josh went to bed and Alex was serving up their lasagne and salad so they could eat it in front of the TV.

Before they chose a programme, Cleo wanted to make her apology. 'Alex, I'm really sorry about getting at you on Saturday morning...'

'Forget it. I've told you it wasn't for me and you'll probably find out about the result soon enough.'

'I've already spoken to Gracie. That's why I was late.'

'Oh, did she tell you she was here?' Alex handed Cleo her plate of food.

'Here? No she didn't mention that. She just talked about her pregnancy.'

'I'll tell you about lunchtime and you tell me how we can help Gracie.'

As they ate, they discussed Gracie and then got onto Cleo's favourite topic of the TeMPS unit.

They had just cleared their plates away when Mum skyped, wanting no secrets about police and pressing Cleo to accept some money from her to tide her over this rough patch.

Feeling relaxed by then, they could honestly say to Teri that things weren't too bad. After telling her about Neil's visit to High Rigg and how Dan had stopped him from taking anything, they asked Teri about her trip.

'What's your news, Mum?' Alex asked and they waited eagerly for Teri's latest adventure.

'I can see you girls are getting on fine without me and I've still not seen everything I want to see yet, so I don't want to rush back for the beginning of September.

'I've found that I love the underwater life in the Red sea. I'm thinking of staying on to travel around a bit more and then finishing my trip off by doing a scuba diving course. What do you say to that?'

'I'm just checking that it's ok to stay a little while longer and leave my flight home until nearer the end of September.'

Cleo and Alex looked at one another; that was new, *more* time together?

'It's ok by me,' Alex said, looking hesitantly at Cleo.

'And me.' Cleo had to agree. She didn't want Alex to feel uncertain; she'd been distant enough to her in the past. 'Don't worry Mum; we'll both be fine. We just miss you.'

'I miss you both too, but it's so exhilarating here and I can see that you two don't need me so I'm going to see and do all that I can before I return. Just one thing, how's my lovely boy?' They used the iPad to pan over to a very relaxed Pharos curled up in the middle of the sofa.

Teri wiped away a tear, 'Oh, I do miss him.'

'Mum, aren't you lonely travelling on your own? Do you want one of us to join you for a week or two in summer, when school breaks up?' Alex asked.

'Of course not. I was thinking that, as you'll be with Cleo for longer, you *could* go with the EllaBella's to France for a couple of weeks. Do you want me to arrange it with Mary? That will give you a break too, Cleo.'

Alex's eyes sparkled. 'Thanks Mum that would be brilliant!'

'Anyway, don't fret about me because I have a travel companion; I'm not going to be on my own,' Teri confessed.

'Who? Alex asked.

'Yes, who?' Cleo was interested in who had persuaded Mum, of all people, to try scuba diving.

'He's called Greg and he's very experienced,' Teri explained and then she was gone mid-sentence. Skype had cut out on her again.

'*Mum?*' Cleo tried to get her back but she couldn't connect.

'So, what do we make of that?' Alex asked, when they were sure the Skype session was over.

'Experienced?' Cleo added.

'Greg?' They both said it together and laughed. Teri would have been proud of them, even though they were laughing about her.

'They'll just be friends. Mum's a bit old for all of that coupling lark, isn't she?'

'Probably,' Cleo said, while thinking, *I wouldn't be so sure.*

Once she was settled into bed, her own room back at last, Cleo thought about phoning Dan. She had saved his mobile number but eleven was a bit late to phone if he was at his parents' house. Well, in Dunleith circles it was late; it would have to be an emergency. She'd like to thank him soon, though.

Her mobile, still in her hand, rang and startled her. She glanced at the number and her hands trembled as she answered the call. Back in the day, they used to be almost telepathic about calling one another.

'Hello, Dan,' Cleo spoke softly.

'Ah Cleo, you know it's me, your burglar-catcher and apprentice locksmith. I guess that there is only one man who would have the temerity to call you at eleven on a school night. I thought you'd want to say thanks, or good luck with your hospital meeting or something.'

'You thought right.' She smiled and snuggled into her duvet, suddenly wakeful enough for a long chat.

27

Cleo woke up the next morning feeling refreshed. As she stretched luxuriously, she glanced at the clock. That couldn't be right, she sat bolt upright and again, eight o'clock. Eight! She should have left half an hour ago. Now she would hit the traffic and be late for the second time in two days. Damn and blast.

Alex knocked, then opened her door. She had a coffee in one hand and a glass of juice in the other, 'Ah, you're awake. I've brought you these.' She placed them on the side table.

Cleo pulled the bedclothes back, 'I don't have time for morning coffee Alex, have you seen the time? We're both going to be late again.'

'Yes, I have and there's no rush. I thought you needed a lie in after the past few days and so I took it upon myself to silence your alarm when Josh got me up at five thirty.'

'Alex, I'm the deputy, I *have* to get into school early or the absence covers don't get done in time.'

'The school won't fall down and Tef can do it himself for once. Anyway, you're one of the absentees today.'

'What do you mean?'

'I've phoned in sick for both of us.'

'You've *what*?'

'I've called and left a message. I was thinking about it last night. This way we both get to meet Marianne and say goodbye to Josh properly and you get a chance to do all of your private calls to the bank and places. I said we'd be back Wednesday... it's just a day.'

'What on earth did you say we have for *one* day?'

'You know the nit epidemic in Year 8 you were telling me about?'

'You didn't!'

'Yup, I said that we were both staying home and delousing today to stop the spread to staff and lower sixth and we'd be back in tomorrow. Tef won't want you near him with nits.' Alex looked jubilant.

Cleo sank back into her pillows. 'You are such a bad influence Alex! This is the first time I've skipped school, *ever*.' It felt quite liberating to have a free day though.

'Don't tell Mum,' Alex said as she got up from the bedside. 'Now I think we'll all have Josh's favourite sc'ambled eggs before we meet *his* Mum.'

When Alex packed Josh's case, there wasn't enough room for all the extra possessions that he seemed to have acquired over his stay; wellingtons, books, pens and more of the plastic figures that he loved to collect. She put them into her school rucksack and then drew a dinosaur on the front as Josh watched, giving advice on the finer dinosaur details. Josh was delighted that she had given her bag to him, he loved all the zips and pockets in it. He had packed and unpacked it all morning.

She was glad that she'd instigated a day off for them both. Saying goodbye to Josh couldn't be rushed and Cleo had been absolutely shattered last night. After breakfast she had shut herself in her office, called school to say she'd work from home and had started to make all the difficult phone calls to the bank and credit companies.

Mum was going to put some cash into Cleo's account and she had reluctantly accepted, insisting it would be a loan. Living with Cleo had brought home the proud traits about her and how independent she liked to be. Alex sort of admired that now.

Marianne was arriving at one and Cleo was now able to pick her up from the airport. Alex and Josh were going to the shops to buy a quiche from the bakery and salad stuff for lunch and they'd look for wild flowers, they were in short supply in the city but there had to be some - to make the table look festive. The errand would take an hour because Josh was insisting on taking his rucksack and he liked to dilly dally. That would give Cleo the peace that she needed to finish her jobs before collecting Marianne.

Alex set the table with a tablecloth bordered with lemons that Cleo must have got from Mum and put a large jar of dandelions in the centre. The quiche was in the oven ready to heat and the salad was prepared. She had just put a jug of water on the table when she heard a yelp from the bathroom, then Josh's wails started. She ran into the bathroom to see the floor flooded, Josh drenched and the newly drawn 'Rucksack Dino' wearing a wet grin too.

'Sorry Alex. It all just spilled when I put my rucksack on.' Josh looked cute with his bottom lip stuck out and a guilty look all over his face.' Alex had to stop herself from giggling at him; so much for keeping him clean for his mum's arrival.

'What spilled?' she asked him, crouching down and taking his hand to show she wasn't angry.

Josh still wasn't sure if he was out of trouble and looked tearful as he explained,

'You see, I had made room for *my* jar. I put the lid back on till I got it home.'

Alex took the sack and found the flowers that Josh had picked for his mum. She had given him a small jar to arrange the flowers in but hadn't filled it with water. He'd done that bit himself.

'Your mummy can see them on the table, Josh, flowers

don't travel well in jars. We'll have to get you cleaned up.'

Josh wiped his eyes with grubby hands that streaked his face and grinned, 'Thanks for not being cross, Alex!' He gave her a hug.

At that moment they heard the doorbell, there wasn't time to clean up, Cleo and Marianne were here.

'Mummeeee!' Josh ran along the hallway with Alex following.

'Josh, hallo mijn kindlief.' He jumped into his mum's arms and Alex was relieved that she didn't seem to notice the state of him or his wet back one bit.

Cleo stood in shock. She'd be wondering how she left a clean little boy and returned to find this damp, grubby urchin. Alex felt anxious until Cleo winked at her.

'The table looks lovely little sis; let's start lunch after someone's washed their hands.'

Marianne was petite, slender and with her thick blonde hair tied back in a long plait she looked about the same age as Alex. They opened a bottle of prosecco and enjoyed Alex's lunchtime spread while catching up on all of the things that Josh had been doing.

When he wandered off to find where Pharos was hiding, Marianne explained more about her father falling ill and how she had little choice but to call on Neil to help her by looking after Josh.

'Neil is always irresponsible, but he loves Josh and I wasn't worried about leaving him for a day or two. When I got there, Dad was in such a bad way so I couldn't really leave him and as you know, Neil let me down badly once again.'

Alex saw the hurt in Marianne's eyes and how she immediately looked older and tired.

'Why don't you two take your coffee and go for a chat in the office while I clear the table and keep an eye on Josh. We'll dry off 'Rucksack Dino' with the hairdryer, he'll like that,' she said.

'What a lovely young girl,' Marianne remarked when they sat in the office and Alex was out of earshot.

Cleo nodded, 'Yes I have to agree; she really is, even though she is my own sister.' She waited a second, measuring her words, before adding, 'Now, if you don't mind, can you tell me the truth about *when* you split up with Neil and some of what has happened since then? He has been so deceitful that I don't know what to believe.'

Cleo was relieved to discover that the couple had split up months before she came along and that Marianne had moved on because of his habit of gambling and spending had destroyed their lives as a family. Marianne had thought that a break might shock him into seeking help but it hadn't and she was really upset to hear of how fraudulent he had been.

'He spent all of our wedding gift money from my father and his own parents but that, at least, wasn't stealing. He isn't a bad man, but he is *so* weak.'

Cleo didn't know whether she agreed with this or not. His actions towards them all had shown no concern for anyone but himself. She suspected that Marianne still cared for Neil, even though he'd messed her around.

'He will get in touch with me eventually because of Josh and I will let you know where he is,' she promised. 'He must face his crimes and put this right with you.'

Cleo liked Marianne, but that shouldn't be a surprise because, after all, Josh was a delight and had clearly been well brought up. She *was* surprised that Marianne was so warm towards her.

'We have met in strange circumstances but you have been so good to my son and so understanding towards me. I do hope that we can keep in touch. Maybe you will visit us if you're in the Netherlands one day.'

'Oh are you going back there?'

'Yes, I want to be near my father until he is stronger

and we can live with him and sell the English house to pay off Neil's debts to you and to other creditors. I'm going to enrol into college there to be a teacher, an English teacher. I had started my course when I met Neil and then...then I dropped out.'

Cleo guessed that Marianne was still dealing with a lot of hurt and it would take her a while to get over Neil.

'Marianne, I'm sure you'll make a great success of what you've chosen to do.'

'Thank you. I'm moving on but I can't ever regret marrying Neil because of our wonderful little boy.'

On cue, Josh opened the office door. 'Mummy come and see my rucksack now that it is dry. It has my best dinosaur on it.' Marianne took his hand and, as Cleo watched them, she felt a surge of longing. Josh was so glad to have his mum here.

She wanted to see her own mum, that was it... or was it? No, her longing was for what Marianne had; she wanted to have her own child run up to her like that. She'd never felt broody before. Cleo sat there and, with a pleasant new sort of ache in her heart, she finished her coffee.

28

The summer break had finally arrived. Cleo felt as though it would never happen but here she was driving towards the Northumbrian border for the summer and the old car was stuffed to the gills. Cleo was using Mum's eight-year-old Range Rover. It wasn't her convertible but at least it was roomy.

They were spending a few weeks in Dunleith. Alex was excited to see the EllaBellas and Cleo relished the freedom of a long summer stretching ahead.

She'd worked solidly to finish the timetable, to finalise the plans for the unit and to work with her bank to get her finances back on an even keel. The credit cards that Neil had used were frozen and he would be charged with fraud, but the bank hadn't confirmed how much responsibility she had to take for the money that had been drained from her bank account.

Her car had been sacrificed to clear the debts, so this summer she was having a 'staycation' but she didn't care, she just wanted to unwind and free her mind from its recent troubles.

Not that she was free at all really. She still had to keep an eye on Alex for a couple of weeks, until she went off to France with the Collingwoods mid-August, and she had offered to have Archie for two nights this week.

All of his grandparents were busy. Heather had booked

a bargain break for Mark and herself before checking with them so, as his godmother, her services were requested.

'Thanks for stepping in. My mum and dad would have had him but they're still away on their cruise,' Mark explained.

'And *my* mum has a ticket to see Erin in 'Sweeney Todd'.

Cleo's eyes widened. 'You must be proud of your little sis. She's doing really well to be in another West End show.'

'She's in the chorus, not a main part, but it's what she loves to do and Mum's excited about going to see her,' Heather said.

Cleo hadn't looked after Archie overnight before, but she owed Heather big time after the child care she'd put in with Josh. Besides, she was confident that she could cope with younger ones now and she missed having Josh around.

Pharos, his cage strapped into the front seat, had wailed several different tones of 'Maam' from the moment the engine started but she had turned the radio up and was happy to be behind the wheel with midget gems, music and her thoughts.

Pharos fell into a snooze first and then Alex snuggled down into her seat. Cleo turned the music down and enjoyed the silence. She'd be able to sleep for hours this week.

Dan came to mind - he was never really very far away. Cleo knew that he had been short-listed after his hospital meetings and that a final interview for the consultancy post was taking place in Newcastle this week, so he was going to be around.

She didn't know if he'd be travelling straight back to Australia after his meeting, or if he'd be able to stay in Dunleith for a while longer. Would he want to?

She blushed just thinking about him. They had phoned

one another a couple of times but in his eyes she must be a real idiot; allowing Neil to fool her and being so stupid for so many years over her sister. Was he just being kind? Did he think that he'd had a lucky escape when they split up years ago?

She sighed and reached for the midget gems to munch on. After the Neil fiasco, she should stay well away from men. She couldn't help thinking, but Dan... isn't he different?

Heather dropped Archie off at High Rigg the following Monday, delighted to be escaping to Edinburgh with Mark for a couple of days.

After waving the carefree parents off, Cleo noticed Archie looking a bit tearful.

She quickly distracted him, 'Hey, Archie, I think you and I will go for a picnic and catch some tiddlers! Would you like that?'

'Tiddlers?' Archie shrugged his shoulders and showed his opened hands. He wasn't impressed.

'You don't know what they are? They're fish... fishies,' explained Cleo.

'Fisheees!' Archie jumped up and down, he knew what *they* were.

'Yes, we're going fishing. First we'll have to see if there's still a fishing net in the garden shed.'

High summer had stretched north to the border. The sun blazed and bees were swarming around the heather by the time they set off with a picnic blanket and an old fishing net. They called at the village shop to buy something for a packed lunch to eat by the river. Cleo opened the door and spotted Dan.

'Yes Dot, I'm back again. I may even be back here for good if my final meeting goes well this week.' It was Dan undergoing an interrogation by Dot Weddell.

'You'd think Australia was just next door the way you young 'uns wander around nowadays.'

'It's a long flight Dot but it's always worth it to get home and...' he stopped as he caught sight of Cleo.

She felt flushed and couldn't think of a thing to say. She managed a smile and then turned all her attention onto Archie, asking him about sandwich fillings and hiding her rosy cheeks with her hair.

'Have you seen who's here, Cleo?' Dot was determined to bring her into the conversation.

Archie saw Dan and ran over, 'Hiya, Hiya Unca Dan,' he beamed.

'Hi Archie, what are you doing here?'

'With Auntie Cloee.'

Cleo grinned, he always got it the wrong way round.

Dan looked at Dot, 'Can't stop, I can't hang around as much as I'd like too, Dot.'

He glanced at Cleo, gave her a wink as he left the shop and she breathed a deep sigh. Why hadn't she said something; anything? Why hadn't he waited?

A few minutes later they left the shop. Archie was carrying a tube of crisps and Cleo had the rest of the day's picnic.

'Hey, Cleo.' Dan was sitting on a bench opposite the shop and beckoning her across.

She took Archie's hand and crossed the road. How do you stop a heart from hammering so loudly? The whole village would hear it.

'They're my favourites.' Dan pointed to Archie's tube of crisps.

'Mine.' Archie clutched them to his chest and grinned.

Cleo's heart had steadied and she found her voice, 'They're to share Archie. We share.' She smiled as he nodded in agreement.

Dan peered into her basket at the crusty bread, cheese, a punnet of plums, juice, haribo gums. 'It looks like a picnic sort of lunch,' he said. 'Where are you off to?'

'We are going to the burn because Archie is going to catch his first tiddlers.'

'That sounds great. I love fishing with a net.' Dan's gaze fell away from her to Archie. 'You'll have fun today, Archie.'

'Dan come?' Archie reached for Dan's hand.

'That depends on Cleo.' Dan looked across to her.

'Didn't you tell Dot you were busy? You don't have time for messing around with us.' She prayed that he did.

'I *said* I couldn't hang about the shop. Fishing, now that's different and it'll stop me over-thinking my big day tomorrow.' Dan's eyes lit up, 'Hey Archie, I have a great idea. I know *the* best fishing spot. We could go there if you want.'

He looked at Cleo to see if she agreed. 'Come on, Cleo; let's take a ride to Ingram valley he'll love it and there are great spots for netting tiddlers.'

'OK then, we'll go.' Had she said that? Dan was up and back into the shop.

He came back with two extra fishing nets, it was that sort of sell-everything shop, a bottle of wine and another tube of crisps. 'Fishing is hungry work so I've got us some extra supplies.'

They rode in Dan's car and Cleo enjoyed seeing the familiar landmarks on the way to one of her favourite childhood haunts. She hadn't been there in years but nothing along the route seemed to have changed. They were over the wooden single lane bridge and into the valley and found the perfect picnic spot. A grassy slope to the river, trees for shelter from the sun and wind and smooth stones to act as natural fishing platforms.

Cleo took Archie's shoes off and put rubber ones on his feet so that he could paddle in the river and led him to the waters' edge with two of the nets.

'Oh, so *I* get the old one and you two get the new. I bet I get more fish than you two before lunch,' Dan called.

Archie was having great fun filling their jam jars with river water. Cleo glanced over at Dan who was studying her with great intensity.

'Thanks for joining us, Dan.' She looked into his eyes and couldn't say anything more.

'The pleasure's mine. I've been wanting to see you all week but your end of term seemed manic. You're the sole reason I'm in Dunleith today. You know I could never change the way I feel about you, Cleo; even if I wanted too.'

'I feel the same.' They walked towards each other and were in each other's arms.

Cleo felt a tug at her shirt, 'Fisheees!' They looked at Archie and then at one another. This reunion was going to have to wait.

And wait.

Dan helped Cleo to unload the car and she had just summoned up the courage to invite him for supper when he said,

'I'd better get a move on. I'm booked into a hotel in Newcastle so that I'm near the hospital tomorrow morning and I'm having supper with someone from the department tonight.'

'Oh... Well good luck for tomorrow. That's if you decide you want the post.'

'I definitely want to come back whether I get this post or not. I decided that the last time I was here. I've been away too long and I had forgotten what I was missing.' He gave her a long look then strode over and brushed her cheek with his lips. She turned to face him and, once more, felt that familiar tug at her shirt.

'Cloee, me hung'ee,' Archie wailed.

'I told you that fishing was hungry work.' Dan ruffled

Archie's hair and was out of the door leaving Cleo wishing her lips had touched his, just for a moment.

Archie was asleep by the time Alex came home, after spending all day with the EllaBella's.

'Come to the window, Cleo,' she said, grabbing Cleo's hand. Cleo admired the flamingo-feathered sky that held the promise of another sunny day ahead.

'It's beautiful to see so much sky out here,' Cleo murmured.

'Yes, but the moon, Cleo. Look at that full moon.'

'You're right, we can make a wish; Mum would like that.'

'You still don't get it,' Alex's green eyes glinted with pleasure, 'It's a *blue* moon. How often do we get to wish on that!'

Cleo stared at the second full moon of July. Some things happened just once in a blue moon and she was going to wish for another chance with Dan.

Heather and Mark arrived to collect Archie after their two nights in Edinburgh.

'Look Daddy, Dan got me fisheees,' Archie was carefully carrying his bucketful of tiddlers to show his daddy. 'They have to go back in the water. Dan said so.'

'Dan said? Heather looked over with interest. Cleo, I think *we* need a coffee while Mark takes Archie to the burn to set those fish free.' Her urge to visit Erin's seemed to be forgotten.

Mark grinned, 'Come on, son. We'll put the tiddlers back in the burn.' He turned to Heather and said, 'You two have half an hour to share news.'

Cleo filled Heather in on what had happened, or not had a chance to happen, between her and Dan and then asked, 'What's your news anyway? Mark said you had something to share.'

Heather beamed, 'You won't find this the least bit thrilling but, over the weekend, we decided to try for another baby. A brother or sister for Archie.'

Cleo hugged Heather and told her that of course she was thrilled. The funny thing was that she *really* felt thrilled. She didn't have to pretend it was good news, it seemed that at the moment, she was loving small people.

BLUE MOON

29

On Wednesday evening, Alex and the EllaBellas were going into Berwick for the evening and Mary was picking them up afterwards. With Alex having a sleepover at the Collingwoods' house, Cleo had a free night ahead of her, for the first time in forever it seemed.

As she relaxed in a bubble bath wondering whether she should read one of the many books she'd downloaded onto her kindle, or start to watch the 'Breaking Bad' box set that she hadn't opened since unwrapping it at Christmas, the landline rang. She grabbed a towel and went to answer it.

'Hi Cleo it's me.'

'Hi Dan.'

'I've just heard that I've been offered the consultant's post and I wanted you to be the first to know. Will you celebrate with me?'

'Wow! Yes, YES! That is great news, where are you?'

'I'm coming up your path now with champagne.'

'What?'

'Shall I ring at the front or come around the back?'

Bloody hell, Dan had done it again! Here she was without a scrap of makeup and wearing just a towel.

'Come to the back.' She flung down the receiver and raced to her wardrobe.

She paused, went back to the hall and leaned over the

banister to call, 'Dan, you know where the glasses are in the kitchen. Just give me a minute and I'll be down.'

After clipping back her damp hair, she pulled on an emerald green maxi dress that she usually kept for holidays, slipped on some Havianas and grabbed her lip gloss. That would have to do. There was nothing she could do about pink cheeks; it wasn't the bath but sheer panic that had brought on this glow.

Dan was in the kitchen pouring two glasses of bubbly. 'Cleo you are truly beautiful tonight. And before you answer back, you are beautiful whenever I see you. Please come over here and take this drink before I spill it.'

Cleo took it and touched glasses with Dan saying, 'Here's to success in your new job.'

'Thank you,' he said as she took both glasses and placed them on the kitchen table. Facing him once again, Cleo put her arms around his neck and their lips were almost touching.

'I'm so glad for you, Dr Collingwood,' she said.

They kissed softly, then passionately and hungrily before moving away from the kitchen into the hallway. Lounge or upstairs? Cleo didn't hesitate, she took his hand and they found themselves back on her single bed.

Dan's fingers travelled up and down her body and his lips trailed kisses from her neck to her breasts and back again. Her skin was on fire; his kisses were taking her on a journey she knew and had yearned for ever since she saw him again. The melting sensation grew and she wouldn't be able to wait; she weaved her fingers into his hair and pulled his head back to give him a pleading look.

'Come with me,' she whispered. He paused and then he stood up and his eyes never left hers as he unbuttoned his trousers and kicked them off. They were together, at last.

Afterwards, there was a peace, a floating sensation before she sank back into herself onto the bed. Dan, I love you she thought.

'What was that you said?' Dan's voice was husky.

Had she said it aloud? She looked into his eyes. 'Thanks for coming back to me, Dan,' she whispered.

'Thank you, Cleo. Thank you for just being you. I love you.'

'I love you too. I always have.'

Within a few moments they were kissing again. This time it was slower and Cleo had more control over her desire but not much, oh how she wanted this man!

The midnight chimes from the church clock roused Cleo. It was dark and they must have dozed off. She quietly climbed out of bed and stood at the window. The moon was bright over Dunleith; she smiled thinking that her blue moon wish had come true.

They spent the rest of the week trying to keep their rekindled love a secret from the village. It was an open secret because everyone they met seemed to be able to tell that Cleo and Dan were head over heels.

The night before she left for France with the Collingwoods, Alex had badgered her into admitting as much. 'The EllaBellas and I *know* you've got the hots for Dan and he's really into you, so just go for it. You want to, don't you?'

'The *hots*? That sounds awful, Alex! But, you're right, we do like each other... a lot.' Cleo smiled at Alex's eagerness for her to confess.

'More than a lot.' Alex insisted.

'Yes, more than a lot,' she admitted.

'Go for it, I might even end up being related to my BFFs.'

Yes, you might... if Dan ever asks.' Cleo grinned at Alex's expression as she leapt up and hugged Cleo.

'I never thought you two were a match but now I think

you *do* go together, somehow. Don't spoil it while I'm away by thinking of work and being sensible.'

'I won't,' promised Cleo. No, she wouldn't be sensible she promised herself.

The summer days before Dan had to leave for a last trip to Australia to pack up his life over there, passed in a whirlwind. They went back to Newcastle far away from the eyes of Dunleith taking a wailing Pharos who had just got used to his old haunts.

They spent their time on day trips out, nights with Heather and Mark and evenings of finding each other again.

Dan wanted to settle somewhere in Northumberland, an easy journey from Newcastle and so did Cleo. They were going to find somewhere together but she'd asked Dan to stay with her in the apartment until the right place came up.

Cleo had always worked hard at her career but, since looking after Josh, Archie and Alex, she knew she wanted her own children as much as she wanted a teaching career and she wanted them with Dan.

They talked a little about the past and how they'd split up. Dan had felt that she kept him at bay and wanted to be free to follow her career without distractions.

'I understood how you wanted to achieve to make your Mum proud but, when work *always* came first, even before family and even though we were still studying and should have some fun times... I thought I was holding you back and should bow out,' Dan confessed. 'I always hoped you'd tell me to stop being stupid and fall back into my arms,' he gave a rueful smile, 'but, you didn't.'

'Oh, I wanted too! I cried rivers when you told me we were through. I blamed Alex of course. I thought it was just because I didn't like her hanging around us when you loved doing things with the EllaBellas.'

'It wasn't just that, Cleo and it wasn't all you, the kids enjoyed winding you up when they were younger and you reacted every time.'

Cleo smiled; Dan seemed to see the best in her. She really *had* hated spending time with the kids then and she had been so set on achieving and proving herself to the world. She hadn't been ready for Dan then, but she was sure that she was ready for him now.

On their last evening together, over a delicious dinner at *Artisan,* Dan said, 'I think we've both come of age again, Cleo. A thirties coming of age. We still want each other, we want the same things, at last, and I hope we can have them together.'

'So do I.' Cleo wanted to be with Dan; she was ready for the house, the kids, the wedding and she wanted them all with this wonderful man.

'It'll only be a few weeks and then I'm back for good and your mother will be back too. I'm going to propose to you properly and we'll tell the world and our families our plans then.' Cleo's heart was full to overflowing, things couldn't be better.

30

Teri rinsed her hair and enjoyed feeling the strong jets of the shower rinse away the sand and salt from the beach. These days were a perfect bubble of happiness, every day stretched out full of a myriad of things to do and see. Days when they could enjoy one another. Hours drifted by slowly yet time flew too fast. Teri would have to start thinking of when she should book her flight home but swiftly pushed the thought to the back of her mind, not yet, savour the moment.

She stepped out of a haze of lemon-scented steam and wrapped a towelling robe around herself. She hardly recognised her own body because, as well as gaining a much needed pound or two, it had turned such a rich golden shade.

She knew something was wrong the moment she moved onto the balcony to dry off her hair. Greg was sitting there with questions written all over his face and a frown darkening his eyes.

'What's wrong?' she asked, gently placing a hand on his shoulder.

'You tell me.' The stern questioning look he gave her made her shiver.

What did he mean? 'You'll have to give me a clue,

Greg. I went into the shower and we were fine and now...?'

'You went into the shower and your phone rang but I couldn't get to it in time. What I did see was that the caller had tried several times over the past few weeks and that there were messages asking you to ring. A voicemail says your caller is from a hospital and they are anxious to talk to you. Why haven't you called back? What's going on, Teri?'

Teri walked into their room, lay back on the bed and closed her eyes. She hadn't told Greg about the tests she had taken before travelling to Egypt.

Greg followed her asking, 'What are you running from Teri?'

She opened her eyes to see him looking down at her with real concern. 'I'm not running; I'm just giving myself some space. I needed space before I heard some test results from the hospital, that's all.'

Greg sank onto the bed next to Teri. 'What sort of tests?'

He took her in his arms and Teri took strength from his embrace and told him about the pains she was dealing with and her fear that they may be related to her cancer, even though it was three years on.

'The pain hasn't been so bad since I came here. I haven't taken half as many tablets,' she assured him.

'You can't hide from things like this Teri, you owe it to yourself and the girls to take such things seriously and to find out your results.'

'Oh, I take them seriously, Greg; I just needed to do a couple of things. I've had two dreams that I've kept in my moondream jar for years and I had to do something about them.'

'Moondream jar?' he looked even more puzzled.

'Just keep holding me and I'll tell you about it.'

They talked, made love, ordered supper in their room

and talked some more. Before drifting off to sleep, Teri promised Greg that she would call the hospital first thing in the morning.

Teri's hands felt clammy as she held the phone and her mouth was so dry that she could hardly speak. She was eventually put through to her consultant's office.

'I'm sorry but Mr Amonkar is on leave, he's lecturing abroad for a month. He doesn't give results over the phone anyway. I can see from your notes that he was trying to get in touch to arrange a follow up appointment right up to the day he left.'

Teri couldn't blame the woman for sounding shirty. She'd probably been the one ringing her number every week and getting voicemail.

'Thank you for letting me know. I've been travelling but I'll call back as soon as I get home.'

'Wait. Have you another number? One that it's easier to get you with?' the woman wasn't going to let her hang up.

'No, no. This number will be fine from now, I'm sorry for your inconvenience.'

'I'm going to look at his diary and give you a priority appointment when he comes back. Can you hang on?' the voice softened slightly.

'Yes, I'll do that.'

She was given the Tuesday after her birthday; that gave her another three weeks. Teri felt Greg's eyes on her as she ended the call.

'What now?' he asked.

'He's on leave so I have a reprieve but I do have an appointment date. Now, let's go diving.'

CORN MOON

31

The summer break always seemed so long to begin with then it flashed by. Cleo picked Alex up from Dunleith the weekend before school started and listened to her chatter away about the brilliant time she'd had in France with the EllaBellas, how she'd enjoyed hanging out with her Dunleith friends but how she would be glad to get back to see Gracie and Lee and the Newcastle crowd.

'Eleanor can be a bit bossy but Isabella just doesn't realise it,' Alex confided. 'I notice it more now that I've matured a bit and I try to stand up to her. She doesn't like it though.'

'Good for you.' Cleo was proud of Alex. It was hard to imagine that their first trip to her apartment just ten weeks ago had been so strained.

Alex had actually *wanted* to spend the first weeks of this term with Cleo until their mum came back from Egypt and, because her coursework was developing well and she was covering the syllabus for her Art, Design and English courses, her own school had no objections. She'd really miss sharing with Alex when Mum got back.

'Now tell me about what you've been doing,' asked Alex. Cleo suddenly felt vulnerable. What would Alex think of her and Dan being a serious couple?

'Cleo? *Hello*? What's hard about that little question?' Cleo flushed and took a deep breath before saying,

'I've been seeing a lot of Dan.'

'I knew it! We knew it; the EllaBellas and I said you both looked like you were falling for each other. Now he's coming back, will you be all serious and getting engaged and stuff?'

'Hold on, I said we had been seeing each other but give it time, Alex.'

'*Time*, you're both getting on! Do you want to be with him, a proper couple, Cleo?' Alex's eyes were shining and she felt? happy for her.

'Yes Alex. Yes, I do. We'll have to decide when to tell the families after Dan gets over here so don't broadcast it.' She laughed as she thought that request would be a lost cause between Alex and the EllaBellas. 'Now let's change the subject so I can concentrate on my driving.'

Alex went quiet and Cleo could see her thumbs working overtime on her phone. She'd be relaying this back to Dan's sisters but that was fine. She didn't really mind who knew now that they were sure of each other.

Alex stayed at the apartment the next morning because it was a training day. Cleo had arranged for a literacy consultant to run a teaching reading workshop for the support staff and, once that was underway, she had a meeting with the rest of senior management to iron out any problems with staffing and timetables and to discuss all of the school's new initiatives. This term the building of the TeMPS unit would get underway and she couldn't wait to see the work finished and the unit up and running by Christmas.

Gracie and Alex had been in touch by text over the holidays and she knew that Gracie was four months pregnant, so this would enable her to carry on studying when she was in her third trimester and after the baby was born.

Cleo pulled in next to Telford as he was getting out of a

shiny new black BMW.

'Good morning Cleo. I see you still have that old banger of your mother's. I thought you were going to get something new over the summer?'

'Good morning Boss. I actually like this one. I don't need to worry where I park it and it holds loads more than the convertible. I *will* get another car but I'm not in a hurry. I see you've changed your car again...very nice.' Already, Tef was grating on her and she hadn't got into the building.

'Every year, Cleo, every year. I couldn't drive a tank like that.' He beamed proudly at his own car and was still admiring it as Cleo went into school.

'Cleo,' hissed Ann, who had the dubious honour of being Teflon's PA this year. Cleo was in the back of the literacy meeting making sure the right staff were there and that the equipment was working for her guest speaker. She slipped out to see what Ann wanted.

'The Boss wants *all* senior management in the meeting room now. He says it's urgent.'

'Do you know what it's about?' Cleo asked, as she followed Ann who was hurrying along and checking rooms to find the other assistant heads.

'No, but he doesn't look happy.'

They exchanged looks. When was *he* ever happy? But, this was early in the term, even for Tef. What had rattled his cage?

They soon found out. A letter had landed in his in-tray informing him that their school was going to be inspected on Thursday and Friday of this week.

'This means that *everyone* will be working flat out to make rooms ship shape, all teacher's planning must be checked by a senior manager, pupils must be warned that behaviour will be judged and we will all have to check that our own areas of responsibility are running like clockwork.'

They all nodded and Cleo started making lists of the hundreds of things she would have to check before Thursday. Whole school literacy in every subject, pastoral care and the start of building the new unit were hers to oversee once she knew her new timetable was running smoothly. No week was a good week for inspection but the first week back took stress to a higher level.

'Who is leading the team, Boss? What's their background?' asked Paul Charlton, looking decidedly grey. He was responsible for behaviour with oversight of the PE and humanities faculties and was known to fly by the seat of his pants. Paperwork was his downfall and he'd be in school from now until Thursday to get through this.

'Interestingly enough, it's a local chap. Well he *was* local. I've just run a check on him and he attended a local grammar school, went on to Oxford in the eighties and has been a head teacher in the South for a number of years. Ralph, Ralph Fenwick, son of one of the old grammar school heads.'

Cleo felt the blood drain from her face and her heart hammered painfully against her chest as she fought for breath. Oh shit, she felt the room swim and had to grab onto Paul to steady herself.

'Steady on, Cleo. It's not that bad - I bet your paperwork is in a better state then mine,' he whispered.

The pounding at her temples made Cleo feel sick. There could be no doubting it; this Ralph Fenwick must be the one mentioned in Mum's diary. She wasn't just preparing for an Ofsted school inspection; she was preparing to meet her biological father.

If Cleo looked tense and worried all day, nobody mentioned it. The school's happy 'just back from holiday' atmosphere had been smothered as quickly as a sea fret could chill a sunny Whitley Bay day.

Lots of staff were stressed when there was no need to be. Cleo knew that the school had produced improved exam results, this year's grades were exceptional for an inner city school and it was outstanding in most areas. The inspection might keep them on their toes until the end of the week but they'd get though with flying colours she was sure. If only *her* nerves were due to this government hoop they had to jump though.

Cleo was relieved to get home and touched to see that Alex had defrosted a large shepherd's pie that they'd brought from Mum's freezer at High Rigg and it was bubbling away in the oven. Over dinner, she explained how everyone was in a 'tizz' about their inspection on Thursday. Should she tell Alex the rest? Why not, Alex had seen the diary at the same time as her.

'You can't be serious? Like your *father*, he is coming to school on Thursday and he doesn't even know who you are? Bloody hell Cleo, how will you tell him?'

'Tell him? Of course I won't tell him. It's none of his business. He lost that right when he dumped Mum and went to Oxford and she didn't get to go.' The tears that welled in her eyes were dangerously close to falling.

'Don't be upset Cleo. I just thought you'd want him to know how well you've done. *He* was a head, his father was a head and now you're a deputy head, it's a sort of family thing isn't it?'

'He's not my family.' Cleo was sure about that.

Whoa! I've just thought, maybe he'll *look* like you? I mean you're dark haired with those dark eyes and look nothing like Mum or me.'

Cleo stared in horror at Alex. 'Bloody hell; I hope it's not that obvious!'

Alex grinned, 'Only you and I would guess because you haven't even got Mum's maiden name. Miss Cleo Moon you will keep your secret until *you* decide!' she added in an excellent impression of TV's 'Big Brother' commentator.

Cleo was usually in school by seven thirty and suppressed a smile when she saw that Teflon's car was already there. He had been hell to deal with for the past three days but she knew he would be oozing buttery charm to today's visitors.

Cleo had just begun to listen to the school's messages, to see who had fallen at the first hurdle and was phoning in sick on an inspection day, when a sleek silver car took up one of their 'reserved for visitors' spaces. She swallowed hard and resisted rushing to the window. It was bad enough facing an inspection but she'd met that particular challenge before. Looking at the other half of her genetics, she couldn't think of him as her father, for the first time was something she had never experienced.

The school door buzzer sounded in Tef's office as well as hers but he obviously wasn't there. For security, the door remained locked until reception staff came on duty. Feeling calm, almost as if this was an out of body experience, Cleo walked into the foyer to release the door.

'Hello there, Ralph Fenwick, chief inspector.'

Cleo took the outstretched hand, gazed into eyes as brown as her own and knew straight away that this really was him.

'Cleo Moon, deputy head.' she matched his firm handshake thankful that her voice sounded normal. 'We have a room set aside for you and your team, if you'd like to wait there, I'll go and find Mr. Teflon for you.'

'Did you say *Teflon*?'

Did she? No! 'Mr. *Telford* is the head. I'll just locate where he is,' she said.

'No, don't bother the head yet. I like to get into schools early to see what goes on so I'll just shadow you, if you don't mind.'

Cleo shot him her questioning look, unsure of how to answer this request and received a similar questioning look in return. Bloody hell. This was a fine start to the day.

'OK,' she nodded. 'It's a busy time for me so, if you don't mind starting without a coffee, you can watch me sort out staff absences. I arrange cover for any absent staff before school starts.'

'You lead on Miss Moon,' he said.

Day one of the inspection went well and Mr. Telford was extremely happy at the senior team's debriefing at the end of the day.

'It's looking like we're going for 'outstanding'. Just need to make sure that inclusion and community cohesion and safeguarding is up to scratch tomorrow and observe some more excellent lessons.

Cleo, I'm giving you the lead man first thing tomorrow morning. You can tell him about your new TeMPS unit, show him the plans and the area that's being refurbished and then pass him along to Paul to find out about sport in the community.'

Next morning, their tour of the new facility went smoothly and afterwards Cleo led Ralph Fenwick to the cafeteria. She would answer any further questions over coffee and then Paul was going to meet him to discuss the school's links with the community.

'I must tell you that you're doing a wonderful job in creating this unit for the area, Miss Moon. It's being refurbished with a donation to the school for this purpose, you say?'

'Yes. We were going to raise funds but the moment the project was mentioned, we got the full amount by an anonymous donor.'

'That's great luck.'

'We would've raised the funds, eventually,' bristled

Cleo. 'But yes, it was lucky to be able to start sooner than we anticipated. The school has planned how to fund the staffing. It's mainly from our school budget but other schools in the area will contribute because they will be using the facility for their own single mothers too.'

'Just so. That's great team work and you must be proud to be leading on such an important initiative.'

'I am,' Cleo smiled and RF, she thought of him by the initials she'd been writing on copies of reports for the past week, smiled back at her, his face warm and open and understanding. Catch on, she told herself, *this* is a man who dumped one of these very girls.

'Things must have changed a lot for pregnant students since *your* schooldays,' she commented evenly.

RF seemed surprised by the comment and sat back in his chair looking at her as if wondering what to say.

'I'll tell you something, Cleo, and then you will know *just* what a difference you're making. I knew a wonderful girl, a real scholar at history and a brain that would take her to Oxford and further. She fell pregnant and every door to education closed. I don't know what happened to her but something like this... it would never have happened.'

Cleo's heart thudded; she bit her lip to stop making a comment, but couldn't help it.

'What about the boy in your story? There must have been one. I suppose he just sailed on with no worries and the girl paid the price?'

RF looked at her intently, 'I think that such a boy could never forget how he'd ruined a life, maybe two, Cleo. But that was the past and now, thankfully things are different.'

Paul came into the cafeteria, pulled up a chair and set several files on the desk as RF and Cleo locked eyes.

'I hope you've seen all you need to see; I'll leave you with Mr. Charlton.' Cleo managed to stay calm and walk sedately off before finding the ladies and bursting into tears. Tears for her mum and for herself and none for the boy who might have had no choice himself all those years ago.

It was an hour after most staff had left the building and Tef was still in a meeting with the lead inspector. The senior management team were all huddled in the staff room. Waiting. Telford burst in shouting,

'We've done it!' Tie loose, jacket off and shirt buttons bulging, his red face had never been so animated with delight. 'We have really done it. *We* are an outstanding school. Grade one across the board. We have got an *excellent* management team, apparently. Now let's all have a glass of champagne.'

Ann came in just on cue with two bottles of the real stuff and real glasses. Tef must be in celebratory mood!

The darkening sky reminded Alex that the days were getting shorter and she needed a school coat. The moon was hidden by cloud and there was that fine drizzle and a chill in the air signalling that autumn was around the corner. Alex sat on the low wall by the staff car park, her hair soaked and her thin jacket giving no protection from the wind that was starting up. She was beside his car waiting for him to come out. It had to be soon and it had to be before Cleo.

Alex had thought long and hard about this. She hadn't talked to anyone else. She didn't want to tell the EllaBellas, she couldn't call Mum without telling the whole story and she knew that Cleo didn't want to tell Ralph Fenwick anything.

Alex had considered it from all points of view and thought that this was a secret that had gone on too long and she might be able to help Cleo to get her real father back. She had to try. Cleo would be glad once it was done, wouldn't she?

His tall figure crossed from the school to the car park

and Alex's heart thudded.

'Excuse me sir,' she stood up and as he looked her way, his eyes widened in surprise. 'Excuse me Mr. Fenwick, could I have a word?' Ralph Fenwick put his briefcase into the boot of his car and walked over.

'And *you* are?'

'I'm Alex; I'm...actually I'm Miss Moon's sister.'

'Oh,' he smiled at her, 'you'll have a delighted sister tonight because the school has done very well. No need to worry. Why are you waiting for her here in the rain? Shouldn't you be inside?'

'I don't want to see Cleo; it's you I want to see. Can we talk for a moment?'

'Hmmm.' He frowned at her.

She waited, fingers crossed in her jacket pockets as he considered her request. A deep frown furrowed his brow. 'Can we sit in your car; I'm freezing?'

'I'm not sure that would be appropriate, Alex; you see-'

'Look sir, I don't want Cleo to see me,' Alex interrupted, 'and I want to tell you about your daughter so it's best that we sit in the car.'

'You're mistaken, I've got sons. I don't have a daughter.'

Alex could see from his concerned expression that he was trying to be polite but she was troubling him. This wasn't going to plan at all.

'You do! Your daughter is in that school now. My sister.'

'Cleo? Miss Moon?'

'Yes, she's *your* daughter.'

That hadn't gone like she'd hoped but it was done now.

Mr. Fenwick glanced around the car park, was he going to call for Cleo? No, he opened the passenger door and turned back towards her.

'You'd better get in and explain.'

Alex sat shivering as he looked at her closely.

'Let me get this right. You are saying that Miss Moon, Cleo, you think she's my daughter?'

'I know she is. We both do, we know who you are because our mother is Margaret Donaldson - aged fifty. Well fifty this month and she went to school with you.'

'My God!'

Alex knew she had his full attention now, '*And* she had your baby, and that was Cleo.'

Mr Fenwick sat rubbing his brow as if he was massaging this news into his head.

'Alex, I don't know what to say. Why hasn't Cleo mentioned this? Where is Margaret? I swear I've often looked for her but never a trace.'

'Margaret's had a name change and she's in Egypt so she doesn't know any of this. Look, I need to let Cleo know that I've told you about her and then, do you want to meet up?'

'I'm not sure what to do, Alex. I don't know what's best. I've got sons and this will be a great shock to them.'

'I can't stay any longer in case Cleo comes out and catches me here. Look, I've written our address and number on here for you so, in your own time but don't leave it. It's not right.'

As he took the slip of paper, he nodded and Alex got out of the car.

She watched him drive off. Was he going to the family who knew nothing about a daughter? She headed for the metro station. She would get home just before Cleo and tell her when the time seemed right. She was sure she'd done the right thing.

32

'We've been graded outstanding Alex. Celebration supper!' Cleo had stopped off for Thai food and knew there was a Riesling chilling in the fridge that would match it perfectly.

'I knew you'd do well.' Alex jumped up and went straight to the cutlery drawer to set two places.

Cleo noticed that Alex's hair was damp; she must have taken a shower before changing into the onesie she was wearing. 'Here, you dish up and I'll slip into something stretchy too. I can eat more then.'

Cleo was back in two minutes. 'Whoa! That's enough for me. I can always go back for more.' She took her heaped plate from Alex and enjoyed relating all the ins and outs of the day and the way her tour of the new TeMPs unit had gone down so well with Ralph Fenwick.

Alex looked preoccupied.

'Are you listening?' Cleo asked.

Yes, of course I am.'

'You look as though you're miles away.'

'I'm not. I was thinking about *him* too, the inspector, I mean. That RF, as you call him, I was thinking about him meeting you and not knowing he's your father.'

'No, he doesn't and he's not going to know either.' Cleo was determined that wouldn't happen. She'd seen him and that was enough. They both had their own lives.

'That *might* not be the case.' Alex looked concerned.

Cleo was puzzled, what was she on about? 'What do you mean, Alex?' Cleo stopped pouring a second glass of wine and searched Alex's face closely, her little sis was acting strangely.

Alex pushed her plate away and grabbed one of Cleo's hands. 'Cleo, I thought he should know. He should know he has a brilliant daughter and you've done *so* well.'

Cleo felt a flush rise to her cheeks and it wasn't the Riesling. 'What exactly are you saying Alex?'

'I told him.' Alex's eyes were looking imploringly at her.

'You *what*?'

'I explained it all.'

'When? *When* did you see him?'

'In the car park tonight. I told him about Mum and you and gave him your number that's all.'

'*That's all?* You stupid, stupid girl! How dare you. How dare you stick your nose in to *my* past like that.'

'Don't be mad, Cleo. He deserved to know and he might get in touch; he said he might.'

'Oh, he said he *might,* did he? That makes it all just hunky-dory, doesn't it! Don't you understand that I don't *want* him to?' Cleo knew she was yelling but, bloody hell, what a thing for Alex to do.

'You don't understand.'

'No *you* don't understand. How can you go totally against what I wanted? What a terrible thing, what a bloody unsisterly thing to do.'

'Don't say that! I'm sorry; I thought you were just saying that.'

'*Sorry?* Sorry isn't enough Alex. You've really excelled yourself this time.'

'Right! Just hate me all over again.' Alex got up and slammed her bedroom door.

Cleo slumped into her chair and burst into tears. This

was their first row since they'd become close. She shouldn't have said 'unsisterly', but could she forgive her? Would they get over this?

A few moments later Cleo heard the front door open and, as she raised her head, she saw the back of Alex leaving with an overnight bag. She ran to the door and shouted after her but she was gone.

Cleo ran down the stairs but it was dark and raining and she couldn't see which way Alex had gone. Slowly she headed back upstairs to the apartment. She'd left the door wide open, it was a blessing that it hadn't slammed shut and locked her out.

She started to clear up the supper cartons and looked around for Pharos; there were a couple of prawns that he would devour. Where was he? Cleo did a quick search of the apartment. He was in none of his favourite nooks. He hated noise, was he hiding? Or worse, had he escaped when she left the door open? She grabbed her coat and went outside. She hoped he hadn't gone far.

Cleo lay on her bed her eyes swollen with crying and wondered what to do next. Alex had sent a text to say she was at Gracie Grieves' house; she was staying there for the weekend and wouldn't be returning to the apartment. That was a worry. A second text stated that she was going to pick her schoolwork up on Monday and then go back to Dunleith and stay with the Collingwoods until Mum came home. Mary had agreed that she could stay as long as Cleo was happy.

Alex didn't pick up when Cleo tried ringing and she knew that Alex would hate her going around to Gracie's house. She could hardly drag her home and, from her school experience, she knew that the police wouldn't take action over a seventeen-year-old.

She was worried about Alex but almost as concerned about Pharos. She didn't know what would happen to an elderly cat out on the busy streets around here. She could hardly call the police about him either but she must do something.

She couldn't call Mum; she'd let her down with Alex and her cat. Would she lose Mum's love too? At a loss over what to do next, she rang Dan and, instead of telling him about her successful Ofsted, she had to confess that she'd chased away her sister and Mum's cat.

It was breakfast time over there and he was rushing to his last stint of duty. She had expected sympathy but all she got was how *she'd* promised Mum to look after them and how she'd have to get them both back.

'I'm aware of what I need to do, Dan. I just thought you might be supportive, maybe have a thought for me.'

'Cleo, I love you and think of you all the time, but Alex is in her teens and you say she's staying in a dodgy area. Your mum idolises the cat and it's missing. You've vented your anger about your father out on them both and your kid sister was trying to help.

I'll get back as soon as I can; I have this one final shift in the outback and then I'm booking my ticket home. Until then, you'll have to sort this out and quickly. Heather and Mark will help you until I get back and... you might not like this Cleo, but I agree that, if you're not getting on, it would be best if Alex returned to her own school and stayed at Fernlea Lodge.'

'Stop it. Stop telling me what to do. *I'll* decide what's best!' Cleo yelled down the phone and cut him off. She furiously chewed on a handful of her least favourite jellies, even her sweet bowl was empty and held no comfort.

Why couldn't Dan have just sympathised with her? And anyway, what did he know, her anger wasn't *at* her father; it was about him finding out about her, wasn't it?

Mac, he would have known what to do. Even as she thought this, she recognised that, over the years, she'd cast Mac as the perfect dad because he wasn't here and couldn't let her down.

Cleo couldn't sleep. She got up again to look for Pharos but she didn't dare call for him as one of her neighbours had shouted an infuriated '*please!*' at two in the morning and it was almost four o' clock now.

She looked out of the window at the courtyard below and there was a sleek black cat slinking along by the cars. The moon shone brightly lighting puddles and pavements but there was no silver dark-spotted boy in sight. It would be the corn moon; she wished on it as hard as she had as a child; Keep Pharos safe, help me to make amends to Alex and Mum and Dan, bring us all safely together.

She couldn't believe she'd reacted so badly to Alex's news. OK she didn't want anything to do with RF but he was hardly going to broadcast news of a long lost daughter. She wasn't likely to cross his path again. She'd been mean to Dan too just because he hadn't said what she wanted to hear. She would try to make it up to them all, once she found the cat.

Posters. That's what she'd do. She wasn't going to sleep. By five thirty Cleo had a photo of Pharos and contact details on a hundred posters. She needed more printer cartridges to do more when the shops opened. She set off to put them on lampposts and through letter boxes and to check the roads, all the time terrified that she'd find Pharos lying there.

An early coffee with Heather and Archie helped to clear Cleo's head. Heather listened to the whole saga of Ralph Fenwick and didn't interrupt once. By the end of the story, Cleo, was crying again, she just couldn't stop.

'You may be annoyed with Alex but she was doing what she thought would help. I don't know how much damage it will do to your new closer relationship, but just give her some space and then talk it over with her. She must know you're sorry because you've tried to call her, so give her a breathing space.' Heather handed her a tissue.

'I'll have to. I don't want a scene in school on Monday so I'll just have to go along with her going back to Dunleith and staying with the Collingwoods until Mum is back.'

'Right, that's Alex sorted. Now what can we do about your missing moggie?' Heather asked.

'We could post more leaflets about Pharos. I think we should call vets and catteries, the police too, just in case he's handed in.'

'I'll do the calls and I'll give my number too for anyone who wants to contact us with news.' Heather volunteered.

Cleo was just hoping it wouldn't be bad news such as he'd been killed on a road. The tears started again.

Heather went on, 'As for arguing with Dan, don't leave it too long before you call. You know he's always on your side. I think he was just trying to be practical.'

A chilly feeling crept over Cleo, it was as if she was made of eggshells and her head was cotton wool. She was dimly aware that Heather was taking her up to her spare room and telling her to take a rest.

'You're in shock and you've had no sleep. It's time to sleep or you'll be no good to anybody.'

Cleo sank into the duvet, felt a blanket going round her shoulders and slept.

Nothing had changed when she woke up in the middle of the afternoon. Heather had no news from shelters and vets and her mobile showed that she hadn't had a call from Alex or Dan.

Cleo set off for her apartment although Heather and Mark asked her to stay. She called at the shops for more print cartridges. The whole neighbourhood would know about Pharos because she just couldn't contemplate him being lost forever.

Back at the flat, the living area was strangely tidy. No magazines, trainers or hair slides lying around and no Pharos lounging on the sofa. Alex's door was open and she could see that she'd been back and taken most of her things.

Cleo walked to the back of the sofa and traced the scratch marks left by stretching cat claws, she looked at her pale grey covers that bore the evidence of many wine, juice and milk stains over the past few months and she walked into the tidy spare room, sat on the bed and howled.

A few months back all she had wanted was her own space in her own beautiful tidy apartment and now she had it, give or take a stain or two, but at what price? She'd lost her sister again and managed to chase away her mother's beloved cat.

She couldn't even get in touch with her boyfriend; his phone had no signal. Maybe Dan had thought about their row and regretted getting back with her. She wasn't going to try ringing him anymore tonight, she couldn't face more disappointment.

What would she do with herself over the weekend? More posters and a trip to the shop to hire an upholstery steamer? She had to keep busy while she was falling apart.

33

After saying goodbye to Gracie on Monday morning, Alex called into the newsagent's and bought an iced coffee and a chocolate bar. There hadn't been much cereal or milk to go around at the Grieves' house this morning and the little ones needed something before school. Gracie was taking them to their primary school but she wasn't going in to Tyneview herself.

She had been sick quite a lot, she thought she was starting to show and she wasn't as focussed on keeping up with her courses as she had been before the holidays. Mrs. Grieves worked in a bar until late so, if Gracie was around, she didn't get up until the little ones were at school. How on earth was Gracie ever going to manage her exam work with a baby on the way? The sooner Cleo had that teenage mums' unit up and running, the better it would be for Gracie.

Alex was going into school early to collect her design work and clear her locker and say thanks to the staff who had supported her and then she was heading back to Dunleith. She had been going to stay at High Rigg on her own but Mrs. Collingwood had insisted that she should stay with them until her Mum returned and she didn't mind doing that.

Anything was better than facing Cleo again after the spectacular mess she'd made of trying to reunite father and daughter. She had palpitations even thinking about what she'd done; she would never forget that row and that night as long as she lived.

On Friday night, after storming out of the apartment, she had walked towards the metro station wondering where on earth she could go and had only come up with one solution, to ring Gracie.

Gracie was with Ty but told Alex she'd be home in an hour and to meet her there so, to kill time, she'd tucked herself into the corner of the tiny café by the metro station and ordered a cup of tea.

She saw Will, the karate instructor, come into the café and wrapped her scarf further round her face. She looked out of the window and hoped that he wasn't sitting in. Through the reflection in the window, she saw him order a coffee to take out and was just breathing out a sigh of relief when he stopped by the door and glanced her way. Oh no, he was coming over.

'Hi there,' he started and then his eyes widened in recognition.' Oh, hi Alex. It's you!'

Shuffling further down the chair, she nodded.

'I was just going to take this onto the platform when I recognised the purple and black colours of my rugby club and had to come over to see who was wearing it,' Will explained.

'Huh?' Alex didn't follow what he was saying.

'The scarf,' he smiled, pointing to the scarf she was still holding tightly to her face.

'Oh!' she blushed bright scarlet and wished herself miles from here.

'Who gave you that Scottish team's rugby scarf, then?' he asked.

Alex searched frantically for an answer. Could she say she found it? Bloody hell it was *his*! How could she forget that?

Will pulled out the chair opposite and sat waiting expectantly then his smile faded. 'Hang on ...' He reached over and stared at the silver Scorpio pin at one end of the scarf.

'It's my scarf, Alex. How did you get it?'

Alex was dumbstruck. This day couldn't get much worse; she'd have to own up to being one of the idiots he had helped in June.

She watched realisation dawn on Will and tried to hold back her tears.

'I think I know who you are now! You saved your friend by calling an ambulance when you were at The Nest.'

Alex didn't see it like that, it was Will who had done the saving, but she nodded.

'You left your scarf under her head and, when I picked it up, you'd gone.'

'Yes, I had to get back to the door. How is she, your friend?'

'Eleanor? She's fine. We haven't touched a thing since then. Lesson learnt and all that'

'So tonight, why are you here all alone, except for my scarf, on a Friday evening?'

'Do you have an hour?' Alex managed a smile and tried to shrug off the fact she had nowhere else to go.

'Yes, if that's what it takes.' Will's warm amber eyes were still looking into hers, willing her to talk.

The story came tumbling out. Will listened and nodded and handed her clean napkins to blow her nose and dry her eyes when she got to the bit about Cleo calling her 'bloody unsisterly'. When she finished, she felt better.

'What would you do, Will?' she asked.

'Go home and make it up with my sister,' he answered.

'I can't do that. She's furious and we'll fight again. I'm going back to Dunleith, that's where I come from, once I've collected my work from school on Monday. It's my only choice, really. I'll just have to find somewhere to stay until then.'

'Have you a friend from school? I'd say stay at mine but I tutor at the school and I think your sister would object to you staying with a nineteen-year-old male.'

Alex thought he'd be older than that because he'd been a doorman and seemed so assured and confident.

'I'm sorted until Monday. I'm going to Gracie's. You know Gracie Grieves from Tyneview? But she's not in until ten thirty.'

'It's that time now,' said Will, looking at his watch. 'Come on, I'll walk you around and, if you still want to go to Dunleith on Monday, I'll take you and your stuff back there in my van. I don't have lectures for another week. I'm just here to sort out my flat.'

'Would you?' Alex felt brighter with someone on her side. They stood to go and impulsively, she gave him a hug. 'Thanks Will! You've just saved the day again.'

When they reached Gracie's, Alex handed him his scarf back.

'No, you keep it. I'll just take this.' He removed the pin. 'This tie pin was a present from my sister for my eighteenth birthday. I hardly ever wear a tie so I pinned it to my rugby scarf for luck.'

On Friday, when Will had smiled down at her, Alex had felt her insides do a peculiar little flip. From the moment he'd taken her arm, her worries had seemed smaller. Alex smiled at this recollection. She had fancied him from the first karate lesson but now she had a mega-crush on Will and he was picking her up and driving her to the Collingwood's this morning. That must mean he kind of liked her too, mustn't it?

34

Underneath her cotton top, Teri felt sweat trickling down her skin. Her linen trousers were sticking to her legs as she walked and her hair felt sticky under the wide brimmed hat that shielded her from the sun. This time of day was suitable for swimming, scuba diving or siesta definitely not for walking about. She'd just been to the travel agents to check the availability of tickets for home around about the eighteenth. She hadn't booked one yet but she'd have to do it soon. The hospital had rung to move her consultation with Mr. Amonkar to Monday, the day he returned to work. Was that ominous or not?

She would have to get back to Dunleith soon. Mary had called to say that the girls were at war again but she didn't know why and that Alex had asked to come and stay with them until Teri came home.

Cleo had phoned in tears to say, 'Mum, I've let you down,' because Alex was with the Collingwoods but *she* didn't say what the row was about either.

Alex hadn't answered her call but sent a text to say she was OK and wanted to stay in Dunleith. She'd always known this holiday couldn't go on forever.

Teri was meeting Greg at their favourite coffee shop but he wasn't there yet. She sat down grateful for the shade and cool air-conditioning inside the shop and ordered water and a mint tea. She felt better after a few sips of water. Oh, how she was looking forward to the cool green of her own garden and sitting in the gentle September sun with Pharos on her lap. The girls weren't talking but that was something she'd lived with forever and if they could get on while she was away then it was possible that they'd patch up their differences again. She'd give them more space in future to do that.

Her thoughts turned to Greg and she looked through the photo gallery on her phone at the recent snaps of him... of them. He was a few years younger but they didn't feel the age difference, it was their stages in life that were different.

Teri had been a mother from seventeen, she was now finding freedom for the first time and she turned fifty on the twentieth. Greg was forty-one, he hadn't had children yet but he still had time to find a wife and start a family of his own and he'd make a great dad. Teri loved him enough to let him go and wish him well but it would be a real wrench.

There had only been three men in her life and she had children by two of them. Greg had been such a wonderful bonus; she tried to keep her thoughts positive. I'm not going to get upset over this because it was a great summer she told herself for the tenth time that day.

A shadow loomed over her and a butterfly kiss touched the back of her neck.

'Hi, sorry I'm late. That's a great pic of us; you'll have to send it to my phone.' He sat opposite her and took her hand.

Teri smiled, 'Yes I will. We'll have to send each other the best ones to remember our Egyptian summer.'

'Did you book your flight?' he asked.

'No, I just looked, there was plenty of choice.'

'What's holding you up?' Greg asked.

'When I think of going back, I'm excited at the thought of the girls, the garden and seeing my darling Pharos but really sad that this, that us being together, is all over.' Teri looked at Greg and tears welled in her eyes. 'Such happy days! I wouldn't have missed being with you for the world.'

'I'm glad to hear that. Maybe, after you've sorted out the girls and been open about your past and you get the results of your tests and we know what we're dealing with, maybe *then* we can go on another trip,' he said.

He didn't understand, why was this so hard? 'Look Greg I... I don't think that's a good idea. I mean, this has been so wonderful and we get along so well but it's a transient sort of thing isn't it?' she clasped his hand hard hoping he would understand that this was difficult for her too.

'What do you mean? What's transient about being together and being in love? You being in England won't change how I feel about you, about us.'

'It won't ever change how I feel either but I'm not right for you long term, Greg. I think you need to move on and find someone your own age or at least your own stage in life.'

Greg looked at her, his dark eyes unreadable. 'There you go. Neferteri Moon running away from her chance of happiness and chasing me from mine. Bloody great. I don't want you to decide what my future should hold for me!'

'I'm not deciding it, Greg, I'm just being realistic.'

'You *are* deciding it. Trying to. You are deciding that I will leave you and find a young thirty-something to have a couple of kids with and then live happily ever after and that's not the life I want.' He was white around the lips and the reproach in his eyes made Teri look away.

'Isn't it?' she asked. He made it sound as though she was telling him what to do? Was she? She just wanted what was best for him. What *she* thought was best for him.

'No, that's definitely not what I want.'

'But you said that your wife was pregnant and you lost your chance of a family.'

Yes, I did. A family I'd love because it was with her. Now that I've met you it's your family I want to meet and love, or not love as they seem a pair of awkward customers.'

He managed a grin, 'I'm a dog man but I'll even take to your cat because I love *you*.' He took both of her hands in his and his eyes held her own. 'I'm not asking for marriage, Teri. I'm just asking that we keep our relationship and our love alive and that you don't kill it off.'

'I don't know what to say.' Teri tried to find the answer he was pleading for but she couldn't.

'Don't say anything and we'll see how it works out shall we?'

'But how? I mean there'll be all that distance between us.'

'There will never be a distance unless you put it there, Teri.' He withdrew his hands and held her glance until she broke away again and looked out of the window.

Sahib came and offered Teri more tea, Greg ordered a coffee and the conversation stopped. The tension eased a little as they looked through and swapped photos from their phones. All the time Teri was thinking, but could it work, could we carry on? Am I being silly over a holiday fling or am I throwing something precious away?

That evening, after they had made love, Teri held onto Greg as he slept. She curled into his back, let her fingers comb through his tousled long hair and inhaled the scent of him and let herself imagine that she didn't have to say goodbye. How wonderful it would be.

She tried to picture the reactions of Cleo and Alex but she couldn't. A tear rolled down her cheeks. She couldn't because they wouldn't ever get to meet him, the very thought of carrying on was ridiculous. She was falling for him too deeply so perhaps it was time she went home and got back to reality.

35

Cleo had to drag herself from her bed on Monday morning. She stood at the sink of her empty kitchen and even the smell of her favourite Illy coffee didn't lift the grey fog over the Tyne mood that had settled around her.

She had a later start than usual because she was going to a meeting at the civic centre. There were papers to sign because the TeMPs building work was starting today. She should feel elated about this, she *was,* but it was hard to concentrate on one positive achievement when the rest of her life was such a bloody hopeless mess.

She checked her answer phone and her mobile and there was nothing. No message from Dan or Alex. How did she chase everything that she loved out of her life? She knew what she'd done to Alex but she was upset that Dan hadn't answered her calls. Sipping her coffee, she walked over to the window overlooking the car park to see if Pharos was about.

She'd have a quick scout around the neighbourhood before she went to her meeting and she'd take a few more of her lost cat leaflets with her.

When the meeting at the civic centre was over, Cleo headed for Tyneview. Just as she was pulling into the school entrance, she saw the karate instructor walking towards an old battered van with Alex. She had a couple of bags and he was carrying her design folder and holdall.

So he was giving Alex a lift, was he? Cleo hadn't even known they had become friends. Was he the someone special that Alex had hinted at? She hadn't a clue; some big sister she'd turned out to be!

'You've just missed Alex,' Ann called as she passed reception to go to her office.

'I saw her getting a lift with that karate chap, what's he called?' Cleo replied.

'Will, Will Campbell. He's doing a sports science degree at Northumbria and he's a karate champion; he's a lovely young man.' Ann had a lot of dealings with their after-school staff.

'I'm glad to hear that,' Cleo said before shutting her office door and slumping into her chair. She could put her head in her hands and cry, but she mightn't stop so she'd be much better going through her in tray and keeping her mind on her job. Picking up the first letter, she blinked back the tears that threatened to fall.

Late in the afternoon, Cleo took a walk across to the TeMPs area after the workmen had left for the day and tried to visualise how the completed unit would look. An airy classroom, a computer suite, a shower and cloakroom area, a shared kitchen for the mums and staff and a nursery; it would link to the main school and be part of their community but would be a haven for the teenagers juggling pregnancy, exams and motherhood. Her heart lifted for the first time that day. She'd get this right.

'Hi, Miss. Can I come in?'

Cleo was snapped out of her reverie by Gracie Grieves tapping on the window. Cleo used her access card to unlock the fire door.

'Hi Gracie, come on in. It'll be out of bounds after tomorrow when the building work really starts but I'll show you how this place should look.'

Gracie's eyes lit up as Cleo explained what would go into each area.

'Will it really be ready by next term? For me and the bump?' Gracie was trying to be upbeat.

'It should be, Gracie. You'll have to keep up with your studies this term though.'

Gracie looked serious, 'I will. I really will now that I know that this will be here and I'll have a place for the littl'un when I'm studying. I couldn't leave another bairn at our house. It's heaving already and my mam hasn't the patience for more.'

'You'll be one of its first students so you'll have to help to make it a success.'

'I will, Miss. And Miss... you know that Alex was with me at the weekend?'

'I do and thanks for that. I expect she told you we had a huge row?'

'She didn't say *what* but she *did* say she was sorry you had fallen out'

'Thanks Gracie. That's good to know.'

Was Gracie just being kind or was Alex regretting their words as much as her? 'Did she tell you who was taking her back to Dunleith, Gracie?' Cleo asked. She wondered if Gracie might know more about the friendship with Will.'

'She just said she had a mate with wheels, Miss.'

'I see. Come on then, I'm going home and I'll drop you off if you like.'

'Thanks Miss, but you can just drop me at the metro station.'

On the drive to the station, Cleo had been tempted to ask more questions about Alex and Will but she knew that Gracie would close up and she knew that it didn't matter anyway. Alex was gone and she'd stay gone until Mum came home.

Cleo searched the nearby streets for Pharos and rang Heather to check on any sightings by vets or catteries.

He hadn't been found but there hadn't been any road deaths reported either so she still had a chance of finding him.

Later that evening, she returned from one false sighting just a couple of streets away when her phone rang again. She rushed to get it, 'Cleo Moon,' she crossed her fingers and hoped it was another sighting.

'Hi Cleo, this is Ralph... Ralph Fenwick.' Oh, bloody hell. Not what she was expecting, what could she say? She put the phone down.

How stupid, but she'd panicked. What if it was about the inspection and not about her? The phone rang again and she picked up. 'Cleo Moon,' she said trying to sound calm.

'It's Ralph again Cleo. Please don't hang up. I wanted to talk and to find out if your unit got started on time today. How is it going?'

Cleo gathered her scrambled thoughts together and told him a little about the unit. He prompted her every now and then with a question and she was just beginning to think that he wouldn't mention the embarrassing elephant of a revelation that was in her living room, when he did.

'I want to apologise to you and to Alex. I didn't take the news about being a father very well on Friday because it was something so long ago that I'd almost forgotten.'

'Mum couldn't forget could she?' snapped Cleo.

'Yes, you're right and I know it seems unfair and wrong that she had all of the responsibility but they were different times and we followed what our parents said. I... I didn't even know if or when you were born.'

'I was born and stayed with Mum because *she* didn't follow her parents. She left home and changed her name and her whole life just to keep me.' Her voice had wobbled but she wasn't going to break down.

'I can imagine she did. Your mother is a strong, fantastic person, Cleo. I can see her doing that. Please know that once I got away from home, I did try to find her and to discover whether she did have our baby... you... but I drew a blank. I have talked it over with my family, I have two sons, and I've told them everything. They would like to meet you.'

'I'm not sure if that's something *I* want. You may be my biological father but I don't need another family.'

'That is entirely up to you, I understand, but the offer always stands.'

'Give me some time?' Cleo asked.

'Of course. Thanks for talking, Cleo. For what it's worth, I'm so glad we met up and I'm proud of what you've become.'

Cleo put the phone down and sobbed. It was all just too bloody much. Lying there on the sofa, her mind was a whirlwind of emotions over finding her father, losing her sister, losing Pharos; she'd happily have the latter two back.

Then she understood. Understood how RF had needed time after Alex talked to him; they were alike in that way. They withdrew, took time to sort out their feelings and then made decisions. She wasn't ever impulsive like Teri or Alex; she was like her father.

If she took him at his word, her father hadn't rejected her in the first place, he'd tried to find her. He hadn't rejected her out of hand on Friday, he'd just needed time to adjust. Maybe she *would* want to get to know him better when she got used to the idea. Cleo knew that she must broach the subject with Mum first. They had to talk about what she'd found out and she had to make sure that Mum was happy about her talking to RF. No way was she *ever* going to hurt her mother by getting to know her father.

36

Cleo liked to take the river route home from school. This followed the Tyne as it flowed by Tyneview High and then passed industrial parks, old terraced houses and new buildings taking her right to her own apartment on Mariner's Wharf. Her apartment, overlooking the Tyne, had always felt spacious until the past few months when it had been stuffed to the rafters. It felt so empty now that everyone had gone and she wasn't in a hurry to get home.

A few times, since she'd read Mum's diaries and seen the address on the inside covers, she had almost turned left at the roundabout heading for Elswick and driven towards Middle Row. She'd searched google maps and knew that the row hadn't been knocked down to be replaced by flats or a shopping arcade but still stood there, close to the river and quite close to where Cleo worked.

She wanted to find out whether it was the house she remembered visiting when she was a tot. Maybe not a tot but she'd have been less than four because she had her fourth birthday with Mac; he'd strung balloons and fairy lights all over the garden making it magical.

How reliable was a three-year-old's memory? She could recall red bricks, a front door leading straight onto the pavement and a red front step with flowers in a plant pot next to it. A tall frowning lady stood in the doorway. She didn't shout but had a scary voice as she ordered her mum to go away.

Even now, the memory brought shivers to Cleo. She'd thought about it a lot since reading the diaries. Thought about how going to live with Mac and being so happy had meant that she put all of the time she was away from him right out of her mind. She had to talk to Mum about that time when she got back.

Why had mum taken off to London with her and why had she then gone back to Mac? They loved one another, she knew that, but Mum and Mac did move away from one another. Was it because of her? *Or*, had she returned because of her? *Or*, was it nothing to do with her at all? She just didn't know because she had blocked any talk about being adopted whenever Mac or Mum had raised it and had never asked questions about her time before Dunleith. When she was younger, she didn't want to know the answers but she did now.

Cleo surprised herself by making a detour and heading back towards Elswick and Middle Row. There was no harm in finding the house, was there?

She drove slowly down a road where children were playing football and toys were strewn on the pavement. The street had speed bumps and she could slowly pass number thirty-seven.

A plant pot stood by the step, dark green and overflowing with geraniums. Cleo wound down her window for a better look. It was one of the few houses in the terrace that looked cared for with a red front step and a shining brass knocker.

She parked a little further up and a couple of little kids, nine or ten-year-olds she guessed, cycled up to the car looking interested.

'Who you looking for missus?' A copper-headed boy with a face full of freckles peered into the window.

Cleo wasn't sure what to say. 'I'm not looking for anybody,' she told the lad, 'I'm just looking at the houses.'

'I'll tell you the ones that's up for rent,' his friend piped up. He was a spelk of a boy with teeth that he hadn't grown into yet. 'The one next to mine is up... number twenty.'

'Aye, and then there's thirty-seven. She's trying to sell that.'

Cleo's ears pricked up, she hadn't noticed that it was for sale. 'Do either of you know who is selling thirty-seven?'

'Aye, me da says she's mental. She's asking thoosands for it and me da says she'll never get that much for a hoose aroond here.' With that, the freckled lad went to join his pal in riding circles a bit too close to her car and doing wheelies.

Cleo took a closer look at thirty-seven and noticed a poster in the front window, it wasn't obvious like a 'for sale' board outside a house. The house was being sold by Pattinson's estate agents.

'Thanks lads,' she smiled and took a giant bag of Haribos out of her glove compartment. 'Take these for your help.'

'We shouldn't take sweets from strangers but I reckon you're alreet,' said the freckled lad holding out his hand.

'Consider them earnings for information,' Cleo said. 'What's the name of the woman who has the house for sale?' There was a slight chance that it still belonged to her grandmother who would have to be in her eighties by now.

'It's an owld witch called Lizzie Donaldson. She hates kids and she double hates me!' the lad doing wheelies butted in and grinned proudly.

'Ta for the sweets missus,' Freckles said. 'Hope you buy her oot but don't pay over seventy. Me da says it's not worth it.'

'Thanks for the heads up,' Cleo called after them as they cycled off at speed.

She slalomed past a scooter, a pedal car and a shopping

trolley to turn around at the end of the row and, as she drove slowly back down the row, her hands were trembling. There in that house was an 'owld witch' who hated kids and that owld witch was her grandmother.

At lunchtime next day, Cleo called into Pattinson's on the West Road asking for details. The girl behind the desk looked doubtful as she handed over the printed details.

'It does need a complete refurbish. To tell you the truth, the street is usually bought up by buy-to-let landlords nowadays but they aren't going to pay that sort of asking price. If you want to buy in this area, we have other properties around about that price that may be more suitable.'

'Thanks, but it is this property that I particularly want to look at,' Cleo explained. She could hardly wait to get out of the shop and go over the details.

She crossed the road and went into the Beacon, an old fire station converted into offices and a café, for a coffee and a sandwich while she skimmed through her pack of information.

It was a nineteen twenties two up two down terrace with a sixties extension on the back that gave the house it's upstairs bathroom and a galley kitchen in the back yard. The original outside toilet and wash-house had been converted into a garage that was accessed from a narrow back lane.

The photos showed old-fashioned rooms that were neatly kept, a dingy looking bathroom suite – was it avocado? and two bedrooms. One looked to be a chaos of floral prints and full of knick-knacks but the smaller room was bare. Mum's room had been left empty.

A hard lump came into Cleo's throat; there was no room for Mum in that woman's house or her heart.

Fingers trembling, she phoned the girl across at the estate agents. 'It's Miss Moon, can you arrange a viewing for me at the weekend please? I'm interested in viewing thirty-seven Middle Row.'

37

Just before bed on Wednesday evening, Cleo went for a final scout around the area to find Pharos. She had intended being a few minutes but couldn't resist turning into another street and then another. At each turn, her stomach clenched in anticipation of seeing a silver streak of fur lying by the side of the road. He'd been gone five nights.

He wasn't the sort of cat who would look for a new home; not when he'd been with them, well with Mum and Alex, for seventeen years. He must have been run over or stolen or he would have shown up for a meal by now.

She headed back to her apartment and was quite a distance away when she saw a dark figure resting against the communal door. Her first thought was that someone was locked out but, as she got closer and the figure lifted his hand in greeting, she realised who it was. She broke into a run and hurled herself into Dan's arms.

'Oh Dan, I've really missed you! Where have you been?'

'Once I finished my last stint, I took the first flight so that I could to be with you. I missed my farewell party because you seemed so panicky over the phone and so down that I wanted to get back as soon as I could.' He hugged her tightly and she felt relief and warmth flood through her.

'Why haven't you answered my calls?'

'I finished my contract with my Australian phone company and I have to set a new one up, so I've had no phone service.'

'Skype?'

'I thought it was best if I just got here and saw you face to face because, if you remember, you put the phone down on me.'

Ah, yes, she had. How could she have forgotten that? 'I'm sorry, Dan. I've not been thinking straight and I didn't mean to be so bitchy.'

'That's a change coming from you... an apology? We'll take it as forgotten.'

'I must catch you up on what's been going on but let's go inside first,' Cleo said and led him up to her apartment.

As soon as the door closed they were back into each other's arms, kissing and peeling off one another's coats and kicking off shoes.

'I've missed you, you can't guess how much. Dan pressed her up against the back of her sofa.

'Show me,' Cleo gasped and unbuckled his trousers as he hitched up her skirt and pulled her towards him. He brushed her hair from her face and kissed her, his nearness driving her wild. Pulling himself free of his jeans, he reached for her and Cleo was ready for him. She just wanted Dan.

Between kisses he said, 'Never... ever...put the phone down and worry me like that again.'

'I won't,' she managed to say before his kisses left her speechless.

They showered together and Cleo tossed Dan a thick grey towelling robe. It was on the small side for Dan but at least it covered him up so that she wasn't tempted to slip back into his arms, not yet anyway.

'A 'drink' drink or a coffee?' she asked.

'I'd love a coffee,' he said, 'We need to talk, I want a clear head and you fluster me enough. Especially in that silk cover thing you're wearing.'

Cleo smiled, she had deliberately chosen something that wasn't a cosy joggers and vest combination.

'What do we have to discuss?' she asked as she set about making two coffees.

'We have to discuss you and Alex, and you and me and where we go from here. What's best to start with?'

Cleo placed the mugs onto the low table in front of the sofa and curled up next to Dan.

'You needn't worry over my feelings for Alex. I know I was annoyed with her when we chatted but I've had time to think and get over what she did. I don't think she should have done it but I can sort of understand her intention. She wanted me to meet that man as a father and she wanted to help. I have to try to get her to talk to me and I'll apologise because I realise that I've needed a sister for a long time and I can't lose that now.

'I thought I'd be arguing the toss with you about that, Cleo. That's great.' He slipped an arm around her.

'You try telling Alex that. She's hurt and being stubborn and hasn't answered my texts.' Cleo sipped her coffee, 'And what is it about *us* that you wanted to discuss?'

'I wanted to say I'm sorry for giving you advice and not letting you think things through and I don't want you to think that Alex is the cause of yet another row.

She's never been the cause you know, Cleo. The real cause has been that, until now, you haven't listened to other points of view or thought you were even the slightest bit in the wrong.'

Cleo drew away. 'Is that what you think? My take on it may be a bit different, Dan Collingwood.

For instance, when you phoned from Australia, straight off it was think of it from Alex's view. *Straight off!* Not for one minute did you say poor Cleo, her sister has acted out of order and she has every right to feel mad. If you'd said that before being sympathetic to Alex, I might have felt heard… felt listened too… not discounted. But no, it was look at the other side straight off.

I look at every side of disputes every day, Dan, it's part of my job. I *know* how to look at other people's points of view but when I'm hurting I want the man I love to back me up first, to understand me.'

Dan looked stunned, 'I didn't think you'd take it like that. I mean, I always have you as number one in my thoughts or I wouldn't try to make it right for you.'

'I don't want the man I love to make things right for me. I want him to listen to me and try to understand my feelings, my hurt or my happiness, whichever comes my way.'

Dan stood up put his coffee cup on the counter and faced Cleo. 'I think I do know your feelings Cleo, sometimes better than you and that's why I try to put things right for you.'

'How patronising can you be? Don't *ever* believe you know my feelings better than me. You who have had a charmed life and never, ever felt unwanted! How noble of you to want to help me understand what I really feel.' Cleo was on her feet, fists clenched and face to face with Dan.

'Hey, hey, that's a bit strong!'

'Oh is it? When we got together and I'd just lost a dearly loved father, you kept pushing and pushing for me to do more with Alex, when I just wanted my life to be as it was. No sister, a mum who spent time with me and a stepdad who was the world to me. You were the one to say 'let's do this with the kids, let's do that.' I didn't want to because I *couldn't*. I couldn't face the fact that my life had turned upside down.

'You were the best thing in it at that time and you didn't just listen or help me to escape the sadness. You just wanted me to adjust. You, who had a mother and father and always had them rooting for you and who had other brothers and a sister, as well as the twins and were used to sharing your parents, were trying to make *me* be like *you* when I wasn't.

I admit that I wasn't keen on my little sister but actually Dan, I might have gotten over it sooner if you hadn't gone on about it and then broke off with me because I didn't have the same interest in kids as you did and I worked hard at my studies.'

'Bloody hell, Cleo. I didn't know you felt like that. I was just helping, I had just left school and wasn't that bright it seems.'

'Dan you hadn't been what I'd been through, that's all. I shouldn't blame you, just like I should never have blamed Alex but it stopped me from blaming it all on myself. I've been feeling guilty ever since I can remember do you know that?

'When I first met you, I just wanted it to stop and it never, ever has.' Silent tears streamed down Cleo's cheeks.

'You never talked about it like this, even this summer.' Dan pulled her into his arms.

'I couldn't. It's hard even now. I thought about counselling but even that was too painful to go through. Why do you think I've chosen a career with kids? Chosen schools in the inner city where there is deprivation? And why do you think I'm hell bent on opening that mother and baby unit? It's all to make me feel better for being born and for being the way I am!' Great sobs engulfed her.

'Oh Cleo,' Dan held her, 'Can you let me in? Can I help? That's all I've ever really wanted. Let me be close to you, let me love you and be there for you.'

'I'm going to try Dan but please remember that when I push you away, that's when I need you most.'

Next morning, Dan got up with her and made their coffee. As she was leaving, he was pulling on running gear. He'd told her last night that he would look out for Pharos when he set off for a morning run and it hadn't been idle talk.

She drove to work, pondering over how wrong they'd been about one another. They'd always been attracted, but just how little they'd understood each other had shaken them both and she hoped their relationship was stronger for it.

As from today, it was going to be based on understanding and love rather than lust and romance and Cleo was a bit in awe of how deeply they felt about one another. It made her feel so much stronger and so wanted and that was something that she hadn't felt since Mac had died. Dan wasn't taking over Mac's place, but last night, he'd listened and given her that same grounded feeling of being loved.

They'd agreed to look for a house together. House-hunting with Dan, it made her smile and forget her sadness about Pharos and Alex for a minute or two.

She had tried to speak to Alex earlier in the week but she'd refused to answer her calls and wouldn't come to the phone at the Collingwood's. She was going to keep trying to get through to her. Dan had been surprised at how stubborn Alex had been. Last night, he'd realised it wasn't just Cleo who could be stubborn and had said 'It's well seen that she's your sister, Cleo.'

38

Dan stayed with Cleo on Thursday but was flying out to a conference in Italy at the weekend. This was to do with his new job in Newcastle and he had planned to go there straight from Australia before coming to the North East but he'd changed his flights to be with her. They had talked a lot so Cleo was happy to have a weekend of rest and time to catch up on her school admin.

She had her viewing on Saturday too and, although they'd talked about RF, Mac's death, the diaries and most other things, she hadn't mentioned her plan to view her Mum's old house and meet her grandmother. This was something that she wanted to see and do for herself and she didn't want to talk through the pros and cons of what she was doing.

The door to thirty-seven opened and an angular woman stood there looking at her without the hint of a welcoming smile. Cleo noticed hooded eyes, a downturned mouth and steel grey hair cropped and curled then hairsprayed into submission. She didn't look frail but she didn't look friendly either. Could she hear the thumping mallet that was Cleo's heart?

'Come in then. You wanted a look around, so don't hang about in the road.'

Cleo walked through the front door that led straight

into the living room. Her first glance took in the net curtains, lace doilies covering every surface and china ornaments galore. Her eyes scanned the room again. No photos; she was hoping to find a clue about her mum.

'You'll want to see the dining room.' The woman stood at the doorway and indicated the next room to Cleo. The smell of polish, dark furniture and a large sideboard with lots of crystal on top of it. No photos.

The kitchen was beyond; functional and clear of clutter. An old gas cooker, a formica table with two chairs and a door to the yard.

The yard was whitewashed and had a row of broken glass and china cemented along the top of its walls to deter intruders, cats or little boys who might want their ball back. Several flower-filled tyre planters graced the walls and stood sentry by the back gate and a washing line, pegged with tea towels and aprons crossed the yard.

'Your flowers make the yard look cheerful.' Cleo felt she had to say something but the woman didn't acknowledge the compliment.

'It's a back yard when all is said and done and there's access to the garage,' she pointed and then stood back clearly expecting Cleo to come back in so that she could close the door.

When she stepped back into the kitchen, the woman gave Cleo a hard stare with slate grey eyes that seemed full of suspicion. 'You look perfectly trustworthy,' she said, 'So if you don't mind I'll let you look upstairs yourself. I get breathless going up them, that's why I'm selling.'

With that, she sat at the kitchen table and Cleo wasn't sure what to do.

'Go on up then, you can't get lost.' She gave a tut of impatience.

Cleo walked back through to the dining room and up the open staircase to the upper floor, her mouth was dry so she found it hard to swallow as she opened the door to the room that she wanted to see first.

She walked across flat brown carpet and stared out onto the back yard. Mum's room, her window, this was where Mum grew up. She scouted around for a sign, anything, but there was nothing to show who had slept here. Plain white walls, flowery curtains and no furniture just as if Mum had never been here.

Blinking back tears, she crossed to the front bedroom. A plain bed made up with blankets and a candlewick bedspread in green. No pictures. Cleo glanced at the dressing table with a hairbrush set and underneath it a linen tray cloth and then looked again. Embroidery, that golden thread; the tray cloth was cross-stitched in the centre and in the corner, in chain-stitch, the same as on the shoe bag containing the diaries, were the initials M D, Margaret Donaldson. Mum, she *was* there.

The smell of bleach led the way to the bathroom. She peered in and saw that the suite was a not quite avocado not quite beige-sludge colour. A cream linoleum floor with a brown bath mat completed the look. Cleo suppressed a shudder, the whole upper floor was cold and cheerless. After one last look into Mum's room, she went downstairs.

'You've seen all that you need to and no doubt you'll make up your mind but I'm telling you now what I've told the others, I'm not taking a lower offer.

My husband and I spent a lot doing this house up and keeping it nice and I'm not being robbed. You're not working for a landlord are you? I don't particularly want it to be a rental either.'

'I'm not working for anyone, Mrs. Donaldson.' Cleo saw a chance of finding out more. 'Did you and your husband buy this a while ago?'

'Yes, I've told you we did all the renovations.'

'Very nicely done and you've certainly kept the place looking smart,' Cleo said.

With a sniff, the old woman agreed, 'It's not modern

but it was in its day and *we* liked it.'

Here goes thought Cleo, 'Is your husband no longer with you?'

'That's right. I lost him years ago, I lost him suddenly.'

'That sounds like you had a tragedy.'

The woman gazed out of the window. 'Tragic wasn't in it. My husband couldn't bear it.'

'What happened?' Cleo hardly dared to breathe.

'Like all men, he was weak. He walked.'

'He *walked*?'

'Yes, he walked out and left me because he couldn't bear to live here anymore.'

'Where did he go?' Cleo held her breathe. Had she asked too much?

'He didn't walk far but he was out of my life.' The old woman frowned at Cleo, 'Anyway that's nothing to you. If you've seen everything you'd better go because I find all of this tiring.'

'Sorry, I was just curious,' Cleo said.

'You know what curiosity did.' The old woman reached for the front door handle.

'Just one thing. Is your husband… is he alive?'

'The house is in my name now so it doesn't affect the sale.'

Cleo had to know, 'But *is* he?'

The woman turned and stared at Cleo. 'Why is *that* important to you?'

'No reason,' Cleo said as walked towards the front door thinking she'd better go.

'Hold on,' said the woman, 'there's something about you, about the way you look. Who *are* you?'

'I'm just a house hunter,' said Cleo. Her voice sounded wobbly and she had to get out of there.

'I've been racking my brains for who you are like and I think I'm onto you. Are *you* something to do with our Margaret?'

Cleo turned and nodded and saw the old lady's face darken to utter hatred. 'Yes, I am.' she said. 'Do I remind you of her?'

'Her?' she spat out, 'No, not her... *them*! When I look at you, you've got that Fenwick hair and eyes and you're the double of his mother. How dare you come to this doorstep? How dare you be so brazen? What are you looking for, an inheritance? Because no bastard grandchild will get my house!'

'No, no that's not it. I just wanted to see where Mum lived. To meet you and hear about my grandfather.'

'You've seen me, you've poked about and now you know that your grandfather left me because he couldn't stand living here without his little ray of sunshine. He spoilt Margaret and look what happened.'

Cleo had to try again, 'Where did he go?'

'Oh, not far. He found digs in Ethel street *and more* I don't wonder from that Lottie Fletcher.'

'Is he... is he still alive then?'

'Not to me he's not. Neither of them are, not him nor Margaret.'

'Is he still alive?'

She gave a cold stare that made Cleo shiver. 'Last I heard he was in a nursing home. When Lottie Fletcher passed, she left him her house so he could stay there, she was that fond of him. When he couldn't manage, he sold up and moved into Sunny Court.

I haven't seen him; it's those that go to St. Michael's that told me he'd moved into care last year.'

Cleo said, 'I'd better get going.' She waited. Was this woman going to ask how her daughter was? 'Do you want to know how Margaret is?' she asked.

'I do not. I don't want you back here ever again, either.'

Cleo turned on her heel and walked towards her car. What a vile, hard-hearted woman! As she slipped behind the wheel, the woman called,

'Wait there a moment. Did your mother eventually marry? Did she have any *legitimate* children?'

Cleo considered whether to answer or not. 'She did, I have a younger sister.'

'That's the one I'd like to meet then. She'll be proper family. She'd be welcome but no one else.'

Cleo left feeling rejected again. 'Why did she feel so bad? Who would want anything to do with that nasty, vindictive creature?'

As she made lunch, Cleo mulled over everything that Mrs. Donaldson had revealed. Her grandfather *had* been alive when they had visited all those years ago but he hadn't lived at that house. She remembered the words '*you killed him*' like it was yesterday. Did her mum know that her father was still alive? They'd have so much to talk about when she got back.

She could hardly video call and say, 'Guess what, Mum, I've been researching our family tree.'

Cleo took her pasta into the office and opened the map app on her iPad. Where was Sunny Court nursing home? She was surprised to see that it was near Elswick and less than three miles from here.

Should she go and visit? No, *when* should she go and visit?

39

Sunday brought clear skies, a slight breeze and sunshine. It was one of those glorious September mornings when summer seemed to call back, just for the day. Mum would say, 'She's forgotten something' or 'She needs one last look at her beautiful work.' Cleo smiled at the thought.

Mum personified all of nature, loved the sun and moon and Cleo had always laughed at what she thought of as Mum's tree hugging tendencies. She really had missed her and with what she knew now, they'd have plenty to catch up on. She realised that she really wanted to get to know her mother better, not just as 'Mum.'

She set off on her early morning walk to call out for Pharos. She knew a lot of her neighbours now because of her week's efforts to find him. If he was still alive, lots of people were looking out for him and there were posters all over the area. Heather had passed his disappearance round on twitter and said that would widen their helper base.

After touring the streets, she stood by the wharf and out over the Tyne. Had he slipped in there and drowned? She shuddered. Here she was wanting Mum back home but how the hell would she tell her she'd lost her beloved boy?

At ten thirty, she set off for Sunny Court. Now that she knew about her grandfather, she couldn't wait to meet him.

Would he want to meet her or would it be 'grannygate' repeated? The home was a modern building with ample parking in front of the main entrance. She buzzed and told the intercom that she was here to see Mr. Donaldson and the door opened to allow her into a large foyer with a reception desk.

Cleo had rehearsed a few stories as to why she wanted to visit and decided that researching the Donaldson family tree was the simplest and nearest to the truth. The young girl on reception didn't even ask.

'Hi, just sign the book and you can go through.'

Cleo signed and explained, 'Mr. Donaldson isn't expecting me. Do you want to let him know?'

'Bobby's always happy to see visitors, he has a regular tribe. He's in the garden pulling a few weeds this morning, maybe you could call at the kitchen and take him a cuppa. Strong tea, a touch of milk and no sugar.'

Cleo walked through and followed the sign saying kitchen. She found a small communal kitchen for residents and visitors to make drinks. She made a coffee for herself and the strong tea that Bobby liked and then wandered out to find him in the garden.

The garden was enclosed by high walls and much bigger than she thought. As she stood by the door, he wasn't in sight. She clasped the mugs tightly because her hands were trembling and she wasn't sure which path to take. She saw someone on their knees in the flower bed at the far end of garden and made her way over there.

As she got nearer, Cleo's throat felt dry. An elderly man with a shock of white hair and a tanned complexion was pulling up weeds and throwing them into a wheelbarrow.

'Mr. Donaldson?'

'Yes, my love, that's me,' he smiled and it reached his eyes, as light and bright as her mother's.

'I've brought you a cuppa,' she said.

'How lovely! I'm in need of that.' He got up slowly and stretched out. 'These knees aren't so good nowadays and I can't kneel for long but I've made good headway with the weeding, don't you think?'

'You have,' she agreed.

He pointed to the two mugs, 'Ah, you've come to join me have you? Well, let's go and sit on the bench in the sun over there.' He glanced at the sun in the clear sky and chuckled. 'Yes, she's back because she's forgotten something.'

Cleo smiled at Mum's saying, it was this man that she had got it from, and followed with the mugs as he walked over to the bench in easy strides. He was fit for an old man.

They sat down at the bench, 'So, are you a new volunteer at Sunny Court?' he asked.

This was it. This was the time she dropped the bombshell.

'No, Mr. Donaldson, I'm not.'

'Call me Bobby; everyone does.' He sipped his tea. 'Perfect. You make a good cup of tea, some of the staff make it like dishwater,' he laughed.

'Bobby, I came to see you because I'm researching my family tree, the Donaldson tree,' she explained.

'How interesting. My branch is pretty thin, one brother killed in the war and me. He was born in '24 and I was born in '26 so I'll be ninety this November.'

'You don't look it,' she said truthfully. Cleo sipped her coffee. How was she going to say this? Would he go into shock? He seemed strong enough.

'You aren't the *last* of your line though are you Mr Donaldson?' she asked thinking, please don't *you* erase my mother's life.

'No, I'm not but I can't help you with that.' His eyes, looking into hers, were so open like her mother's. She liked what she saw, would he like her after this?

'I don't need help with that, Bobby. I've got all of Margaret's details.'

'You have? You've traced her?' Bobby's eyes widened with delight. 'I searched for years and got nowhere. Is Margaret alright?'

'Yes, she's fine. She came back to find you, once. She visited Middle Row and was told that her leaving had killed you, so she thought she'd lost you.'

'What? When was that?'

'It was four years after she left.'

'That woman! She made both our lives a misery living with her and she still had to do that when we left her.' He put his empty mug on the arm of the bench and turned to face Cleo.

'Tell me, my love, how do you know all this about my Margaret and how did you find me here? Are you a Donaldson, too?'

'I'm her daughter, your granddaughter... the one she ran away to keep,' she admitted stiffening for the backlash. She didn't expect his arms to be flung around her and to be clutched to his scratchy woollen sweater, it took her breath away.

'I've prayed for this day. I've knelt in St. Michael's and asked and asked to be forgiven and here you are.' Tears glistened in his eyes and Cleo knew that he meant every word.

It had been a marvellous visit, better than she could ever have hoped for. Grandad Bobby, he'd asked her to call him that, was full of questions about her and Alex and how her mum had done. He was delighted that she was exploring Egypt because she'd always loved ancient history and he was full of stories of Mum as a girl.

He'd laughed at Mum's choice of name saying that he might have guessed she'd pick an Egyptian theme. He'd spent years trying to trace Margaret Donaldson but never in his dreams would he have looked for Neferteri Moon.

Cleo had told him all about her project to support pregnant students and their babies and he'd told her he was proud of her. Her grandad was proud of her and that made her extraordinarily happy.

She'd been kicked out by the staff at lunchtime but promised to meet him on Thursday after school. Every Thursday, he played bowls and she was going to pick him up from his club and they'd go out for an early dinner. He'd told her 'It's not a hospital here you know, I can come and go as I please, but I get all mod cons.'

There was only one dark cloud. She had a grandad who wanted to know her and who was proud of her and she so wanted to tell Alex and share him with her. When would Alex talk to her?

40

Cleo left school late on Monday. It was a progress meeting about the unit with Jim the caretaker and the workmen, so she didn't mind. The project was taking shape and the building would be complete and ready to furnish after half term. The builders had kept to every deadline so far. Jim had told Cleo that her enthusiasm had rubbed off on them and they didn't want to report back that they were behind schedule. It could be that but she knew that Jim kept a close eye on them, too.

Back home, she played George Ezra and had a long soak in the bath, washed her hair and defrosted chilli for supper. She put on a new fine knit top and trousers in a silver grey, too good for bed but lovely for lazing about. The faded teddy pyjama look wasn't happening tonight when Dan returned from his conference. He was staying with her for a couple of nights before going to see his parents in Dunleith. She had so much to tell him and couldn't wait to hold him.

After pouring herself a glass of pinot, she sat in her office dealing with emails she hadn't had a chance to respond to while she waited for Dan.

'You look like a silver moon goddess in this,' he said as he stepped through the doorway and proceeded to remove the top. 'But you look much better now,' he added when he had her stripped naked. Taking her hand, he led her to the bedroom saying, 'Much, much better.'

They sank onto the bed more hungry for one another, than the chilli that waited on the bench.

Teri needed to talk to Cleo. She took a deep breath and turned on her laptop. She had left Greg chatting to some of their scuba diving friends in a bar of the Jasmine Palace hotel. He had suggested earlier that she should either phone or video call Cleo to see if she would open up about what the girl's big fall out was about and, after mulling it over, she thought she'd give it a try.

She sat at the desk come dressing table in their room and adjusted the screen so that she'd have a good view of Cleo's expressions and took another calming breath. She felt edgy. Would Cleo pick up or avoid her call? Did she *want* to know what this row had been about? Definitely. She practiced a smile; it felt a bit forced but she wanted to start the conversation in an upbeat way and try to get Cleo to open up.

She called and there was no response. It was late evening in the UK and Cleo should be home but she might not be plugged in, or whatever, because they usually planned their Skype sessions for a certain time. Maybe she should use the phone? Or text and arrange a session for later? She would have liked to see Cleo face to face as they talked. She sat there, unsure of what to do.

It was after ten when Dan and Cleo finished their supper and Cleo popped into her office to pack up her laptop for work in the morning. She noticed that she'd *just* missed a video call from Mum. They hadn't planned one, was she OK?

'Dan, I'm just going online to chat to Mum. Won't be long.' She would never sleep if she didn't know Mum was fine.

Teri was sitting at the desk lost in thought when the video call tone startled her. Cleo was calling her back.

'Hi Mum, I was in the living room and just missed your call. I wasn't expecting you to log on for a chat tonight. Is everything OK?'

'I'm fine darling, nothing to be anxious about. How are you doing after all this silly business with Alex?'

Cleo breathed a heavy sigh, 'I feel dreadful, Mum, just dreadful. You know that she's gone back to Dunleith and we still aren't speaking? I've tried to call her but she's having none of it, she won't even pick up her phone or come to the house line so, Mum, I've huffed her big time. We were getting on *so* well too! I'm sorry, I really am.'

This was a surprise; Teri had expected the same negative reaction from Cleo as she had received from Alex. She had thought that Cleo would be up there on her high horse about her little sister.

'Oh... so *you* want to make up, do you, Cleo?'

'Yes Mum I do, but it won't happen. I lost my temper over something she'd done and I'm still really angry with her but I don't want us to be at loggerheads like this.'

'Oh Cleo, sweetheart, that makes me so pleased. If you are wanting to make amends, then we'll just have to wait until Alex sees sense. She needs a big sister so it's lovely to hear that you're willing to try.' Teri could see shadows under Cleo's eyes and she seemed tearful. 'Do you want to tell me about it darling. Maybe talking would help?'

'Has Alex told you *anything* at all?' Cleo was guarded.

'No, but she said that you wouldn't appreciate her input about the situation any further, or something like that, so I presume she's *said* or *done* something that you didn't like.'

Cleo's weak smile showed she was right and so she urged, 'Do you want to tell me?'

'No Mum. It's between Alex and me and I don't want

to involve you, yet. I'll tell you when you're home. I've talked it all over with Dan. He's here right now actually.'

'Oh is he? That's lovely, I'm so relieved you're not all alone with this, whatever it is.'

'You'll be back at the end of the month won't you, Mum? We'll all need to sit down and chat then. I have so many things to tell you but it can all wait until you're home.'

Teri heard the wistfulness in Cleo's voice, she was missing her. She wanted to keep her Saturday arrival a surprise but couldn't help saying, 'Yes, I might fly back a bit earlier than that; I'm missing you both *and* my Pharos of course. I can't wait to get back for hugs.'

Cleo looked alarmed, 'I have to rush you off here, Mum. I...I need to visit the bathroom!' and she zoomed out of sight.

That was brief, did Cleo have a bug? Teri got up and walked to the window to look out onto the lush dark-leafed gardens. What moon was shining down on them tonight? She couldn't see it from here. Her head was in a spin, weighing up all that Cleo had said, or not said, when she heard her computer splutter to life. Cleo's voice came back into the room.

'Bloody hell, Dan that was *so* hard. What am I going to say? Sorry Mum but I've lost your cat and, by the way, Alex told Ralph Fenwick that he's my Dad. That's why I lost my temper and now he wants to meet up again. Imagine if she heard...'

Teri stared at the screen. It had gone dead. Nothing else, Cleo must've moved away or closed her laptop. Usually Teri initiated and logged off their video chat sessions and Cleo mustn't have logged herself off earlier.

She sat back at the table and willed the screen back to life. Should she call back? Should she call Alex and say she knew what all this was about? Chin in hands, she tapped her temples trying to think of how this had happened. How the hell had Alex traced Ralph? How the hell had they lost her Pharos?

Greg came in. She didn't know how long she'd been sitting there.

'Why are you looking at a blank scene? Didn't you get through?' he asked.

She got up and pulled him to her. 'She *was* there and I heard more than I bargained for. It's a good thing I've booked that Saturday flight home Greg.'

41

When Alex finished school, she slipped out of the back gate to take the bus home on her own. Once she reached Dunleith, she decided to take a walk by the river Tweed. She had avoided meeting up with the twins because she wanted to be by herself for a while. She'd been staying with the EllaBellas since Monday and had started back at her old school but she felt unsettled.

The truth was that she missed Cleo. She was annoyed and hurt by her but she couldn't summon up a great hate for Cleo like she used to. It really irritated her when Ella called Cleo names too; she wasn't *her* sister to be rude about.

In the summer, and again over the past couple of days, Alex had noticed that Ella was a bit full of herself compared to Bella and it grated on her now. She was 'off' Ella and felt like taking her down a peg or two or telling Bella to stop just going along with everything. Bella needed to stand up for herself more but it wasn't really the right time to say this when she had to lodge there until Mum came back.

She sat on the river bank, pulled an apple from her bag and enjoyed being alone to be miserable in peace without anyone nosing about what was wrong. She missed seeing Gracie and Lee, she missed Cleo's company and she missed seeing Will. Dunleith without Mum was dull; she missed Mum.

A tear squeezed out of one eye and she felt better. She took a bite of apple, concentrated on how awful this week was and a few more tears came.

She took out her phone to check for texts. She had one from Bella saying 'where are you?' She sighed and tapped a reply saying where she was and that she'd be at Fernlea Lodge in half an hour.

It was Will's name that she wanted to see. Will had sent one text asking how she was and she'd sent him a long reply back but, since yesterday, nothing. They'd chatted all the way from Newcastle to Dunleith on Monday. He'd told her about his studies and how he worked the door some weekends at his uncle's club to help fund his karate.

She thought that he liked her but he was starting his second year at Uni and she was still at school, so he probably thought she was too young. She put her earplugs in, wrapped herself in Will's scarf, and nibbled at her apple.

She was engrossed in Ed Sheeran and just about to toss her core into the bin when a black creature bounded up and high-fived her hand for the core. It was Shadow closely followed by Scout. Alex pulled her earphones out of her ears. Which Collingwood had brought the dogs out?

'Hi there, Alex.' Dan gave her a wave and came towards the bench.

She was relieved it was him and not the twins. 'Hi Dan.'

'Mind if I join you for a bit and let the dogs do all their sniffing down at the river?'

'No,' she forced a weak smile.

'Got the miseries?'

She nodded, slumped further down into the bench and stuffed her hands in her pockets.

'I came to find you. Bella said you'd be here. I wanted

you to know that Cleo has the miseries worse than you and to tell you what I told her.'

'What was that?'

'That you're both far too stubborn.'

Alex laughed, 'Bet she didn't like that.'

'I took my life in my hands but she agreed with me. She really is sorry and she has lots to tell you but you're not talking, so she can't.'

Alex said nothing. Dan just sat watching the spaniels paddling and sniffing along the bank.

'She can't have anything *that* interesting to tell me.'

'Oh she does; she says you're not the only super sleuth in the family and she's been investigating your family tree.'

Alex shot up. 'She's what? What tree? Her tree? Or our tree? What's she been doing Dan?'

Dan smiled and raised his eyebrows.

'Come on Dan, you know!'

'I do, but Cleo wants to tell you herself and you're not speaking. She still thinks you meddled, and you did, but she's over it. She also said you were the one who told her that families can fight and disagree but it doesn't mean that they hate each other.'

'She's right, I did say that. You're right, I am stubborn. I'm nosey too so come on Dan, tell me what's going on.'

'I'll tell you one thing, just to whet your appetite, if you promise you'll call round and see her tomorrow night when she drives over to High Rigg.'

'She's coming tomorrow?'

'Yes, she misses you.'

'I promise I'll go over and I'll make up, if she's not too snotty.'

'She won't be. I've told you she's sorry.'

'What's she been up to?'

Lots, but I'll give you one clue and that's it.'

'OK.'

'She decided to pay a visit to your Mum's childhood home, Middle Street wasn't it? The address that's at the front of her diaries.'

Alex's eyes widened, 'Middle *Row*. And?'

'*And...* You'll have to ask her about it.' Dan stood up and whistled to the dogs. They bounded up and sat at his feet ready for him to put their leashes on. Alex took Shadow's leash and set off with Dan.

'Dan Collingwood, you're so unfair! If you know then I should too,' she urged.

'Ah but I'm on friendly terms with your sister and you're not... until tomorrow. Have patience.'

Alex felt happier by the time she got back to the house. Mary Collingwood had made pie and peas, she was going to see Cleo tomorrow and she decided that Ella wasn't *so* bad after all. As she took her coat off, her phone made its hunting horn call. A text from Will.

'*Driving to Edinburgh for weekend. Shall I stop by to see you on Sunday? Will* x'

'Who's that from?' Ella peered over her shoulder to read the text, 'Don't you answer straight back, Alex. Keep him waiting.'

Alex smiled, Ella was becoming bossier than Cleo.

42

On Thursday, after school, Cleo parked outside the bowling green on Summerhill Grove. As Bobby Donaldson strode out of the gate, she thought he looked marvellous for his age. He was in an open-necked shirt with a tweed jacket and carried his bowling bag with ease. Where should they go to eat? She hadn't booked because she wasn't sure of her grandfather's taste in food. She had so much to find out.

'Hello, my love, here I am being picked up by my granddaughter for the first time and nobody has come out of the club so I can brag about it.' He smiled and his eyes lit up his whole face.

'I'm sitting here wondering about what food you like. I haven't a clue.'

'I like anything that's nicely cooked. I'm not a fussy chap at all but I do have one favourite,' Bobby said.

'What's that?' Cleo asked as she opened the car boot and put his bowling bag in there.

'I was in Italy for a while, during the war you know, and I love their food. Not what passes for it at Sunny Court but the proper stuff - garlic and herbs and a good sprinkling of parmesan. I reckon you'll know a good Italian or two round here.'

'I do, I'll take you to my favourite. They don't take

bookings but they open from 5.30 and their food is *the* best.'

Cleo headed for Jesmond and hoped that a queue hadn't already formed at Francesca's.

It was almost full, but they got the last table for two tucked into a quiet corner. Cleo watched Bobby sniff at the mouth-watering aroma from the kitchen and knew she'd made a good choice.

They chose specials from the blackboard with tomato garlic bread as a starter because Bobby hadn't tried that.

'Now what about a drink, Cleo? I know you're driving but can you raise a glass with me? I *do* like a prosecco,' he said.

'Me too, and I could have *one*, Grandad,' she said.

'*Grandad*. Do you know, that's music to my ears. I can't wait to see Alex, the young one, too. Has she spoken to you yet?'

'No but I'm going to see her tomorrow.' She'd told him that they lived on the border at Dunleith.

'Tell her a bit about me, and give her my love.'

'She's just like Mum so you'll love her.'

'That's as maybe but I can see myself in you and I love that, too.'

Cleo felt choked and blinked back a tear as she raised a glass.

The time flew by. After their main course, they ordered dessert then coffee and never stopped chatting. Bobby insisted on paying the bill.

'I never expected to see my grandchild in this lifetime and it makes me happy to be able to treat you to your supper. I hope it's the first of many.'

Cleo took her grandfather to Sunny Court and he sat there quietly for a moment in no rush to be leaving the car.

'Cleo, this is the best night I've had since your mother left home. Lizzie was right in a way because it did kill me to lose my girl. Leaving her at that home, I didn't know what to do for the best for her or for her bairn. I just wish I'd been able to talk to her but I couldn't. I was treading on thin ice with Lizzie and I handled it all wrong. I made a life for myself after she left but never a day has gone by that I didn't wish her well or worry about her.'

'She'll understand, Grandad. She's very understanding, my mum.'

'Let's hope she will. I've written her a letter in a card every year for her birthday. There's thirty-three of them that have never been posted. I've just finished this year's effort for her fiftieth on Sunday.

There are some things she never knew and I've always wanted to tell her. I told her what she needed to know for her age, you know. The first birthday letter I ever wrote, the one for her turning eighteen, I explained why I went along with Lizzie.' He patted Cleo's hand. 'I'm leaving the letters with you for safe keeping. I'm leaving nothing to chance and I want to make sure she gets every one of them. Is that alright with you?'

Cleo nodded, 'Of course. You'll see her yourself though, Grandad.'

'I hope so. Goodnight, pet.'

Cleo leaned over and gave him a kiss on the cheek. 'You get yourself in, Grandad or they'll be locking the doors on you. It's after ten.'

He chuckled and got out, giving her a cheery wave.

Cleo watched him into the building before driving off, her heart singing. She loved having a grandfather.

HARVEST MOON

43

By Friday, Cleo had to accept that Pharos was well and truly gone, she'd scoured the area again that morning and there had been no sign of him. He had been missing a week and she missed both him and Alex. Dan had called when she got in last night, and told her that Alex had thawed out and was willing to talk. That was something. She didn't want to lose her new close relationship with Alex without giving it her best shot.

If they were speaking, they might Skype their mum together on Sunday because it would be her fiftieth birthday. Her only worry was that she couldn't mention Pharos to her while she was so far off. She was concerned that when she told Alex about his escape, that would start another row. Would Alex share the blame? They'd both left the door open.

After school, Cleo picked up food for the weekend and, when she put it in the boot, she noticed her grandfather had left his bowling bag there. She'd have to drop it off at Sunny Court before his bowls next Thursday.

She stopped off at home for some clothes and hastily picked up her mail, glancing at the envelopes without opening them until she came across a handwritten padded envelope. It bore an Italian stamp and she knew that writing.

Dear Cleo,

You'll be surprised to hear from me. I know that I haven't behaved very well and I left things in rather a mess but by now you'll realise that I have a need to gamble and don't always win. I want to say thank you for keeping Josh safe. Marianne sings your praises. She won't let him out of her sight now but I've phoned Josh. I am sending you some cash while I have it. It's not a lot but I give you my word that I will try to repay what I owe you eventually.

It was a great surprise to 'bump into' your fiancé at San Siro race track this week. He kindly promised not to track me down again as long as I apologise and repay you a.s.a.p. Please assure him that this is just the beginning and you'll be repaid in total when the UK house is sold. Marianne is dealing with that.

Kind regards,
Neil.

Inside the envelope was a wad of cash and a pawn ticket for her watch.

Dan was a dark horse! Had he really tracked down Neil when he was over in Milan? Now Neil obviously wanted to keep Dan off his case. Neil had made a start in paying her back but she felt better about getting her money back now that Marianne was in charge of the house sale.

Cleo couldn't stop thinking about Neil on her way to Dunleith. 'I give you my word' he'd written; she didn't have much faith in that but, with Dan and Marianne both putting pressure on him to do the right thing, maybe he would try. He was charming and clever but he used those gifts to be devious and dishonest to feed his addiction. She felt really sad for what he was missing out on with Josh and Marianne, that upset her as much as her own financial loss.

Neil's letter stopped her thinking of Dan for a while but he was never really out of her mind. He must have had it in mind to hunt for Neil but he had said nothing about it to her. It felt good to have Dan on her side; she'd like to have him by her side forever.

On the final stretch of the road to High Rigg, Cleo's thoughts turned to what she could say to Alex. She'd apologise for being so angry when Alex had been trying to help her to get to know her father. She hadn't meant any of the mean things she had said to Alex and she hoped Alex hadn't meant what she'd said to her.

It was dusk when she pulled into the drive and, as she got out of the car, a flash of silver landed with a thud onto her car bonnet. She turned to see what had dropped and was startled by the loudest yowl. Locking eyes with a gooseberry glare, she gave a sharp intake of breath. She didn't dare hope, surely it couldn't be?

'Pharos! How on earth did you get back here? You clever, clever boy.'

He allowed Cleo to pick him up from the bonnet; he felt light but he was Pharos all right. He yowled to be put down and then led the way around the back to the kitchen door where he slid through the cat flap.

She looked up at the Harvest moon and said a big thank you. One wish granted! She didn't know how that old cat had found his way fifty miles back to Dunleith but he was here and he was shouting for supper, so he must be OK.

Stretching out by the fire with Pharos lying on her chest and purring louder than the crackling logs, Cleo felt her eyes grow heavy and her body relax for the first time in a week. A noise in the hallway made her sit bolt upright, her heart thumping. Had someone broken in? The door opened and Alex's silhouette was framed in the doorway.

'Cleo, I saw your car but the houselights were all off. Why are you in the dark?' She switched a lamp on.

'Hi Alex, I must've dozed off. You gave me a shock there.'

'I've popped in to say hello and sorry.' Alex knelt down and cuddled Pharos.

'Hello old boy, have you missed me?' She turned towards Cleo, 'He feels scrawny, is he OK?'

Yes, he is now. There's a nightmare of a story to tell you about him but, first, I want to apologise to you about last weekend.'

'No, I think I need to say sorry for meddling, Cleo. I shouldn't have done it.'

'Maybe not, but it was for the right reasons so I'm sorry I had such a go at you.'

Alex grinned, 'Oh OK then, I'll let you apologise most because it doesn't happen often.'

Cleo threw a cushion from the floor at her.

'I've hated this week,' Alex confided as she plonked onto the cushion and sat beside Cleo.

'Me too, It's much better when we are both on the same side.'

'Look, I'm going to ring Mrs. Collingwood and say that, while you're here, I'm staying over. Is that ok?'

'That would be lovely,' Cleo assured her.

'We can catch up.' Alex grinned at her and added, 'Dan tells me you've been investigating the family tree and have lots of news, so it had better be good.'

Before bed that evening, Alex took a post-it and scribbled on it for a while.

'It's not a new or a full moon, but I need to put a fresh wish into our moondream jar.'

'Can you pass one over? I'll do one too,' Cleo asked.

'Shall we swap to read them like we used to with Mum?' asked Alex. 'Or do you want to keep yours private?'

'Here, you can see mine.' Cleo passed hers over.

They both read one another's and smiled at each other. They'd written the same wish.

'We won't have Mum home for her birthday but what do you say that we prepare a celebratory lunch for Sunday and invite all the Collingwoods for being so lovely to us?' Cleo suggested.

'We can put up balloons and we'll make a chocolate cake to eat in Mum's honour,' Alex said.

Cleo was glad that Alex was taken with the plan.

'Could I invite someone else? If they could make it that is?' Alex asked.

'Yes, whoever you want. Who are you thinking of?'

'Will, the karate guy.' Alex flushed.

'Oh yes, I saw you, on Monday, getting a lift from him. I think it's my turn to listen to your tale now. Are you two an item?

'Cleo!' Alex yelled, then shrugged, 'I wish...'

Before going to bed, Alex slipped another note into their jar. Maybe Will would stay for lunch on Sunday and, for once, he would see her when she wasn't in crisis. She'd phone him tomorrow and try to sound cool about it.

44

Cleo listened at her sister's door. She felt happy just hearing her steady breathing. She was here and asleep and they were under one roof with Mum's silver boy safely tucked up in the garden room. Family was more important than anything else; she had learnt a hard lesson over the past few months and she knew that she wanted to be part of this and part of Dan's family.

Things would work out. Even if Mum was away, they could talk and she'd see that they had celebrated her birthday on Sunday. Tomorrow was going to be a busy day of shopping and preparations but it would be fun.

She'd just switched off her light and was snuggled under the duvet when she heard a sound, almost like the pattering of rain. She waited; there it was again against her window. She smiled as she leaned over and looked through the window to see Dan waving her down. As she went downstairs to open the door, she knew that he'd be cock-a-hoop to catch her in her faded teddy ensemble again.

Dunleith church bell struck one as Cleo studied the contours of Dan's face in the firelight. He dozed peacefully with Pharos stretched out over his legs. Lying on her tummy, by Dan's side, she enjoyed the dwindling glow from the logs on the fire.

The ring of her phone startled them both out of their loved-up relaxed state and, as always, Cleo's immediate thought was about her mum. Was she safe? She checked her phone but it was an unknown number.

'Hello?' she kept her voice down even though Alex had been asleep for a couple of hours.

'Am I speaking to Miss Moon?'

'Yes, I'm Cleo Moon. Who is this?'

'I'm ringing you from Sunny Court, Miss Moon. Robert Donaldson, Bobby, gave us your name as his next of kin just this week.'

Goosebumps and shivers made her voice tremble 'That's right, I'm his granddaughter. Is something wrong?'

The last ember of the fire flickered and died as she heard, 'I'm sorry but it's not good news. Bobby's been having chest pains and we think it's his heart. He's in an ambulance and on his way to the Royal Victoria Infirmary as we speak.'

She managed, 'Thanks, I'll be there.' Grabbing hold of Dan's hand, she sobbed, 'It's Grandad.'

This is surreal thought Alex. She'd been woken by Cleo and was sitting in the back of Dan's car in a jumper and joggers heading for the hospital to see a grandfather that she'd never met. She had the choice to go with them or stay at home but Cleo so upset and she wouldn't have gone back to sleep so she agreed to go. Cleo looked dreadful; this had really upset her. She'd talked for ages about their Grandad Bobby tonight and had been excited about taking Alex to meet him; not like this though.

Alex felt strange. It *was* sad, but he was ninety and she hadn't met him. You'd think Cleo had known him for years. It could be like that with some people because she felt like that about Will.

The roads were absolutely empty; just the odd truck but no real traffic so they'd be at the RVI in an hour. She hoped, for Cleo's sake, that their grandfather wasn't dead when they got there. She concentrated on catching sight of the harvest moon as it slipped in and out of view and pleaded, 'Work your magic for just a bit longer on the old man.'

They were directed to intensive care and Alex could hardly look at the still figure with tubes and machines all around him. This was her mum's father but he wasn't familiar to her. It hurt her to see Cleo, looking so full of sorrow and gently massaging one of his hands. She was whispering and talking as if willing him to awaken.

'I'm going to go and get a can of coke or something, Dan,' she whispered and made for the door.

'Wait a sec,' he walked over, said something to Cleo and then came back to the door. 'I'll come with you.' He put an arm around her and they went in search of a drinks machine. They found a machine by some sofas and decided on hot chocolate.

'Dan, I'm sorry for Cleo but I don't really know my grandfather and I feel awful. I'm just numb and sad for Cleo,' Alex confessed as they sipped their drinks.

'That's OK. That's why I'm here too. *We* don't know him but we can support Cleo and hope he turns a corner.'

'Will he, Dan? Do you think he will?'

'Alex, I'm a doctor but I'm not a psychic,' was his gentle reply. 'All I know is that he's in great hands here.'

After an hour, they left the hospital and drove to Cleo's apartment so they'd be nearby, as they waited for news. Alex was bone weary and ready to roll into bed just as she was. She reached the door and caught a glance between Dan and Cleo. Too good to miss.

'I don't mind you two sharing tonight but mind you, no gross noises while I'm here.'

'Go to bed, Alex. We're all too tired.' Cleo managed a

smile.
    Hmm, her big sister was catching on to her wind ups.

45

By mid-day on Saturday, Teri could hardly contain her excitement. She was waiting at Heathrow for her flight to Newcastle and it was time to phone Cleo's apartment. She would call Cleo and then ring the Collingwood's to speak to Alex.

To her surprise, Alex picked up. 'Hello Darling. What are you doing at Cleo's? Have you two made up?'

'Oh, hi Mum, yes we're sound. I'll just go and get Cleo to speak to you.' Teri was delighted that Alex was there but, from her tone, she didn't seem to be herself.

Cleo came on the line. 'Hi Mum.' She didn't sound grand either.

'I'm glad you two have made up, sweetheart, but why do you both sound so glum?' This wasn't the homecoming that Teri had expected.

'Oh Mum! It's bloody awful here, but you're so far away and I don't know where to start.'

Teri hated to hear Cleo upset, 'I was about to tell you that I'm waiting at Heathrow for my Newcastle flight. Does that help?'

'Oh yes, Mum. Thank goodness you're back. We're both in Newcastle so we'll pick you up from the airport'

'What's going on?'

'Just get here, Mum,' Cleo begged, 'we'll explain it when we see you.'

Teri put her phone in her pocket. What a welcome after twelve weeks away. There was nothing wrong with the two girls, she'd spoken to them both but she'd couldn't wait to get there to see what was upsetting them.

'Did you get through?' Greg asked when he came back with two coffees.

'There's some sort of emergency, they didn't say what it was. Sorry Greg, this wasn't the way I wanted you to meet my family.'

'I'm just glad to be here with you. Come on, let's find the gate.'

Teri was surprised to see that it was Dan, on his own, who met them from the airport. She watched closely but he didn't flicker as she introduced him to Greg - just a handshake and a friendly smile and then he led them to the car park saying, 'Wait until we get to the car and I'll tell you what's been going on,'

As they walked along, Teri broke the silence by asking about Pharos, since the last Skype session, she had steeled herself to hearing that he was lost and her heart soared when she heard that he had made the long journey home.

'He's heard me read 'The Incredible Journey' to both of the girls. He just knew it was time to stop being a city cat and went on his own trek home.'

Dan looked at her with a puzzled frown and hadn't a clue what she was talking about but Greg just smiled and gave her a wink and said, 'Clever cat, can't wait to meet him.' She loved Greg because he just *got* her.

Taking Greg up on his offer to travel back with her had crept up on her quite surprisingly. She had tried to imagine going back to a world without him but couldn't deny that Greg had become a part of her life. She couldn't just cast him off and she realised that she didn't even want to. Her only concern was whether her girls liked him and why shouldn't they? He was wonderful to her and he made her happy. Cleo was often teasing her about finding a new man; well now she had.

She was feeling tense and still waiting for Dan to break some sort of serious news to them because he looked preoccupied. Deciding that she couldn't wait a moment longer, she asked him,

'Dan, I have to know. What's up? Who's in trouble? What are the girls upset about?

'I've been trying to find the right words. Sorry to be so blunt, Teri, but Cleo has tracked down some of your relatives, her grandparents... *your* mother and father and now your father is in the RVI. It's his heart and it doesn't look great. They want me to take you right there.'

'Say all that again.' Teri was stunned.

She had heard correctly. Here was Dan Collingwood telling her that Cleo had visited Middle Row. Cleo had talked to her mother and had discovered her dad was actually alive. *Alive.* She'd blamed herself for giving him a heart attack years ago and her mother had lied. Well, if not an outright lie, she'd been mean enough to deceive her. Right now, her two girls were sitting by her father's bedside and she was going to see him. She would never, ever have guessed that she'd see this day.

It took Dan a while to find a parking space. The RVI had been modernised and she didn't know her way around this massive complex. Where was her dad? Now that she was so near, she couldn't wait another minute. They stopped at a café in a large atrium; Greg would wait there while she went with Dan to intensive care. It seemed to take forever to get to the wing that they needed.

Teri looked into the half-shuttered window. Alex and Cleo were sitting side by side and Alex had her arm around Cleo. This was her moondream jar wish come true. It had finally been granted but was there a price for that? Had the jar finally spilled out *all* of her secrets?

She could hardly comprehend who she was about to see, the father that she believed she'd killed by grief or shame.

She tiptoed in and there were whispered hellos and hugs. It was so good to hold her girls again but her eyes were drawn to the bed in the centre of the room.

She walked to the bedside and looked down on Dad's face… she drank in all the details, studied the lines that had appeared over their years apart, noticed how his hair had turned white. She was pleased to see him looking peaceful. He wasn't in pain.

'Hello Dad,' she said and took his hand. She squeezed it and sat by him. 'It's …It's Margaret, Dad.' She glanced at the girls but they didn't seem surprised by her using the name. *Well, they wouldn't, clearly they'd read her teenage diaries.*

Kissing his cheek, she explained, 'I'm sorry that I haven't seen you, Dad. I really thought that you were gone. Mum told me, she was so angry and she blamed me for being… for being the death of you. I never imagined her lying.' She thought she felt a squeeze on her hand. Could he hear her? Oh, she hoped he could.

'I'm glad you met Cleo,' she whispered. 'She's brought Alex, her sister, to meet you today.'

There it was again. That was a definite squeeze of her hand. 'Alex, come over here,' she called. 'I think Grandad is saying that he wants to meet you.'

Alex, who had been looking out of the window, turned and walked over to the bedside.

'Look who's here, Dad.' In her heart, she was begging. *Please wake up, please say hello.*

Her eyes never left his face and she sat forward the moment her father opened his eyes, they glazed but then brightened when he looked up and focussed on Alex.

He smiled, 'Ah, Margaret my sunshine, you're back. So, so glad.'

He was looking at Alex. He'd heard *her* voice and he thought he was seeing her- the teenage Margaret - when he gazed at Alex. He gave her hand a tight squeeze before he let out a quiet sigh and closed his eyes. Dad was very tired; she knew that this had been an effort.

A machine emitted a strange beep pattern and then one long tone. Keep clutching Dad's hand. Hearing is the last thing to go. She'd read that somewhere.

'It's all right Dad. We're all here and we love you so very much. Just you rest and we'll stay by you. We love you, Dad. We really do.'

'Get someone!' Cleo stood up but Teri stretched her hand over the bed, lay it over Cleo's and shook her head. He'd gone. Dad was at peace.

Alex started to cry, 'He thought I was *you,* Mum, didn't he?'

'Yes, and that made him very happy.' Teri sobbed.

'No Grandad, not now!' Cleo called out and buzzed for a nurse but Teri knew that Bobby Donaldson had gone.

She was lucky that she'd been just in time to see him with her girls, just for a moment. So many wasted years due to that bitter woman. Her regrets wouldn't bring back Dad.

Teri held his cool hand in both of hers, it still had the callouses from working with tools. She closed her eyes and silently thanked him for being her father and for acknowledging Cleo. *He* hadn't turned her daughter away.

She leaned forward and kissed his brow. In a few minutes, she would leave the dad that she had loved and she would introduce her girls to Greg, the man she loved now. She didn't know how they'd react but she would love them all and leave the three of them to find their own place with one another. Life was finite and fragile and she was determined to make the most of every last dram of hers.

Alex was glad that she could shed tears over her

grandfather at last. When he'd looked at her and called her Margaret she'd wanted extra time with him; time to get to know him just a little. Her grandmother must be a very cruel woman to have done what she did to the family.

They left the ward and headed for the café where Mum's friend, Greg, was waiting. The minute she saw Mum with Greg, she knew that they weren't *just* 'friends'. He hugged Mum and kept looking at her in such a concerned way. Greg seemed OK. Fancy Mum going for someone with a ponytail. She was glad he wasn't an old man; she already had a Mum who was a bit older so it was good to see that Greg had a bit of life about him.

She wasn't sure about how she'd feel about her mum having a boyfriend staying over; that hadn't happened before. Maybe, at last, Mum would agree to her having the spare bedroom in the barn beside the workroom? Her own space in the barn; that would be really cool.

It wasn't going to happen this weekend anyway because the grownups had decided that Teri would go to High Rigg and spend time there with her and Cleo while Dan and Greg stayed at Mariner's Wharf for the weekend to give them some space.

She was going to text Will and ask him to call into High Rigg tomorrow but there'd be no party after all. So much for him meeting her for once when there wasn't a crisis.

46

In the following two weeks, Cleo came to accept losing her grandfather almost as soon as she had found him, but her sorrow still felt raw. She had taken time off work to grieve and help her Mum to arrange the funeral; Teflon just had to manage without her. Three months ago she would never have thought of doing that.

She'd moved Grandad's bowling bag from the boot and it was lying in the corner of her room. It had been a surprise to find that it wasn't just his bowls that were in there. Under his cap, there nestled a bundle of envelopes. All were addressed 'To Margaret' and she realised that these were the birthday messages he had wanted her to look after. He must have intended leaving them in her keeping that Thursday.

She handed the bundle straight over to Mum. Cleo would have read them straight away but her mum put them away saying that she would read them, when the time felt right.

Now, on the day of the funeral, lying in her bedroom she thought of how some things, like her love for her job, were still the same yet she had changed so much. She'd learned a lot this summer and she felt as though there was *more* to her; she was more substantial, more herself.

Was that thanks to her mum for taking a risk in leaving her with Alex? Or, was it due to Alex and Dan bringing out the best, and worst, in her? All of her ups and downs had made her face who she was and appreciate what she had. Maybe it was because she knew more about where she had come from.

The brief time with her grandfather had been bittersweet. She held onto her memory of him saying that he was proud of her, that he saw something of himself in her. Now she had to make the best of whatever lay ahead.

Would she arrange to meet up with her father again? Who knew? Would she marry and have children with Dan? Yes, she was certain of that. Now that Mum was home, her one moondream wish was to live her life happily, with Dan.

Time had flown by, once Teri arrived back home. She had caught up with her girls, taken Greg around Northumberland and helped to arrange her father's funeral. With Greg by her side, she'd faced up to her hospital consultation too.

Mr. Amonkar had looked so grave when she walked into the consulting room. He explained that she had both osteopenia and osteoarthritis in her hips. The arthritis was giving her the pain and stiffness but she needed medication for the osteopenia.

'Is that it?' Teri asked him and he looked perplexed.

'It's quite enough to contend with. We can treat you with medication and diet but, unfortunately, you may be a candidate for a hip replacement in the future.'

Teri beamed, 'That's fine as long as I *have* a future, Mr. Amonkar.'

She could live with her aches if they weren't life threatening.

It was wonderful having Greg with her during these difficult times and oh how she'd miss him when he flew off to Turkey. He was going over there on an archaeological dig next week but he was coming back to her for Christmas.

Teri felt calm as she got into the funeral car that would carry her to St. Michael's in Elswick. She had her family and friends with her and she was ready to face any folk that would be in the church. She was aware that people she hadn't seen for over thirty years would have read about Bobby Donaldson's death in the Evening Chronicle obituaries column but, as he was eighty-nine, there couldn't be that many friends left to attend.

Sunny Court contacted all of Dad's regular visitors and Teri arranged a decent spread with money behind the bar at a pub near to Dad's bowling club for afterwards; Dad would have expected that. She hoped that some of his friends from the club *would* come to the service, because St. Michael's was a big old church to fill.

She opted for a white coat and a black pill box hat and shoes because they were the magpie colours of Newcastle football club, Dad's team. There was only one thing making her apprehensive but she was ready for it, if it happened.

She had her eyes closed as the car hummed along behind the hearse and was deep in thought when she heard a gasp from Cleo and a cry of, 'OMG!' from Alex.

Teri's eyes shot open and she caught her breath as she saw the crowd at the gates of the church. Their car crawled through the gates after the hearse and the crowd followed them. They *were* here for her dad. As she got out of the car, she heard,

'Bobby's had a great turn out, mind.'

'He has at that. There were a lot of folk waiting at the gates for him, nearly as many as there were for Declan Donnelly's wedding.'

'He's got the weather for it n'all. It's warm for October.'

'The sun always shines on the good'uns, that's what I say.'

Teri smiled; it felt so good to be among kind people who liked her dad.

It took a while to shake hands and share a few words with everyone leaving the church after a wonderful service. There were the bowling club 'boys', his gardening club, staff and residents of Sunny Court, Lottie Fletcher's extended family, churchgoers who'd known her dad and then every shop, pub and café in the neighbourhood seemed to have given someone time off to see Bobby Donaldson on his way.

Everyone looked at the flowers outside the church and then walked over to the pub, with Lottie Fletcher's family leading the way. Only immediate family were going to be at the burial.

The churchyard cleared and that was when Teri saw her, the woman who she couldn't call mother, standing by a tree near the newly dug grave. Although she had been armed for this moment, Teri trembled as, for the first time, she drew down the lace veil on her pill box hat so that it covered her face. Looking straight ahead, she strode past her foe without even a glance.

After the burial, Teri stood by the grave alone. Greg, Dan, Alex and Cleo wandered back to the car to wait for her there. As she sensed footsteps approaching, a cold sweat caused her to shiver.

'Trust you to turn up in white for a funeral and make a show of yourself.' The voice hadn't changed or faded with age. 'So you saw him, before he died, I take it?'

Cleo turned around and stared into the cold, hard eyes of her nightmares. Her veil hid her own face and gave her some protection from the bitter stare.

'Say whatever poison you've got to say. You can't hurt

Dad or me now.'

'Oh, can't I? Well, understand this, I'll be contesting his will because we were still married. We never divorced. It should still be *me* who is next of kin.'

Teri walked past her without answering.

She'd been at the reading of her Dad's will earlier in the week and, quite rightly, he had left what little money he had to Lottie Fletcher's family with donations going to a couple of charities.

Lottie had been generous and left her house to him and, in turn, he had left his small estate to her relatives. Teri would never have contested Dad's wishes and she would make sure that nobody else fought against them. She'd have to get her solicitor, George Moore, on the case to help the Fletchers. Lizzie Donaldson had turned into a bitter old crone.

Teri was pleased that they had catered generously because everybody had stayed to eat, drink and remember Bobby. With the addition of a bunch of non-churchgoers who had by-passed the service but come along to the pub to celebrate his life, the room was packed.

Hours later, when the family set off for Dunleith, Bobby's farewell party was still in full swing.

Teri felt at peace. She may have said goodbye to her dad but she sensed he was with her and he still had things to tell her. It made her content just to know that he had never given up on her.

She had his bundle of letters, one for every birthday, waiting to be read. She could not open them yet, but, one day she would be ready.

If you enjoyed reading, 'A Jarful of Moondreams', a short review would be greatly appreciated.

You can meet up with some of the characters again in 'The Barn of Buried Dreams'.

Heather, Cleo's friend, Heather's younger sister Erin and Jackson McGee, a handsome Texan who has business interests in Dunleith take take centre stage. The Moon family, along with other Dunleith characters, make an appearance.

THE BARN OF BURIED DREAMS

-isn't it time they saw daylight?

Two sisters are struggling. Erin, who left a blossoming stage career, has buried herself and her dreams in Magpie's Rest, the family home. Heather is running on wine as she juggles children, work and marriage. She has lost sight of the woman she liked to be.

As Erin and Heather face rocky relationships, betrayal, mistakes and heartache, they learn a lot about themselves.

Can a letter from the past help them to rescue their buried dreams?

Available October 2018. Try the preview chapter.

Chapter 1

FEBRUARY

Erin had never understood how anyone could be totally surprised by their pregnancy.

Until today.

She stared at the stick in her hand in utter disbelief. Two stark lines...the test couldn't be clearer. How had this happened? Well, she knew how, of course she did, but what were the odds? Wow.

Bloody wow. She bit her knuckle and checked the tiny screen again. Wasn't she supposed to be doing a happy dance? Maybe. When she got over the shock. It was such bad timing. This was meant to happen in the future, very far into some fuzzy future, when it would be a thrilling moment with Damien doing the test with her. They had a wedding to plan and their careers to establish before this bit of the story. Erin felt guilty immediately. How could she feel that way? She had created a new life with the man she loved and here she was thinking it was inconvenient. She hoped the tiny being that was beginning to grow inside her couldn't hear her thoughts.

Her life hadn't been her own this year and now it looked like it wouldn't be ever again. She'd spent years working hard to get where she was but now her stage career was drifting away like an unattended beachball, bright and enticing but moving further and further out of her reach. Would it come back to her on another tide or crash on the rocks?

'Erin, our programme will be starting soon.'

'Just coming, Mum.' She placed the confirmation of her future on the bathroom window sill – nobody else came up here – tied her long copper hair up into a ponytail and hurried downstairs to make a pot of tea before *Happy Valley* started.

Mum was soon engrossed in the episode, making comments about the murder case and cursing human traffickers. 'Sergeant Cawood won't let them get away with this trafficking scam, will she, Erin?'

Erin tried to keep up but her mind churned away at her own inner drama. When would she tell Damien? She'd have to tell him first, even before she told her mother. What would they do about a wedding? Rush into a small ceremony before or wait until after? They would both just have to get used to the idea of parenthood. There was never a perfect time to have a baby but she was twenty-seven and they had talked about starting a family, one day, so they'd just have to put their wedding plans on hold and become a family sooner than they thought.

'Erin?' the credits were rolling and her mother was studying her closely.

'Yes, Mum. What is it?'

Liz Douglas leaned forward in her chair, her pale face showing how easily she tired. 'You haven't followed that episode at all and your mind seems far way. Is everything OK?'

'Everything's fine.' Erin managed a smile.

'Are you sure?' Mum could be a mind reader at times.

'I was just thinking about Damien coming at the weekend and wondering how to keep him entertained. You know how quiet he thinks it is around here.'

'A night at the Bridge Inn isn't his idea of fun is it? How about the Red Lion at Alnmouth? That's livelier.'

She caught Mum's wicked smile and laughed. 'Yeah, he'll have to make do with that, or watch TV. He's just here for a couple of nights anyway.'

Erin helped her mother up from the chair and across to the single bed that was set up in the corner of the living room.

It was good to see her regaining her sense of humour and watch her getting stronger every day. In a month or so, she might be back to normal. Bloody hell, she hoped so. Poor Mum, she was really working at her recovery from a stroke but she was nowhere near to being independent again.

Erin was anxious to get back to London, the sooner she could get back to work, the better. Her agent couldn't put her forward for auditions when she was tied up here and she missed Damien. Mum came first, though and, until she had made a good recovery, Erin would stay here. Remembering the baby cells that were multiplying minute by minute, she drew in a sharp breath. She would be limited in getting any roles once this baby started to show.

'What's startled you, Erin? You look like you've seen that Tommy Lee from *Happy Valley*.' Mum looked at her curiously as she slipped off her dressing gown and sat on the bed.

Erin shook her head. 'It's nothing. I've just remembered something I need to do tomorrow.' The phone rang, freeing Erin from any further questions as she crossed over to pick up the call.

'Hi it's me. Is Mum still up?' It was Heather, Erin's sister.

'Yes, she's right here... Mum, here's Heather, for you.' She passed the phone over and took the chance to escape further questioning by slipping into the kitchen to prepare a night time tray with water, a flask of tea, a plate with two shortbreads and her mother's tablets. Heather would be chatting to Mum about *Happy Valley* for a while; they both loved a crime series.

Bracken barked at the door to go outside. Erin smiled as he sat smartly with his head cocked to one side waiting for her to let him out into the back garden. As she stood in the open doorway and watched the silhouette of the Welsh terrier snuffling in the bushes at the far end of the garden, Erin thought about what Heather would say when she heard her baby news. She was longing to tell her. Heather was already eight months along with her second and would be full of advice, but it was only fair to tell Damien first. A few more days until he arrived on Friday and, after she had talked to him, she would break the news to Mum and Heather then her friend, Darcy. She just couldn't imagine Darcy's response. They had both shared dreams of stage careers and of finding love, but they had never talked babies.

***

Lying in bed that night, Erin counted backwards to work out just how many weeks pregnant she was. She'd already done this a dozen times since taking the test and the answer didn't change. She'd run out of pills soon after dashing home to look after Mum in November and hadn't been too concerned because Damien had a busy filming schedule and was going to see his parents in Kent for Christmas. He wouldn't be visiting for a while so there was no rush to renew her prescription when their only contact, video call or text, was a hundred per cent conception proof.

Damien had missed her over Christmas and arrived at the door of Magpie's Rest to surprise her on New Year's Eve with presents and champagne. She hadn't expected this extra surprise… she really hadn't. Just one careless night? Hell, she must be eight weeks pregnant.

She glanced at the time, waiting for Damien to call. Last night, he said if he didn't get in touch by midnight, it meant he was delayed at the promotion event he had to attend. There was a minute or two to go but she was tired. She decided to ring him.

'Hi Damien are you still tied up with work?'

'Erin! Hi babe. Yeah, can't get away, I'm afraid.'

'Never mind. It's not long until the weekend and we can catch up then.'

'Weekend? Oh…the weekend. Listen, I need to talk to you about that. Look, I can't chat now, babe, but I'll call in the morning.'

He wasn't coming. She knew it. She could tell by the tone in his voice. Damien was going to cry off and use work as an excuse but really it was because he thought it was too deadly dull in Northumberland. He loved the bright lights and buzz of the city but she was here; wasn't that enough anymore? Did he think she was dull too? Tears welled up and she turned her head into her pillow.

She was tired, she was shocked by that test result and her hormones were all messed up. Worries about the baby, Damien, Mum, and her career fought with each other for pole position in her racing thoughts. Her life seemed like shifting sand beneath her feet.

She reached for her phone and called Heather.
'Hi Sis, it's me.'
'What's wrong? Is Mum OK?' Heather's voice was croaky.

Blast, she must've woken her up... never a good thing. 'Yes, she's in bed. It's me, I'm not OK.'

'What do you mean? You're crying...Who has upset you? Is it Damien?

'Sort of,' Erin admitted.

'Sort of?'

'He's trying to put off coming and I haven't seen him since New Year. We're growing further and further apart and I just need to see him. I want to go to London. Heather, could you take over here this weekend?'

'No way. Archie has a party on Saturday and Mark's playing rugby on Sunday. Sorry Erin, I know you miss Damien but, right now, it is up to him to make the effort to travel to see you. You know Mum comes first until she's recovered.'

'Of course, I do. But it's all down to me at the moment. Fraser's always working and you hardly vis—'

'I was there last week.' Heather jumped in. 'No. maybe it was the weekend before. Anyway, this pregnancy is leaving me exhausted and I phone Mum every single day!'

'That's fine, Heather, but I do everything else. This arrangement was supposed to be weeks not months. There are three of us, you know.'

'Come on Sis. It won't be that much longer. Mum's improving all the time. I can't do the full weekend, but I'll bring Archie over on Sunday afternoon.' Heather sounded gracious like she was bestowing a favour.

'That won't help me to travel to London for an overnight stay, will it?' She should have known better than to ask. Heather was always busy.

'Shall I ask Fraser to look into getting a relief carer? He offered to sort it out right at the beginning but, oh no, you wanted to do it. You did, Erin.' Heather was getting on her high horse and Erin wished she hadn't said a thing.

'I still do want to help out. I don't want Mum to have a carer but I wish you or Fraser would come more often, that's all.'

'Erin, *we* both work and *we* both have families. Think about it… You're the one with free time and no responsibility. God…look at the time! Can we please have this conversation when I'm not so bloody tired. Archie wakes me up at six, you know!'

'OK. OK. Goodnight Heather. Sorry for disturbing you.'

'Don't get all 'woe is me', Sis. I don't mind being disturbed if it's a true emergency, I really don't.'

'Goodnight then.'

'Goodnight.'

Erin sat up and searched for a tissue to dry her eyes. She shivered but it wasn't the chill in the bedroom that wrapped icy fingers around her heart and left her desolate, it was the growing distance between her and Damien and an uneasy feeling that he wasn't going to take this baby news very well.

***

Heather gave up trying to sleep. She flung back the duvet and grappled for her dressing gown on the bench at the end of the bed. The baby's kicking and Mark's snores were driving her mad and Erin's call had left her head spinning. She crept past Archie's room and made her way down to the kitchen in the dark so she wouldn't wake him.

She sat at the table with a cup of tea and a packet of digestives. She'd stopped smoking when she was pregnant but she really felt like lighting up at this moment. Fraser and her, were they were asking too much of Erin? She knew Mum's recovery was taking a while but Erin had no work lined up at the moment. Heather's hands were already full with work at the newspaper and caring for Archie.

Erin was qualified to take over Mum's Pilates classes and keep the business up and running and she had no ties; a fiancé, yes, but he could visit her. OK, Damien had not been supportive about the arrangement but maybe this would show Erin his true colours. Heather wasn't keen on him. He was full of himself now that he was a regular in a soap. His talk usually centred around Damien Swift and, in Heather's opinion, Erin could do much better. Erin would be fine if only Damien would bother himself to spend a couple of weekends a month at Magpie's Rest. Just until Mum was well again.

Mum! Tears pricked at Heather's eyes when she thought of her active, vivacious mother losing her independence in one fell swoop. Who had a stroke at fifty-seven? She seemed so healthy. She was sure that if anyone could make a good recovery it would be Mum. When they spoke every night, it was as if her Mum was as good as new but when Heather visited she could see she was still frail.

Heather wasn't as hands on or as good at the carer role as Erin was and she had to admit that her visits had tailed off now that her mum wasn't in danger. She used her pregnancy and the distance as an excuse, but the truth was it broke her heart to see her mum struggle to do the simplest tasks.

Half the packet of digestives had been dunked. That had put a hole in her diet and she was determined not to gain a mountain of blubber with this second baby. As she put her cup into the sink, she decided to leave Archie with Mark's parents on Sunday. She would visit Mum and Erin early, help out and stay the whole day. She would take Erin something nice to make up for being a bit sharp with her tonight.

She trudged back upstairs and, as she passed the landing window, the birds were already singing and the sky had turned silver grey. In a while, Archie would be awake and the morning merry-go-round would start. If Erin thought she had it hard, she should try being heavily pregnant and juggling a day's work, a husband, and a toddler on half a packet of digestives and a couple of hours sleep.

About the Author

Chrissie lives in the North East on a beautiful stretch of coastline not far from the city of Newcastle with her husband and their Welsh terror of a Terrier, Oscar.

Oscar makes an appearance, as Bracken, in her second novel, 'The Barn of Buried Dreams.' Bracken is much better behaved!

She had an Egyptian Mau called Pharos and loved giving him a cameo role as Teri's cat in 'A Jarful of Moondreams.' All her other characters are entirely fictitious!

She is a member of the Romantic Novelists' Association and won their Elizabeth Goudge Trophy in 2016.

Chrissie has a Chrissie Bradshaw Author Facebook page and an nstagram account

You'll find her on twitter @ChrissieBeee

Her website is www.newhenontheblog.com

'A Jarful of Moondreams' is Chrissie's first novel.

'The Barnof Buried Dreams' is available in October 2018

Join her mailing list for news about forthcoming books by sending an email to chrissiebradshaw@hotmail.co.uk

Printed in Great Britain
by Amazon